## PRAISE FOR A KILLING IN COMICS

"Collins's latest is great fun . . . enlivened b~ ~~~~~~ ~~~ ects and illustrations by Collins's long-ti~~ ~~~~~~~ ~~~~~ Terry Beatty. Readers familiar with the ~~~~~~~~ ~~~~~~ ~~~~l have an especially good time with this ~~~~~~ ~~~ ~~~~~ ~omic book heroes and their creators."

*~ystery Scene*

"The well-executed plot and the Phil~~~~ ~~~~~ ~ype protagonist make this an excellent historical mystery. The illustrations by Terry Beatty are fantastic."

—*Midwest Book Review*

"This fast-paced, outrageously entertaining romp from prolific Max Allan Collins is a great addition to the comic-noir world of mystery fiction. Crisp, wry, and sardonic, Collins has adroitly blended the fictional and real-life worlds (of comics publishing) into a terrific tale full of twists, turns, and plenty of suspense. Read it and enjoy!"

—*BookLoons*

"With references to Dick Tracy and Mickey Spillane, the author is working within a world he loves, and it's hard not to let his enthusiasm rub off."

—*Bookgasm*

"An amusing effort interspersed with good graphics."

—*BookBitch*

"[Max Allan Collins is] the American master of historical crime fiction . . . *A Killing in Comics* is superbly researched, informative, and loads of fun."

—ILoveAMysteryNewsletter.com

## PRAISE FOR MAX ALLAN COLLINS

"Collins has an outwardly artless style that conceals a great deal of art."

—*The New York Times*

"Max Allan Collins blends fact and fiction like no other writer."

—Andrew Vachss, author of *Terminal*

"A terrific writer!"

—Mickey Spillane

"Collins's blending of fact and fancy is masterful—there's no better word for it. And his ability to sustain suspense, even when the outcome is known, is the mark of an exceptional storyteller." —*San Diego Union-Tribune*

*continued . . .*

"Collins displays a compelling talent for flowing narrative and concise, believable dialogue." —*Library Journal*

"No one fictionalizes real-life mysteries better." —*The Armchair Detective*

"An uncanny ability to blend fact and fiction." —*South Bend Tribune*

"When it comes to exploring the rich possibilities of history in a way that holds and entertains the reader, nobody does it better than Max Allan Collins." —John Lutz, author of *Chill of Night*

"Probably no one except E. L. Doctorow in *Ragtime* has so successfully blended real characters and events with fictional ones. The versatile Collins is an excellent storyteller." —*The Tennessean*

"The master of true-crime fiction." —*Publishers Weekly*

"The author makes history come alive . . . The details of life, the dialogue, and the realities of living in London during wartime are meticulously set out for the reader. The nightly blackouts . . . make the perfect setting for criminal activities. The mystery [is] well crafted and quite interesting . . . A new Collins novel is a treat for lovers of history and mystery alike." —*The Romance Readers Connection*

"Entertaining . . . Full of colorful characters . . . A stirring conclusion." —*Detroit Free Press*

"Collins makes it sound as though it really happened." —*New York Daily News*

"Collins does a fine job of insinuating a mystery into a world-famous disaster . . . [He] manage[s] to raise plenty of goosebumps before the ship goes down for the count." —*Mystery News*

"[Collins's] descriptions are so vivid and colorful that it's like watching a movie . . . [and he] gives the reader a front-row seat." —*Cozies, Capers & Crimes*

# STRIP
# FOR MURDER

## MAX ALLAN COLLINS

BERKLEY PRIME CRIME, NEW YORK

THE BERKLEY PUBLISHING GROUP
Published by the Penguin Group
Penguin Group (USA) Inc.
375 Hudson Street, New York, New York 10014, USA
Penguin Group (Canada), 90 Eglinton Avenue East, Suite 700, Toronto, Ontario M4P 2Y3, Canada
(a division of Pearson Penguin Canada Inc.)
Penguin Books Ltd., 80 Strand, London WC2R 0RL, England
Penguin Group Ireland, 25 St. Stephen's Green, Dublin 2, Ireland (a division of Penguin Books Ltd.)
Penguin Group (Australia), 250 Camberwell Road, Camberwell, Victoria 3124, Australia
(a division of Pearson Australia Group Pty. Ltd.)
Penguin Books India Pvt. Ltd., 11 Community Centre, Panchsheel Park, New Delhi—110 017, India
Penguin Group (NZ), 67 Apollo Drive, Rosedale, North Shore 0632, New Zealand
(a division of Pearson New Zealand Ltd.)
Penguin Books (South Africa) (Pty.) Ltd., 24 Sturdee Avenue, Rosebank, Johannesburg 2196,
South Africa

Penguin Books Ltd., Registered Offices: 80 Strand, London WC2R 0RL, England

PRINTING HISTORY
Berkley Prime Crime trade paperback edition / May 2008

Library of Congress Cataloging-in-Publication Data

Collins, Max Allan.
    Strip for murder / Max Allan Collins.
        p. cm.
    ISBN 978-0-425-22139-6
    1. Cartoonists—Crimes against—Fiction.  2. Syndicates (Journalism)—Fiction.  3. Murder—Investigation—Fiction.  4. Manattan (New York, N.Y.)—Fiction.  I. Title.

    PS3553.O4753S88    2008
    813'.54—dc22

                                                                                            2008004474

PRINTED IN THE UNITED STATES OF AMERICA

10  9  8  7  6  5  4  3  2  1

FOR DENIS KITCHEN,
NATCHERLY

*"Goodness is better than evil
becuz it's nicer!!"*

Mammy Yokum


*"Hatred is idiotic, crazy,
low-grade gorilla thinkin'!"*

Joe Palooka

*. . . but with two r's: Jack Starr, vice president, chief trou-bleshooter and occasional bottle washer for the Starr Syndicate.*

*That's short for Starr Newspaper Syndication Company, headquartered just a block and a half off Broadway on Forty-second Street. We do have a road show Winchell on our roster—Lou "Eyeful of Broadway!" Eiful—but the "theatuh" isn't what we are about: we distribute a lovelorn column and a crossword puzzle and a bridge-tips panel and more . . . though what we are mostly about is comic strips.*

*Still, a small syndicate like ours benefits from its proxim-ity to Broadway—clients and talent alike are impressed, not the least by the Strip Joint restaurant on the Starr Building's ground floor (best strip steak in Manhattan), with its striptease photos, and drawings on the wall by famous cartoonists, and of course its owner, the diva of the comics world, my step-mother, Maggie Starr, president of Starr Syndicate and the only ecdysiast whose fame arguably eclipsed Gypsy Rose Lee's, if momentarily.*

*More about Maggie later. There's a story to tell, with a murder mystery of course, and lots of characters, Maggie and me included. But we really need to start with the most important character in this book—Broadway.*

*Note that I call it a character, not a street. And, yes, there is a thoroughfare known as Broadway, but it's more a state of mind that a stretch of concrete. The literal truth is a meandering former cow path demarcated south of Forty-second by the bustling garment district, and north of Columbus Circle by Central Park around Fifty-ninth Street. The so-called Great White Way can only lay claim to three-fifths of a mile—twelve blocks.*

*Columnists Lait and Mortimer don't work for us, but they said it well, in* New York: Confidential!—*a book published five years ago (1948) and still apt—describing Broadway as "a street of a million lights, of a broken heart for every bulb, and more bulbs every night."*

*They also acknowledged that these days (and nights) only four theaters devoted to the legitimate stage can literally be found on Broadway, and even that number fluctuates. The state of mind that is Broadway, however, numbers twenty-five legit theaters, mostly located east and west of Broadway in the narrow side streets of the forties and fifties.*

*The "real" Broadway—where not so long ago a dozen fabled theaters held sway—has a split personality now. During daytime hours—when the only bright lights are the sun and its reflected rays and maybe a traffic light or ambitious neon sign—Broadway is still the capital of show business. Starr Syndicate is a part of that, but maybe more to the point, so are the offices of agents, theatrical producers and song writers, as well as the studios of scenic artists, costumers and set designers, with the occasional rehearsal hall for hoofers and thesps tossed in.*

*After dark, when lights are flashing and neon is pulsing, the Great White Way (street-level, anyway) is nowadays (nowanights?) home to dime-a-dance halls, flea circuses, shooting galleries, hotdog stands, movie grindhouses, souvenir shops, orange juice counters and army and navy stores. You'll meet an assortment of charming characters right out of Damon Runyon, assuming you find a pickpocket snagging your vacation dough charming or enjoy dating a surprisingly friendly doll plucked right off the street whose bachelorette apartment is nearby, as is her guy with a blackjack.*

*This is Broadway, for real, and on the map, but not Broadway the state of mind that seizes every tourist and, truth be told, most everybody in Manhattan and its greater environs, which you might as well define as the USA.*

*By eight* P.M. *or so, commuters and cliff dwellers have largely disappeared, and a swell of suburbanites and out-of-towners have invaded, looking to establish a Broadway beachhead. This often starts with swarming and swamping the el cheapo ticket outlets, which is fine, just don't expect to get in to* The Teahouse of the August Moon *or* The Pajama Game.

*Behind the Astor Hotel beats the unlikely heart of Broadway, Shubert Alley, a slender private lane that runs from Forty-fourth to Forty-fifth, a three-hundred-foot radius within which the state of mind flourishes. Here are the most important theaters, as well as the offices of the biggest big-shot impresarios and agents. Here, too, you'll find Sardi's, a meeting place for lunch, dinner and after* theater (no such thing as breakfast on Broadway, except at mid-night). The established stars and playhouse patriarchs still seem to prefer the pillars and linen tablecloths of the Astor Hunting Room, while kids trying to make it can only afford (barely) the Walgreens lunch counter at Forty-fourth and Broadway, sipping Cokes (not cocktails) and smoking Lucky Strikes like the grown-ups.

All of these Shubert Alley denizens—including the tourists, suburbanites and even Manhattanites—hold the Broadway show in high regard, no matter how many stinkers they may see. Somehow they know, in their hearts, in their souls, that theater is on a higher plane than movies or radio or (God help us) television. This is art. This is highbrow stuff. Like Guys and Dolls and South Pacific and The King and I. Okay, maybe not highbrow, but high-class and better than Arthur Godfrey's Talent Scouts on the tube (TV's new, after all, and low-rent junk like stupid talent shows are to be expected, and will surely fade as the medium grows).

If you aren't in the mood for song and dance, you can Dial M for Murder or sit in on The Caine Mutiny Court-Martial. Uncle Miltie and Joe Friday have their appeal, but this is Broadway, alive and vital and expensive as hell. Radio and TV are free—how good could they be?

By now you're wondering what this has to do with comic strips and a murder mystery. Plenty. For the first time in the twenty-year history of the Starr Syndicate we were working legit-imate Broadway—involved in the biggest, splashiest musical comedy of the season, the as-sure-a-surefire hit as the new Rodgers and Hammerstein (actually, surer: the new Rodgers and Hammerstein was Me and Juliet—hum something from that and get back to me).

This was October—Halloween to be exact—and opening for previews on Friday, November 6, at the newly renovated St. John Theatre on Broadway (yes, one of the four theaters actually on Broadway), would be the musical version of the fabulously successful satiric comic strip Tall Paul, everybody's favorite stupid hillbilly, eternally pursued by blonde and buxom Sunflower Sue, who once a year chased her feller in the annual Batch'ul Catch'ul race in Catfish Holler (a place at least as imaginary as Broadway and a state of mind only the legendary cartoonist Hal Rapp could have conjured).

You may think you're ahead of me. You figure the Starr Syndicate distributed the Tall Paul strip. Well, we didn't. We wanted to. But we didn't. And yet we had a major connection to this particular Broadway musical. Namely, my boss and stepmother, Maggie Starr, a woman pushing forty who men under twenty would still gladly pay money to see naked, though she'd given that up. I wonder if anybody ever said that about their stepmother before? In public, I mean.

How exactly was Maggie married to Tall Paul?

Well, that's where the story starts.

This was only the overture.

I can't say Halloween had made the Waldorf-Astoria give up the ghost.

Those palatial fifty stories—between Forty-ninth and Fiftieth streets, Park and Lexington avenues—just weren't up for being haunted. The mile-long lobby was not festooned with cardboard skeletons and lithograph black cats and accordion-paper jack-o'-lanterns, the marble and stone and bronze insisting on more dignity than that; same went for the museum's worth of paintings by renowned artists overlooking eighteenth-century English and Early American furnishings, none of which bore a filigree of cobwebs, true or false.

Earlier in the evening—from around six thirty to eight—the hotel had allowed any children who dwelled (presumably with their parents) in the high-tone residential suites in the twin towers to become proper little ghosts and goblins and go door-to-door trick-or-treating, but only in those towers, and always with a parent along.

A kid asking for candy in Manhattan always called for having a parent along.

Up on the twenty-fifth floor, however, another sort of renowned artist in residence at the Waldorf (albeit one whose work was unlikely to grace a gilt frame in the lobby) had really taken Halloween to heart—a costume party had turned cartoonist Hal Rapp's swanky digs into the funny pages come to life.

No skeletons or black cats or spun-sugar webs here, either, though several grandly carved pumpkins were spotted around, sporting the fiendish features of Grotesque Gertie, the *Tall Paul* strip's resident witch. Mostly the suite was Rapp's Catfish Holler in the flesh, and I do mean flesh, as "gals" in short ragged skirts and low-cut bare-armed blouses mingled with hillbillies in overalls, including affable Roger Dodge, Tall Paul himself, the army talent show winner whose *Ed Sullivan* TV spot won him the coveted role.

The occasional interloper from another strip rubbed shoulders with Catfish Holler "sassiety"—Mandrake the Magician in his tux and cloak, Buck Rogers in tights with raygun on his hip, Popeye the Sailor with cap and pipe (but no visible spinach), Dagwood in his bow tie and Blondie in her apron, and best of all an unlikely Little Orphan Annie, that is, a showgirl in frizzy red wig and little girl's short white-trimmed red skirt—enough to make me wish I'd come as Daddy Warbucks.

This wasn't exactly a cocktail party; though the hors d'oeuvres were plentiful, no bar had been provided. The guests were sipping punch from one of two bowls (spiked and un), both labeled "Mingo Mountain Moonshine" in Rapp's own distinctive lettering, after the white lightning brewed up in the *Tall Paul* strip by

that unlikely duo, Choctaw Charlie and Bald Moe, both of whom
were in residence at the party, or at least the Broadway actors
playing them were—a little Jewish guy as the diminutive Indian
and a big Jewish guy as his big, bald backwoods buddy, carrying
his prop caveman club.

Most of the attendees of this shindig, you see, had a leg up on
the costume bit: they were members of the *Tall Paul* musical's
company. They'd been allowed—actually, encouraged—to come
in their character's wardrobe to give this "Come as Your Favorite
Comic Strip Character" party a predominantly Rappian theme.
Mixed in with these hillbillies, many last seen in the road show of
*Guys and Dolls*, were other Broadway guys and dolls, including
some press types, literary lights and TV personalities.

Most of these wholesome comic strip heroes and heroines
were smoking and if the smoke had been any thicker in there,
you'd have needed to install a foghorn. Instead, light jazz from a
hi-fi made itself barely heard. Here and there cardboard "wooden"
signs were stuck on walls or doors in comical Rapp-lettered Catfish Holler fashion: OL' FISHUN HOLE, INDOOR OUTHOUSE, NO
SMOKIN' (OF HAMS) and other such whimsey.

Otherwise, Rapp's suite was typical of the high-priced residential layouts at the Waldorf, modernly appointed in shades of tan
and brown with an off-white fluffy carpet. I was in the living room,
a fairly narrow area dominated by a fireplace on the right-hand
wall, near which two brown-leather sofas faced each other over
a low-slung glass coffee table. Toward the end of this room, down
by the big picture window onto the city, was the left turn into
the dining room, where the "Vittles" platters and "Mingo Mountain Moonshine" punch bowls could be found—and opposite was

the bedroom, which Rapp had converted a portion of into a mini-studio.

A balcony fronted the living room and extended to the bedroom (I knew this from past experience in a similar Waldorf suite) and the crisp fall night had some hillbillies and other cartoon characters out enjoying it, against a geometric skyline in black and white that might have been drawn by *Batwing* cartoonist Rod Krane, if Rod Krane had known how to draw (his assistants did the artwork).

Lanky, sleazily handsome Rod was among the attendees, dressed in a rather lumpy, wrinkly Batwing costume, a sight made more ridiculous by his cigarette in holder. He wasn't speaking to me, because the Starr Syndicate had dropped his strip six months ago (the comic book was still doing okay, but we had only a tiny piece of it). Right now Rod was putting the moves on a curvaceous, short-skirted Nancy, with Sluggo nowhere in sight.

You're already wondering what comics character I came as. I'd come as a guy six feet tall with dark blue eyes and dark brown hair and not repulsive to women. Not enough clues?

Here's what I was wearing: a charcoal pin-striped worsted, single-breasted, with a blue shirt and a snappy tie whose red and blue dots on a stitched gray pattern had a certain comic strip flavor, and black leather slip-on shoes that had no flavor but were damn comfortable. Also, I was wearing a light gray hat with a black band and narrow brim.

I had found a hunk of wall to lean against between a bric-a-brac cabinet and the door to the kitchen ("Slop Shoot") and was sipping my unspiked moonshine when who should saunter up to me but the voluptuous embodiment of cartoonist Rapp's character Bathless Bessie . . .

. . . a black-haired young woman in a wisp of tattered black dress, covering only enough to make her legal and with splashes of artificial dirt and grime that had been artistically applied onto that pale creamy skin (who had *that* job?).

We had not met, but I'd been around the St. John Theatre enough lately, talking to my stepmother about this and that, to know Bessie's real name was Misty Winters. Anyway, her stage name.

"Who are you supposed to be?" she asked, in a breathy, over-enunciated Marilyn Monroe–ish manner that must have taken some real effort.

"You're Bathless Bessie."

She had big dark blue eyes under thick black brows provided by God but shaped by somebody else, and a little wisp of a nose also given by God but with finishing touches by a plastic surgeon, and lush, full, moistly red-lipsticked lips on which God had collaborated with Max Factor.

"You're evading the question," she said. That's "quest-i-yun" in Marilyn-speak.

I touched the snap-brim in a little salute. "I'm supposed to be a detective. . . . Haven't you ever heard of Dick Tracy?"

"Dick Tracy wears a yellow hat."

"Maybe I'm color-blind."

The big blue eyes narrowed suspiciously. "Where's your trench-coat?"

I gestured vaguely across the comics-character-littered room.

"On the bed, with all the other coats and most of the hats. Too warm to wear indoors." I indicated the snap-brim again. "You don't really think I'd be rude enough to wear this indoors, if this wasn't my costume, do you?"

"You think you're funny."

"I am funny."

She arched an eyebrow and half smiled.

"You're smiling," I pointed out.

"Maybe I'm mocking you."

"I don't think so. I think you'd have moved on by now, if you weren't interested."

Half a smile blossomed into a full one that seemed about to let out a laugh and instead gave me: "Oh, you think I'm *interested*."

"I'm a detective. I can read the signs."

She sipped her punch. Pursed the full moist red lips. "Your *costume* is a detective's. You aren't *really* a detective."

"Sure I am. Want me to prove it?"

Both eyebrows went up now. "What, are you going to show me your gun?"

"My gun's at my apartment right now, but we can go over there."

She chuckled and shook her head, black locks bouncing off mostly exposed shoulders. "Try again."

"Okay. Prove I'm a detective. Let's see . . ." I put on a mulling face. ". . . your name is Misty Winters."

Her chin lifted, her eyes narrowed. "That one wasn't hard. I've been in two other Broadway shows."

I raised a finger. "Ah, but you were in the chorus. This is your first time with lines. Your real name is Ethel Schwartz and you hail from Bear Springs, Minnesota, where what you're wearing now may well be in fashion, for all I know."

She was really smiling now, and impressed, despite her best efforts. "What else do you know about me?"

"I know that I just lied, sort of."

"Oh?"

"Well, actually, I'm *sure* I lied."

Her eyes tightened; her forehead didn't furrow—like a lot of actresses, she had learned to minimize wrinkling. "Explain."

"I lied unless you recently went to court and made Misty Winters your legal name. Did you?"

"No. Someday maybe, but . . . no. Why?"

I shrugged. "Then your real name is Ethel Fizer. Your *married* name, I mean."

And I took a sip of punch and let her think about that.

"We're separated, Sam and I," she said, quietly. Then the volume came up a little: "None of this takes a detective to know. It's been in the columns."

"I know. I syndicate one of them."

Now her eyes widened. She shook a finger at me. "*I* know who you are!"

"Yeah, I'm a detective. Supposed to be."

She was grinning; she had nice teeth, on the large side but white and straight up top and crookedly attractive below, and this was a genuine Bear Springs grin, not some studied hip Broadway ironic facsimile.

"Jack Starr," she said confidently. "Maggie's stepkid!"

"Not really a kid. I have a driver's license and everything."

She leaned in accusingly; her nose was inches from mine, and it was one of the more pleasant accusations I've withstood. "You're not a detective! You run that syndicate with her! You sell comic strips to newspapers!"

As she backed confidently away, I admitted, "Right now I do, 'cause I'm sitting in for Maggie while she trods the boards. But normally Maggie runs the syndicate and I'm a kind of a . . ."

She leaned in again, our noses almost touching. "Pain in the keister?"

"No, I do that full time." My God those blue eyes were something; endlessly deep—you could dive in and forget to come up for air.

She backed away and my pulse rate steadied and she said, "How's that pay, being a full-time pain?"

"It's not my official title, or even my job description. I'm the vice president of the company—my late father, the major, founded it. Maggie inherited it."

Teasing but interested, she asked, "Why didn't Daddy leave it to Sonny?"

I shrugged. "Maybe because I was a wastrel or possibly a ne'er-do-well. One of those. Anyway, I straightened out. This punch? It's from the kiddie bowl."

Her eyes widened, just a little this time. "You don't drink? I don't drink, either."

"Why don't you?"

"Too many calories." She tapped her noodle. "And a girl in this business can use every brain cell she's got. What's your excuse, big he-man detective like you?"

"Not as good as yours. I used to drink too much—there's a certain medical condition you may have heard of. . . ."

"Alcoholism?"

"Falling-down drunk. Hard to believe, but I was once a spoiled rich kid who went to college and majored in booze."

Another eyebrow arched; she was ambidextrous that way. "And minored in necking?"

I grunted a laugh. "Too much booze to maintain a minor in anything. Then I went to war and wound up an MP and spent too much time throwing other drunken soldiers in the stockade to consider the hobby an appealing one anymore."

". . . War, huh? My older brothers were in the war."

"Did they make it out okay?"

"Yeah. Alive and well. Where did you serve, Pacific or Europe?"

"Oklahoma."

She giggled.

"Don't laugh," I said. "The Nazis never got past Tulsa. Let me ask you one."

"One what?"

"A personal question that's none of my business, like the last couple questions you asked me."

"Okay."

"What is Sam Fizer's wife . . . all right, *estranged* wife . . . doing taking a part in a play based on *Tall Paul*?"

Everybody in New York—almost everybody in America—knew the basic story: back in Depression days, fabulously successful syndicated cartoonist Sam Fizer had hired young unknown Hal Rapp as an assistant on the popular boxing strip *Mug O'Malley*, and a year later Rapp quit and started his own successful comic strip. The two artists had feuded ever since, often lampooning each other in their respective features.

"You *are* a detective."

"Naw. The Fizer/Rapp dustup is common knowledge. Like you said, it was in all the columns."

Her head tilted back. "How did Mrs. Sam Fizer get a part in Hal Rapp's play? By *trying out*, Jack, at an open audition."

The Marilyn over-enunciation was long gone by now. We were actually talking, Misty and me. Her breathiness remained, however—a quality of her alto, not an affectation, I was relieved to learn.

"I'm not kidding anybody," she went on. "I got a shape and a nice face and I can sing in key and don't trip over myself when it's time to do some simple dance, okay? But that describes half the girls on Broadway."

"And three-quarters of the girls in Hollywood."

She nodded; no argument there. "So I know I probably got this role 'cause Hal wanted to rub Sam's face in it. But I *got* the role, didn't I? And I'm doing fine."

Now it was my turn to nod. "I've sat out in the darkened theater, admiring your work."

She liked that. "You've been over to the St. John for some rehearsals?"

"I have. You're good, Misty. Funny as hell, and real easy on the eyes."

She gave me another Bear Springs grin. "Thanks. Couldn't ask for a better review, Jack."

"How is Sam taking it?"

She rolled the big blues. "Sam is livid. You do know what that means, don't you?"

"I could always look it up."

"It means white with rage."

"It also means red with rage."

She rolled them again. "Oh, first his face turns red, all right, but then white. Like a blister."

"Does that make you happy? Sad . . . ?"

She shook her head, black curls flying. "Listen, I gave three good years to Sam Fizer. I put up with more than you could ever guess—he's a mean, selfish little man who can be kind and generous, when he feels like it . . . but mostly he doesn't feel like it. He's paranoid and jealous and I will be divorcing his wealthy rear end very, very soon now."

"You were a Copa girl when you two met, right?"

"Right." She gave me a funny look, as if she weren't sure whether to smile or frown. "You said that like . . ."

"Like what?"

"Like it didn't matter."

"It doesn't matter."

She studied me. "You don't have a low opinion of good-looking women who make their money showing their legs and whatever?"

"I'm a big fan of good-looking women's legs and whatever. Anyway, remember, Maggie Starr's my stepmom."

"Oh. Yeah. That's right." She studied me some more, but with her face half turned, as if she could only risk one eye on me. ". . . That must be weird."

"Why?"

She nodded across the room toward Maggie, red hair piled endlessly up, a slimly shapely vision in a scarlet low-cut gown, talking to a couple of Broadway hillbillies over cups of Park Avenue moonshine. "Having a 'mom' who's a living doll like that."

I shook my head. "Not that way between us. We're business associates and it ends there."

This astonished Miss Winters. "Don't you like her?"

"I think she's aces. I just don't want to sleep with her."

"Why not?"

"Maggie's my stepmother."

She squinted, like she couldn't quite make me out. "Well, your father's dead, isn't he?"

"Yeah, over ten years, but—"

"So there's no law against it."

Now I squinted at her. "Listen, if you're interested in finding me a good-looking woman to sleep with, there's another way we could go here."

She chuckled and it was throaty, a kind of purr. "Don't get cocky, Jack. Say hi next time you drop by the theater."

And she hip-swayed off. I watched Misty Winters till she took the left turn into the adjacent room, and did my best to figure out if that was her natural gait, or if she was trying to impress me. Either way, she did.

Maggie came over, her own gait nicely swaying if diminished by the needs of the very tight, low-cut gown she was wearing. In the musical she played seductress Libidia Von Stackpole, whose gown was a shade of red the costumers had matched to Maggie's hair, a color that did not exist in nature unless you considered Lucille Ball's hair color natural.

"You two talked awhile," she said. Her voice had a throaty Lauren Bacall timber.

Let's get this out of the way: my stepmother, as you've no doubt gathered, was a knockout. Almost forty, she looked maybe thirty. Maybe. She'd have looked twenty-five if she hadn't been in full battle array, phony long eyelashes playing second fiddle to those incredible green eyes, face powder obscuring her freckles, her bee-stung mouth a scarlet kiss, like a calendar girl.

Right now she weighed 118 pounds. I knew that because that was her fighting weight. She rarely emerged in public if she was an ounce over 120, and currently any time away from the theater she was spending not in the office (where I could have used her) but in her private gym, working her lovely ass off, or I should say keeping her ass lovely.

The cut of the gown put half of her full bosom on uplift display, and those famous breasts seemed larger than they were on that slender five-foot-nine frame. I liked her better in no makeup and jeans. She was distracting, this way.

"You know who she is," I said, referring to my recent conversation partner.

She gave me the glamour-girl deadpan. "Of course I know who she is."

"I don't mean who she is in the musical, or at this costume party . . . I mean—"

The green eyes regarded me unblinkingly. "You mean, she's Sam Fizer's wife."

"They're separated."

One well-plucked eyebrow rose. "But not divorced. Did you pump her?"

"In front of God and everybody?"

No smile. "Did you pump her about her husband? His state of mind. You know—vis-à-vis the Starr Syndicate?"

We were in a potential jam with Sam, and that was no Dr. Seuss deal: *Mug O'Malley* was still our number-one comic strip, even though circulation was down from the war years. And Sam Fizer knew we were thinking of doing business with Hal Rapp, who had offered us a new strip, a sort of *Tall Paul* spin-off called *Lean Jean*.

"Listen, Maggie," I said, "you're over at that theater all day, rehearsing with Misty Winters. Why don't *you* get close to her, you want her pumped?"

"I had the oddest feeling she'd prefer to get close to you. Anyway, we aren't in any scenes together, except the Batch'ul Catch'ul Ballet, and we don't have lines."

Brother was she wrong; did they ever both have lines.

"All she said was, Sam is livid."

Her eyes widened, just a little. "Turning beet red, you mean?"

"Yeah, on Sundays for the color section. Daily, he turns white."

She got thoughtful, making the tiniest furrow between her eyes. "I don't know. Sometimes I think this was a mistake."

"Talking to Rapp about a new strip?"

She sighed, shook her head; her pile of red hair stayed in place. "No. Taking on this musical. I haven't been on Broadway in something like five years."

"Twelve. *Starr in Garter* was '41."

The green eyes drilled through me. "Thank you for the math lesson."

"Hey, what are vice presidents for?"

She put her hands on her hips, like Wonder Guy, except not at all like any guy. "One of the things they're for is keeping the peace where our talent is concerned."

"Nobody this side of Jehovah Himself could keep peace between Sam Fizer and Hal Rapp, and . . . Do you mean you wish you hadn't taken this Broadway role because it leaves *me* in charge of the syndicate? That's a low blow."

She touched my arm briefly, which was something of an event. "I didn't say that. We're a good team. You can't separate Martin from Lewis, you know."

"Sure you can. Martin sings, Lewis mugs. What did you mean?"

Both eyebrows went up. "You want to know the truth?"

"Sure."

Her voice was cold: "I weighed one-twenty-one this morning. Can't you see me bulge?"

"No comment."

"Damnit, I'm eating carrots and celery and working out three times a day and I'm not drinking anything but water . . ."

"And a gallon of coffee."

"But what calories are in that? And I'm at one-twenty-one."

I shuddered. "You know how I hate being seen in public with you, all fat and sloppy like this."

"Shut up. It's the role. I don't do anything but stand there and look glamorous."

"But you do that so well."

She shook her head again, slowly this time. "I've done that since

I was sixteen. But these chorus cuties are running and jumping and square-dancing, while I'm standing there polishing my nails and cracking wise."

"You do that well, too."

Her expression turned businesslike; funny how she could modulate what was basically a deadpan into so many shades. "Are you up for this?"

"What?"

"Finessing the situation."

"What situation would that be?"

She leaned in and, despite the noisy party around us, whispered: "Holding on to Sam Fizer as a client, *and* taking on Hal Rapp. Those two on the same roster is like booking Jack Benny and Fred Allen on the same radio show."

"That's a fake feud, Maggie. This is a real one. But, yeah, I'm a big boy. I'm up to it. I'll pander and get tough and everything in between. Because the big prize, if we're lucky enough to win it, is syndicating *Tall Paul*."

And *Tall Paul* was in a third again as many papers as *Mug O'Malley*, and was the hottest strip in the business, with a list that was growing, not shrinking.

"Well, let's start with pandering," Maggie said. "Here comes our host."

I was not the only one here who was cheating on the favorite-comic-strip-character-costume score, coming as myself and pretending to be Richard Tracy. Hal Rapp had also come as himself, in a yellow sportshirt and tan slacks and brown loafers; about five-ten, Rapp had India-ink hair and dark, cartoony slashes of eyebrow over laughing, squinty eyes, a Bob Hope–ish nose and a seemingly ever-present, infectious grin in an elongated oval face. He looked a little like Tall Paul, actually, if Tall Paul hadn't been an idiot.

Rapp moved with confidence for a man who was missing a leg—his left limb had been lost in a freak childhood accident—and his gait was herky-jerky, as he made his wooden leg do its duty.

"Ha ha ha," Rapp said, putting one hand on Maggie's bare shoulder and the other on my clothed one, "I've never seen a *finer*-looking mother and son."

It was a running gag that he pretended Maggie was my real mother. We played along.

"Yeah," I said, "I didn't stop breast-feeding till I was eleven."

Maggie pretended not to be amused, and Rapp roared.

"Listen, this is a *great* shindig, isn't it?" he said, gesturing. "*Everybody* came!"

As if the cast of Tall Paul had any choice. But he was right: a Saturday night in Manhattan was not spent foolishly, and any number of celebrities were present.

Candace "Candy" Cain, the lovely blonde playing Sunflower Sue (at the St. John *and* this party), had even lassoed her popular comedian husband Charlie Mazurki into coming. Dressed as the comic strip kid Henry, including a bald cap (but incongruously retaining Mazurki's trademark mustache and ever-present Havana), the droll, sleepy-eyed, surrealistic comic stayed at his knockout bride's side, standing protective watch.

"Did you see Mel *Norman?*" Rapp asked, referring to the director of the show, a Hollywood veteran making his dream of doing a Broadway show come true, thanks to *Tall Paul*. "He showed up as Dennis the *Menace*, ha ha ha, right down to the *slingshot!*"

Rapp was a commanding presence, and his style of speech was oddly hypnotic and as herky-jerky as his gait. He overemphasized words, sometimes seemingly inappropriate ones, like the bold-faced bursts of text in his comic strip, a graphic technique he used to attract attention to the feature on the funnies page. Right now he was lighting up—like Krane, using a cigarette holder. Like me, he didn't drink.

"So where's your *costume*, Jack?" Rapp demanded jovially.

"Can't you see the hat? I'm Dick Tracy."

"*I* would have guessed Kerry *Drake*, ha ha ha. How do you like *my* selection?"

I said, "You came as your favorite fictional character—yourself."

He grinned within a wreath of his own cigarette smoke. "And *how*, pray tell, Jack, just how do I *justify* that?"

"First, it's your party and you can damn well dress as you please. Second, you write and draw yourself into the strip, at least twice a year."

"*Yes!* Paul and Sunflower Sue and Mammy May and, ha ha ha, Pitiful Pa come into my *studio* and *insist* I draw them out of their latest *scrape* . . . and I tell 'em they're *on* their *own!*"

"Life is hard for us comics characters," I admitted.

"Listen, Maggie," Rapp said, smoke pluming from his nostrils, "I've been *wanting* to bend your *ear*."

Maggie's expression turned businesslike again because she, like me, thought this meant he was going to get into the *Lean Jean* comic strip we were negotiating with him.

"I always *admired* you on the *stage*," he said with a good-natured leer. "I saw you at *Minsky's* when we were both *kids*—I was too *young* to get in *legally*, and nothing *you* were doing, ha ha ha, was even *vaguely* legal."

"Right," Maggie said, with remarkable patience.

"But when you were on Broadway, in *Starr in Garter*," he said, "and when you did your *nightclub* routine, everywhere from Vegas to Hollywood to Tucumcari, ha ha ha, you had *such* a satirical *touch*."

"Well, thank you. That was the point."

"Otherwise it would just be *bump* and *grind*, ha ha ha, but you transcend the form. Why I bring this *up* is I've taken some barbs from little Miss *Cain* over there and her, ha ha ha, illustrious husband, the *intellectual's* answer to Groucho *Marx*."

I said, "I always thought Groucho Marx was the intellectual's answer to Groucho Marx."

Rapp snorted. "Come to think of it, I didn't know Groucho Marx was a *question*, ha ha ha . . . but Maggie, dear . . . I've been told the book just isn't *satirical* or *sharp* enough."

By "book" he meant the script for the musical, which he'd written himself; the music and lyrics had been provided by a top Hollywood team who director Norman had brought aboard.

Maggie said, "I disagree—I think you take on all the usual *Tall Paul* sacred cows—big business and government and advertising and the rest."

His smile blossomed into an ear-to-ear affair. "Well *thank* you, dear, *thank* you, because I *admit* I may have relied more on *slapstick* than satire. It's this goddamned *McCarthy* nonsense, *blacklisting* and what have you, these nincompoops make it seem *unpatriotic* to lampoon *America*, when we all know there's *nothing* more patriotic, ha ha ha, than making *fun* of your *leaders*."

I said, "It's a hilarious show. The strip jumps right out of the funny pages onto the stage."

Not pandering. Much.

"Can I *quote* you in the ads, Jack, ha ha ha . . . but look at what *Fizer's* doing in that *imbecile* comic strip you syndicate—his boxer doesn't get in the *ring* anymore, instead he dukes it out with *Commies*, who he, ha ha ha, finds under the *nearest* bed."

"We've noticed the shift, of course," Maggie said.

"Hard to *believe*," Rapp said, as if sorrowful and not gloating, "that Fizer used to be an FDR *liberal*—now this *conservative* nonsense he's wrapped himself *up* in, along with the *flag*, of course."

I said, "Hal, Mr. Fizer is on our talent roster. I may agree with you—you'll have to read between the lines for that—but I don't think it's right to discuss the content of one strip with the creator of another."

"Creator of *another* strip *also* on your list? Not yet, Jack. Not yet. But, ha ha ha, I'm *pretty* sure it will be. I like the way you stand up to *authority*, Jack, even, ha ha ha, when that authority is *me*. . . . Excuse me."

The door buzzer was making itself known over the din. Our host kissed Maggie on the cheek, patted my shoulder and disappeared into the throng of guests, navigating effectively on the artificial limb as he made his way toward the front door.

"Did I piss him off?" I asked Maggie.

She was watching him go, as well. "I don't think so. He's too much of a gadfly himself to take offense. Anyway, he was just answering the buzzer."

"Little late for trick-or-treaters—or a new guest, either. What is it, ten o'clock? Everybody else was here an hour ago, or more. . . ."

I gazed over the heads of assorted comic-strip characters and saw Rapp in the entryway at the door, where a small man in a white shirt and bow tie was speaking quickly and gravely.

"Maybe it is a trick-or-treater, at that," I said. "That may be no goblin, but it definitely is a ghost. . . ."

The new arrival was Murray Coe, officially Sam Fizer's assistant, more accurately his "ghost" artist. That Fizer drew almost none of his own strip was the worst-kept secret in comics.

Maggie said, "Sam Fizer's assistant, at a Hal Rapp party? How unlikely is that? And he's not in costume, either, unless he's come as the Timid Soul."

"Fizer has his studio and apartment just one floor down," I reminded Maggie. Another irony in a situation fraught with the stuff: Rapp and Fizer were neighbors of sorts in these Waldorf towers.

Then Rapp came threading back through toward us, proving that his smile wasn't ever-present after all, because that was one long, drawn-out somber mug he was suddenly wearing.

Again he positioned himself between us, and stared right at me. His face looked like melting putty.

"You're a kind of *cop*, aren't you, Jack?" he asked.

"Licensed private investigator." With one client: the Starr Syndicate. "Why?"

Now his smile returned, but it was flickery and nervous, as if it were shorting in and out. "I think *you* should handle this, Jack. . . ."

Maggie asked, "What's happened, Hal?"

"There's been a suicide or a killing or . . . Could you go down there with *Murray*, and check it out?"

"Okay," I said. "Don't call anybody yet, not the desk or the cops, either. Let me handle that."

He nodded emphatically and a dark comma of black hair tumbled down onto his forehead. "I'm in your hands, Jack. . . . Maggie, maybe you oughta go with Jack and Murray."

She frowned at him curiously. "You're not coming?"

"I . . . I need to stay up here. I shouldn't be *seen* down there."

"Down where?" she asked.

But I knew.

"Down in Sam's suite," Rapp said. "Sam Fizer?"

As if we'd been thinking he meant some *other* Sam. . . .

The Starr Syndicate's business relationship with cartoonist Hal Rapp had begun only a few days before—Monday to be exact.

I'd been manning the woman-in-charge's desk for just over a month. The *Tall Paul* musical had been doing its pre-Broadway stint on the road, starting in Washington, D.C., and moving on to Boston. That run ended Saturday night, with only days of rehearsal in New York remaining before preview performances.

Sunday evening, coming down by train, Maggie had returned to Manhattan, and to the Starr Building; but we'd spent only forty-five minutes together, having dinner in her private alcove in the Strip Joint.

The Strip Joint, by the way, is the restaurant Maggie owns, having refused to renew the lease of the Chinese restaurant that had been in that space when we moved in. Maggie used to have a yen for Chinese food, till said restaurant served her up a fingernail in an egg roll. She replaced her evicted tenants with a steak house and bar, hiring a chef from St. Louis who almost never included fingernails in his recipes.

Surprisingly, in a town as wide open as Manhattan—I've already mentioned the sleazy, cheesy nature of much of nearby Broadway—the long-ago ban on stripteasing, courtesy of Mayor La Guardia, remained in force. So Maggie, in a typically astute combination of compassion and business sense, hired New York–based striptease artistes to work as waitresses at the Strip Joint, when they weren't on the road raising the artistic awareness of their mostly male audiences.

In addition, retired strippers from Manhattan were hired as permanent staff—some of these ancient retirees were all of thirty or even thirty-five—so you might guess (and you'd be right) that the Strip Joint was a popular lunch spot for businessmen. Don't get the impression that the waitstaff served in pasties and G-strings—strictly black tie, white shirts and black tuxedo pants. But in the bar at the front of the place, fairly racy photos of these same women did adorn the walls.

Not that the Strip Joint didn't attract families and tourists—opening night in '42, Maggie had invited many of the most famous cartoonists in America to dine on her, imposing on them only to decorate the walls of the rear restaurant area with grease-pencil renditions of their famous characters: Dick Tracy, Little Orphan Annie, Nancy and Sluggo, Wonder Guy, Alley Oop, Mug O'Malley, and many more. And anytime cartoonists visited the Starr Syndicate offices upstairs, they were encouraged to stop downstairs for a free drink or meal and to add a new addition to the comic art gallery.

On top of this, the Strip Joint served up the best strip steak in town, doing steady business, lunch, dinner, after-theater. The darn place turned a profit. Still, I suspected Maggie got in the restaurant game so she could quietly sneak downstairs during her not-infrequent reclusive phases; she didn't keep a cook on staff, after all, and was hardly known for her prowess in the kitchen.

By the way, here's a little geography lesson: the Starr Building is a six-story brick structure on Forty-second Street a block and a half off Broadway. Street-level is the restaurant, the first floor houses the editorial offices of the syndicate (eight employees), the second floor is distribution and sales (twelve employees), the third is given over to my digs, the fourth includes a reception area, Maggie's office and her private gym, while the fifth is Madame Starr's suite of rooms.

While we're doing this, I might as well give you the office layout—the long, narrow dark-paneled room has a parquet floor with an Oriental rug; a wall of leather-bound classics provides a library feel, made less stuffy thanks to framed posters of Maggie's trio of Hollywood movies, burlesque bills she'd headlined (above Abbott and Costello in one case) and other stripper-a-bilia. A dignified portrait of my pudgy papa, the major, resided on the rear wall above some filing cabinets, while at the other end of the room, behind Maggie's desk, a full-figure fancy-framed pastel portrait of herself in feathers and glittery stuff loomed over her desk—which she kept obsessively neat, piles of this and piles of that. The desk was cherrywood and about the size of a twelve-burner stove.

But the office wasn't where we were meeting, which was good, because I kept a somewhat messier desktop—aftermath-of-a-hurricane messier. We confabbed instead in that little private dining room at the rear of the Strip Joint, a compact space just big enough for a table that could sit no more than six.

This alcove was decorated—one per wall—with framed black-and-white portraits of Maggie, no stripper schtick, strictly glamour poses, mostly shoulders up. If she was entertaining a guest or guests (I did not count), a single signature rose might grace a slender vase on the linen cloth.

No rose that Sunday night.

I sat with Maggie (in jeans and plaid shirt and recently washed hair in a turbaned-up towel—her, not me) and we talked as I dug into a rare strip steak, a baked potato with butter, sour cream and chives and a side of onion rings (a boy needs his vegetables). She was poking at a salad that might have delighted Bugs Bunny, but nobody else I can think of. Not even any dressing—if Maggie had been as bare at the end of her act as those lettuce leaves, she'd have still been in jail.

It wasn't like we'd been out of touch—a nightly long-distance call had become de rigueur, with Maggie on the road. But just to be polite, pretending we were catching up, I said, "The critics love you."

She had no makeup on, not even a dab of lipstick; in her natural freckle-faced state, she looked like a teenager. "In Washington they did. They loved the whole show, all of the songs, everything about it and everybody in it, even a fat old hag like me."

That was where I was supposed to say, "Nonsense—you look great."

"Nonsense," I said. "You look great."

The green eyes rose from the salad to shoot daggers. "And in Boston—did I tell you about that one review?"

"Yeah." I gnawed at an onion ring. "Guy loved it—just said the show ran a little long."

"Long? He suggested the audience pack a lunch." She shuddered. "Some nasty things on the horizon."

"Oh?"

"I can almost guarantee Lucille's going to lose her song." Lucille Rayburn was a very funny actress playing the diminutive Mammy May. "And one of Candy Cain's numbers is bound to go. Those two keep making the mistake of asking the director what their motivation is."

"And right now *his* motivation is to come up with a shorter show."

"Half an hour shorter." She chewed salad and allowed herself a swallow. "Thankfully I don't have a song to cut. But it will be brutal this week. We start previews before you know it, and open the week after that."

We ate in silence for perhaps a minute.

"Listen," I said, "has Hal Rapp been around much?"

She shrugged. "He caught the show in Washington, D.C. Said he adored it—you could hear his cackle in the audience a mile away. He's given the director carte blanche to cut and revise the book, you know."

"Really?" I sipped my drink, a rum and Coke without the rum. "He's that cavalier about it?"

She raised an eyebrow; without eye goo, those green lamps were something. "He seems mostly interested in putting the make on the girls in the chorus. He's a lovable letch, our Mr. Rapp."

"Has he bothered you?"

"A woman my size? My age?"

This was where I was supposed to say, "Don't be silly. You are young and beautiful."

But all I mustered was, "Don't be silly." May have hurt her feelings.

"I only bring this up," I said, after enjoying a bite of rare steak, "because he called and made an appointment through Bryce."

She frowned, eyes tight, forehead smooth. "Who did?"

"Hal Rapp."

"What *kind* of appointment?"

I shrugged. "He asked to see me. Didn't specify, but a guy running a comic strip syndicate doesn't exactly turn Hal Rapp away."

Both eyebrows went up. "Is that what you're doing? Running a syndicate? I told you just to keep my desk clear and keep things moving."

Well, I'd done the latter, but was hoping she didn't actually take the time to step into her office and see how I'd done on the former.

"I merely wondered," I said, "if you knew what it was about. . . ."

We ate in silence some more.

Then she said, "You mentioned Bryce. How is he?"

Bryce was the former Broadway dancer who some years back, after suffering an injury, had become Maggie's major domo around the office; he was handsome, bearded, prone to black clothing, with a persona somewhere between Satan and Joan Crawford, if there's a difference.

"Oh, he's *thrilled* to be stuck at his reception desk," I said archly, "when you're going to be over at the St. John Theatre, starring in a new musical. Why don't you take him with you, and let him do your hair or something?"

"Just because Bryce is gay," she said with regal condescension, "that doesn't mean he is a hairdresser. That's a dreadful cliche, and you know it."

I bit into another onion ring, and talked and chewed, just to annoy her a little. "What's dreadful is what you show people are doing to the perfectly respectable word 'gay.' "

She smiled icily. "Yes. Why couldn't we have just stayed civilized and stuck with 'queer' or 'fairy.' "

"Whatever happened to 'fop'? I always kind of liked that one. . . . You should take Bryce with you. He's your personal assistant, isn't he?"

Green eyes flashed. "What, and leave *you* in charge? . . . No, Mr. Rapp said nothing to me about anything regarding business, and we sat together in the theater in D.C. several times and chatted. He did rest his hand on my shoulder a few times and once on my thigh, which I decided to take as a compliment."

"You should ride the subway. You'd get lots of compliments. What if he pitches a strip?"

She shook her head, and the towel turban almost toppled. "That won't happen. It's not exactly like he can bring *Tall Paul* to us—he's been with Unique Features since 1934."

"I know. Plus he writes *Amy and Slip* for King Features with Van Allen drawing. How does he do it?"

She shrugged. "I think he considers himself mostly a writer. He has those two assistants out on Long Island who do almost all of the drawing these days."

We both knew this was not unusual in the world of comics.

"No," Maggie said, in her *I'm-never-wrong* voice, "Hal is just dropping by Starr to pay his respects, because the musical's opening and I'm in it. After all, he *knows* we distribute *Mug O'Malley* . . ."

"By Sam Fizer," I said, "his fiendish foe." Work in comics long enough, you start to sound like the comics.

". . . and Hal probably just wants us to know that even though we do business with Mug O'Malley's maker, Tall Paul's papa bears us no grudge."

"Fine." I cut meat. "What if he offers us a new strip?"

"You're just filling my chair. Don't overstep."

"I promise. But what if he offers us a new strip?"

"He will not offer us a new strip."

The next morning, Hal Rapp, in that drag-a-leg-along gait so at odds with his exuberantly confident manner, was accompanied by man-in-black Bryce to the wine-colored tufted leather visitor's chair opposite Maggie's desk, behind which I stood at the moment, grinning like a goof at my famous guest . . . knowing that the brown-paper-wrapped package he bore was exactly the shape of original daily comic strip art.

"*Jaaack,*" Rapp said, in that familiar nasal voice. He wore a beautifully tailored brown pinstripe suit with a matching vest, pale yellow shirt and brown striped tie. Saville Row, I would say. "Ha ha ha, you must feel pretty *uneasy*, with your mother looking over your *shoulder* like that."

He meant the huge framed portrait behind me.

"Mr. Rapp," I said, since I really only knew the cartoonist from National Cartoonists Society events and other social occasions, "you know very well Maggie is my stepmother. Otherwise, she'd've had to be ten when she bore me."

"*That* woman doesn't *bore* anybody, ha ha ha." He gazed up at the pastel, which was the size of a dining-room table standing on end, with the leaves in. "That's a Rolf *Armstrong*, isn't it?"

"Yes."

"Fine artist." He hadn't sat down yet; Bryce hovered waiting for our guest to do so, and looking irritated about it (but he'd been looking irritated about everything for weeks).

Rapp was saying, "*Back* when illustration had its *place* in this country, men like Armstrong were *gods*. Not like this *abstract* art of today—a product of the *untalented*, ha ha ha, sold by the *unprincipled*, ha ha ha, to the *utterly* bewildered."

I'd heard him say that before, on a television show, but I chuckled like it was fresh.

"Take a look at *these*, Jack," he said, and dropped the brown-paper-wrapped package on the desk.

He sat, the wooden leg squeaking a little. With both hands, he arranged his good leg to cross his artificial one.

Hands clasped behind his back, Bryce leaned in and asked, "Mr. Rapp, may I get you anything? We have coffee ready, soft drinks, a fairly complete bar?"

"No, no, *thank* you, *thank* you. Too kind, too kind."

Bryce nodded and exited, without bothering to see if I might be dying of thirst or anything; he was on a major pout.

I was already seated, unwrapping Rapp's package, and saw—in the twice-up size common with original comic art—samples of two weeks of a daily comic strip labeled *Lean Jean*. The setting, like *Tall Paul*, was backwoods, though none of the familiar Catfish

Holler characters were present. The art was slightly more realistic than Rapp's norm, which was explained by a credit box that included both Rapp's name and that of Lou Roberts, the latter an old pro who been an artist on such established strips as *Tarzan* and *Secret Agent X-9*.

"*Read!*" Rapp insisted, eyes glittering. "Read."

I read the strips. The "gal" was the opposite of Tall Paul, who hated women; she was a hillbilly lass whose mammy had kept her isolated from men until her eighteenth birthday, and now she was boy crazy, to her mammy's dismay.

The ponytailed brunette, Lean Jean, was tall but not willowly—she had the same kind of voluptuous pinup shape as the "gals" in *Tall Paul*.

The samples were funny and exciting, Rapp's patented combination of cornpone humor, social satire and hair-raising adventure. Like Tall Paul in the early days of the famous strip, Lean Jean was heading into the big city; unlike Tall Paul, she was pursuing the man of her dreams, who unbeknownst to her was a multimillionaire, who'd gone hiking incognito in the Ozarks. As the second week of dailies ended, Lean Jean—who had never seen a highway—was crossing one, a cement truck bearing down upon her.

"That's kind of a *specialty* of mine," Rapp said, gesturing, "the *innocent* in the *metropolis*. Like Tall Paul, Jean will be a picaresque novel in pictures—*Candide* in black and white, ha ha ha, and color on *Sunday*. You are *familiar* with Voltaire, aren't you, Jack?"

"He should have kept working with Ginger Rogers," I said, not giving a damn what high-minded goals Rapp was shooting for in the strip—I knew it was a winner, beautiful women, funny gags, cliffhanger endings and the Hal Rapp imprimatur.

"*Well?*" Rapp asked, leaning forward, eyes eager. "Do you *like* it?"

"What's not to like?" I met his gaze. "Can you deliver another strip? Doesn't this make three?"

He sat back, shrugging elaborately. "Well, *frankly*, Jack, that's *my* problem, isn't it?"

I shook my head. "Not if we sell this to two hundred papers, which incidentally we could do by a week from today, and you can't make deadline."

He pointed to the strips, curling on the desk. "You're *familiar* with this boy *Roberts's* work, right?"

This "boy" Roberts was maybe five years younger than Rapp.

"Yeah," I said. "He's pitched in on any number of long-running strips who lost artists. And he's ghosted lots of big strips. He's very good. How much would you be involved yourself?"

He waved a dismissive hand. "All the writing. The layouts. I'll ink the faces—pretty much what I do on *Tall Paul* except there I do most of the inking of figures, too."

Pretty standard stuff for a stellar comics feature. More went into the process than most people knew: after scripting, comic strips were drawn in pencil and then inked; the Sunday pages were also done in black and white, with the color applied by the artist or an assistant to a photostat for the printer's reference.

"Well, it's a great property," I said. "Obviously we're interested."

Half a smile dug a groove in the famous face; a comma of Tall

Paul–esque black hair drooped down his forehead. "Two *hundred* papers, Jack? Is that all *Starr* could *manage*, you think?"

"That's what I know we could manage." I sat forward. "You see, any paper already running *Tall Paul* is unlikely to pick this up."

"But the *competition* will!"

Most major cities had at least two papers; plus, some towns had morning and evening papers from the same publisher—*Des Moines Register* in the morning, for instance, *Des Moines Tribune* in the afternoon. One might run *Tall Paul*, the other *Lean Jean*.

"Yes," I admitted, "but are you prepared to piss off some current clients? Take Chicago—you think the *Sun Times*, running *Tall Paul*, would love you for giving the *Tribune Lean Jean*?"

He shrugged grandly. "That's Unique *Features's* problem, isn't it, Jack? And, ha ha ha, it *couldn't* happen to a *nicer* bunch of *thieves*."

I did wish Maggie were here; I was out of my depth. "Is this new strip designed to get back at Unique? You're . . . *unhappy* there?"

With both hands, he uncrossed the leg and he sat forward and the normally smiling face now wore a scowl that I'd last seen on a villain in *Tall Paul*.

"Jack," he said, "I've been *screwed* by those bastards for almost *twenty* years, and I've had my *goddamn* fill. They could at least, ha ha ha, offer me a postcoital *smoke* now and then!"

I squinted at him, as if that would improve my understanding of this situation. "What's your complaint with Unique?"

"For *all* these *years* I've had the, ha ha ha, same *lousy* terms

I negotiated when I was a *wet*-behind-the-ears *kid*. It's a fifty/fifty split, which I *know*, I *know*, is standard. But it's a *net* split, Jack, not gross, although it is grossly *unfair*, as they've been *killing* from the *start* on the *expenses* they levy against *Tall Paul* and me."

"What about licensing?"

That meant comic books, toys, radio, movies, whatever— including the musical Maggie was costarring in. (God! Don't tell her I said "*co*starring.")

"They get *half* of that, *too*," he said, and shook his head bitterly. "But they can't *screw* me in the accounting as easily in *that* department, ha ha ha, and we've been *very* lucky on that end of things. We had a motion *picture* in the '40s, you'll recall, terrible, terrible, but profitable, profitable, and a *radio* show and all sorts of *comic* books and games and puzzles. And I won't *lie* to you: I made a *fortune* off the Shlomozel."

The Shlomozel was a mystical little wish-granting banjo-shaped critter that had first appeared in *Tall Paul* about five years ago, and had taken the country by storm—generating dolls and clocks and soap and just about anything you could imagine. (The actual continuity in the strip had ended with typical Rapp dark satire, however, with the Shlomocide Squad shooting the generous little critters for fouling up capitalism.)

"Then why spit in Unique's eye?" I asked. "They've made money, but so have you."

He grinned and it was devilish, eyes sparkling. "They made *one* mistake, twenty years ago, when they signed me. Like *any* fool in my position, I sold the strip to them, lock, stock and barrel. But when they tried to sign me to a lifetime contract to write and draw it, like they offered Faust, ha ha ha, I dodged the *bullet*. Jack—my *contract* is up next *year*."

The back of my neck began to tingle. "Meaning . . . ?"

"Let's put it *this* way," he said, with cosmic smugness, "Unique Features owning *Tall Paul* without having me under contract, ha ha ha, is like CBS having the rights to do the *I Love Lucy* show, *without* Lucille Ball *or* Desi Arnaz."

"Unique could find a ghost. . . ."

He nodded emphatically. "They can find people who can *draw* the thing—they could hire my own *assistants*, if they, ha ha ha, waved enough *money* around. But who could *write* it?"

"*Terry and the Pirates* is doing okay without Milton Caniff," I said, referring to a similar situation where an artist had walked, leaving his famous creation behind him.

"Yes," Rapp granted. "An adventure strip that's being adequately continued. But consider two things—Milton is doing better with his *new* strip, *Steve Canyon*, than his old syndicate's doing with its pale-shadow *Terry*."

"True. What's the other thing?"

He beamed with sinister confidence, gesturing to himself with both hands. "Hal Rapp *is Tall Paul*. Could you imagine *Krazy Kat* continuing without George Herriman?"

"No." In fact it had folded, a classic strip that was uniquely the creation of a singular artistic vision.

"How about *Pogo* without Walt Kelly? *Dick Tracy* without Chester Gould, *Annie* without Harold Gray? This kid *Schulz*— already you can tell this *Peanuts* is his alone. A *handful* of us are so *ingrained* with our creations, our personalities so *interwoven*, that those creations cannot *breathe* without us. I'm the *brain* of that strip, and its beating *heart*, and Unique *knows* it."

He was right.

I asked, "So what are you going to do?"

Now Rapp's smile took on a pixieish cast, the eyes sparkling. "If you'll *help* me, I'll hedge my *bets*."

"How?"

He flipped a hand. "We'll *start* with Starr syndicating *Lean Jean*. I won't *wait* a year like Milton did with *Canyon*—I'll have *my* replacement strip, ha ha ha, *already* running in *hundreds* of papers."

"All right . . ."

He flipped the other hand. "Then when my contract is up with Unique . . . I'll *refuse* to sign."

I thought about that. "What would happen then?"

"One of *several* things—Unique could offer a *new* contract, *extremely* favorable to me, giving *me* ownership of *Tall Paul*, granting them, perhaps, another, ha ha ha, *ten* years."

That was unlikely. Syndicates just didn't make deals like that. We were small enough that we might have considered it, but the big boys like Unique and King Features and the *Chicago Tribune–New York News* Syndicate? Not a chance.

"*Another* possibility," he said, his tone falsely light, "is that they continue *without* me, and fail *dismally*, ha ha ha . . . while *you* sell *Lean Jean*, the genuine Rapp article, to *every* paper dropping the cheap imitation."

I nodded, liking the sound of that.

But he wasn't finished. "Then, when *Tall Paul* is in enough *trouble*," he said, "I'll do what I *always* do, ha ha ha—get him *out* of it. I, or you, or we, will go to Unique and *buy* the property back . . . and *Starr* will syndicate it."

That I loved the sound of. "What about *Lean Jean*?"

"What *about* her? You'll have *two* top strips, and *I'll* have an income, ha ha ha, that would make *Croesus* green with envy."

I was thinking of somebody who would be green with envy, all right, but his name wasn't Croesus.

"Hal," I said, gently, "you have to've noticed there's an elephant in the room."

He shrugged like an Arabian carpet seller making a concession at a bazaar. "Sure. A short, fat, *obnoxious* one named Sam Fizer."

I sighed. "The Starr Syndicate goes back almost to its beginnings with Sam and *Mug O'Malley*. The major bought that strip, after Fizer himself went out and sold it to thirty papers, and it practically *made* the syndicate. We're not without a certain sense of loyalty."

"Understood." He arched a cartoonish black eyebrow. "But hasn't Sam's strip *slipped*?"

"Somewhat," I allowed. "This anti-Communist tear he's off on doesn't sit with the more liberal editors, and he's been dropped here and there."

Rapp grunted. "Over a *hundred* heres and theres, I hear."

"But that still leaves a list of five hundred dailies and three hundred Sundays. It's a big strip. Still our biggest. We can't afford to antagonize him."

His eyes narrowed to slits. "You'd let Sam *Fizer* reject my strip?"

"No. I think a relationship with you would be healthy for

Starr Syndicate, Hal—I believe *Lean Jean* could do very well, and the prospect of winding up with *Tall Paul*, down the road . . ."

"Currently in *eight* hundred dailies and *five* hundred Sundays."

"I know. I know. But I need to talk to Maggie, and I'm sure she . . . we . . . will want to talk to Sam. I don't want him hearing about this from anybody but us—not you, Hal, not Winchell or Ed Sullivan or even Eiful. That would be a deal breaker. Understood?"

He nodded with enthusiasm. "Understood. Business is business." Then he shrugged. "But you and Maggie should *know* something—Sam Fizer is *not* a *stable* man."

"Hal . . ."

"This isn't the twenty-five-dollar-a-week *assistant* that monster treated like a *slave* talking—it's a cartoonist who has some *inside* information that you *don't*."

I studied him. "You're saying you have inside info about Fizer's mental health?"

Describing that smile as smug was like saying the *Mona Lisa* was a pretty fair painting. "Let's just say he's *not* the horse you want to *back* in this race. I can't say more. I have to be *discreet*."

I shifted in Maggie's chair. "Look . . . I understand your bitterness. Everybody in the business knows Fizer's been going around bad-mouthing you to editors—"

His eyes and nostrils flared. "*More* than *editors*! He's been showing selected *panels* from my strip to *legislators*—this New York state legislative inquiry into comics and juvenile delinquence, you *know* about that, Jack? Telling them *Tall Paul* is smut, and . . . well, I'm just giving you a *word* to the, ha ha ha, *wise*— he's dug himself a *hell* of a *hole*."

"Comics are coming under fire," I said, gesturing with open palms. "Obviously. But it's mostly comic *books*, not strips, getting the slam. Still, nobody in this business appreciates Sam going around denigrating another cartoonist and his strip, no matter what bad blood may be between them."

I figured Rapp would take the bait, but he was frowning and shaking his head. "I can't say any more about the subject. I'd *love* to, ha ha ha, *believe* me! But I just *can't*."

I sat up. "Listen, maybe Maggie can make peace between you two. I know, after all these years, it might seem—"

"Too late for that."

I tried again: "What if Maggie and I meet with him, discourage him from these attacks on you and your good name and—"

He raised a traffic cop's palm. "I appreciate the *thought*, Jack. But you *really* don't need to bother. Sam Fizer isn't *going* to be a problem much longer."

No smug, self-satisfied "ha ha has" had interrupted those words, surprisingly.

I asked, "No problem for you?"

"No problem for *anybody*." He smiled in a friendly if businesslike manner. "*So*, Jack—are you *interested* in the new strip?"

"Sure. Of course. I'll show it to Maggie right away."

He tilted his head, raised a hand. "I can walk it over to King Features—"

"We *are* interested. You'll have a decision this week."

"Good." He grinned, eyes twinkling. "Could make a nice *publicity* splash, ha ha ha, around the opening of the *musical*."

"Sure could."

We chatted awhile about the show, and he said many compli-
mentary things about Maggie, most of them vaguely suggestive,
and finally he got himself to his feet, or foot anyway, and we
shook hands. His grasp was firm. I may never have met anybody
more confident.

After Rapp had gone, Bryce came in and stood before my desk
like a bearded Greek chorus of one, to let me know what was really going on.

"He's a *loathsome* creature," Bryce said.

"I rather like him," I said. "But I don't disagree, really. A guy
like that, so talented but with such a handicap . . ."

"You mean," Bryce said dryly, "his inflated ego?"

"I mean he lost his leg when was a kid. All that confidence, that
nervous laughter . . . he tries a little too hard to make up for it."

"Now there's an idea."

"What?"

He placed a finger alongside a bearded cheek. "A new column
for the Starr Syndicate to distribute, all across this great land—
*Dime-Store Psychology*, by Dr. Jack Starr. You can buy a doctor-
ate over on Broadway, you know—next door to the flea circus."

I suggested that Bryce do something physically impossible,
though he seemed to be considering it as he went out.

Then I just sat there at Maggie's desk, with her picture looking
over my shoulder, as I wondered how Hal Rapp could be so sure
his longtime enemy, Sam Fizer—one of America's most popular
comic strip artists—would soon no longer be a problem.

To Rapp.

Or anybody.

Jack Dempsey's Restaurant on the west side of Broadway between Forty-ninth and Fiftieth streets was touted as the "Meeting Place of the World." And this was where comic strip boxer Mug O'Malley's papa, Sam Fizer, had wanted us to meet for lunch, when I called asking, a day after Hal Rapp had made his *Lean Jean* pitch.

Even though the Strip Joint was just downstairs from my office, and I could just sign for whatever chow and drinks we blew through, I said yes to Fizer's request. I knew he took real pleasure eating at Dempsey's, where he could play the boxing world star.

I got there first, stepping in from the crisp October weather, and was greeted by Dempsey himself, who rose from his window booth at the left as you came in, to extend a hand the size of a frying pan.

"Hiya, pally!" he said in that familiar, squeaky tenor so at odds with his intimidating physique.

"Good to see you, Jack."

He and the major had been friends; I'd been Dempsey's "pally" since I was shorter than a fire hydrant. In his late fifties now, the champ still had his blue-black hair, and the dark blue eyes had no punch-drunk film over them, set as they were in the high cheekbones and under thick, arching eyebrows.

No maitre d' at Dempsey's—a good enough restaurant, but not that kind of place. If anybody sat you, it was the champ himself, looking quietly dapper today in a blue suit and blue-and-red-striped tie; but he didn't necessarily have to know you, as he had me and my father, to do so—you might just be a teenager whose grandpa saw Dempsey fight Gibbons in Shelby, Montana, or an old boy from Dallas who'd heard the first Tunney fight on the radio.

Dempsey chatted with me while I checked my trench coat and snap-brim, then ushered me into the spacious dining room with its linen-covered tables and over to the prime real estate of a red-leather booth underneath the colorful if fading James Montgomery Flagg mural of my host knocking out Jess Willard in 1919.

The room wasn't full yet—it was noon now and the place had just opened—but other booths were already taken by sportswriters, managers and fighters who were enjoying Dempsey's standard boxing-pro discount, a shrewd move that kept the restaurant brimming with gawking tourists. The ventilation was good in there, otherwise all those cigarettes and cigars would have created a blue-gray fog.

"By yourself today, pally?" Dempsey asked, raising thick fingers to summon me a waiter.

"No," I said. "Sam Fizer's meeting me."

"We got an original page from *Mug O'Malley* framed in the bar, y'know," he said with a grin and nod in that direction. "From the first time he stuck me in the strip."

Fizer made a point of putting real boxers and boxing-world celebrities into *Mug O'Malley*.

"I'm sure that pleases Sam," I said.

"Oh, I know it does. He always mentions it. . . . Bring Mr. Starr a Coca-Cola with a twist of lime, on ice." He was talking to a gray-haired red-vested waiter now.

I had to wonder if this was Dempsey's way of telling me that just because he'd called me "pally," he nonetheless remembered my name; hell, he even knew I was permanently on the wagon and addicted to the drink I liked to refer to as rum and Coke without the rum.

Dempsey wandered off and I considered the menu, which the waiter had dropped off before doing his boss's bidding. The shades of red cover depicted my host thirty years ago, in trunks, poised to punch, next to an elaborate JD monogram.

Steaks were good here, but not as good as the Strip Joint, and soon I had it narrowed down to the fish cakes with spaghetti at a buck or the pricier Jersey pork chop with sweet potato for a buck fifty. I was leaning toward the fish, not because of the half-dollar at stake, but out of a weird sense of guilt. I was Jewish but not Jewish enough to snub pork; the major hadn't practiced Judaism and out of respect to the old man, I worshipped at the same altar as he did, church of the First National Bank.

Still, I always felt funny about eating pork in front of a real Jew like Sam Fizer. Almost . . . guilty.

Maybe I was a Jew at that.

Fizer had grown up in Wilkes-Barre, Pennsylvania, his father a successful local businessman, a dry cleaner; an older and younger brother went into the family business, but the closest aspiring cartoonist Sam came was designing some signs and posters for the store. Right out of high school he'd joined the army to do his bit in the Great War, but the armistice was signed soon after and he'd strictly served stateside. He'd got work locally doing editorial and sports cartoons. Then in the early '20s, now a sportswriter, he met a dumb, good-natured prizefighter and got the idea for Mug O'Malley.

Over a several-year period, the comic strip samples Fizer sent around to all the top syndicates were rejected. He'd gone in person to the fledgling Starr Syndicate and pitched *Mug* to the major, who did not buy the strip but was impressed by Fizer's enthusiasm and salesmanship, and sent him out on the road selling other features. At the same time, Fizer—without the major's knowledge, much less blessing—offered potential clients *Mug O'Malley*. Fizer sold twenty papers in three weeks, and the major signed Sam and his strip, which became Starr's first hit property.

So I'd known Fizer a long time, since I was a kid hanging around the major's offices. My childhood take on Fizer was that he was smart and energetic and a force of nature. As I got older, I came to see him as a pushy, conceited loudmouth. That he was heavily art-assisted was well known in the comics world, and his prickly insecurity about his lack of any real artistic ability was legend. He tried to offset his heavy use of assistants by insisting only Sam Fizer himself could pencil and ink the faces of the main characters.

When I was in college, I had a conversation with the major

about Fizer, who I'd come to cheerfully, patronizingly despise, having encountered him at various nightclubs around town, the rotund cartoonist inevitably accompanied by some bosomy showgirl towering over him.

"Starr Syndicate owns *Mug O'Malley*, right?" I said.

"Right," the major said in his boomy baritone.

"And his assistants do all the drawing, right?"

"Right."

"So why not can Fizer, and hire the assistants, for less dough?"

"Wrong."

"Wrong?"

"Story strips aren't about art."

"Are you kidding, Major? What do you call *Terry and the Pirates* or *Prince Valiant*?"

"Good stories. You can always find somebody who can draw, son. Finding a top writer, like Fizer? That's where the magic is."

"Well, it *is* a good strip. Corny, but . . . the stories *do* keep you reading."

"Right. And Fizer writes them all himself. The only person who ever ghosted a *Mug O'Malley* script was Hal Rapp, and after the fiasco that ensued from *that*, Fizer never let anybody else touch the scriptwriting again. Say what you will about that fat little bundle of neuroses, Sam Fizer is a first-rate storyteller, as close to Damon Runyon as the funny pages have ever come."

Now that I'd been in the syndicate business some years myself, I'd come to appreciate Fizer's work. Mug was a sweet, good-natured palooka, but his manager Louie was a Broadway cigar-chomping wise guy. The dialogue was snappy, the plots involving, the cliffhangers masterful.

And Fizer's prizefight sequences were particularly compelling, championship bouts that lasted for week upon exciting week, the exchange of blows and the literal ups and downs of a heavyweight fight parceled out in little four-panel daily doses, with narration echoing the way radio sportscasters reported fights on the air.

I was asking for a second Coke when Dempsey came over with Sam Fizer himself in tow. The little guy was beaming, shooting waves and nods to the boxing pros in the booths, damn near strutting.

I say little, by which I mean how many hands high Fizer was, which wasn't many. If he was taller than five-four, I'd be flabbergasted, though he was about half again as wide, one of those round guys who somehow didn't look fat, the way a beach ball doesn't look fat—just round. Plus, he was a dapper gargoyle, his suit a yellow herringbone and his tie striped gold and white and yellow, his shirt a paler yellow; his brown Florsheims were polished like mirrors.

Fizer, like a lot of cartoonists, had a sort of caricature face— under suspiciously black, slicked back, receding hair, a somewhat Neanderthal brow with very dark India-ink slashes of eyebrow lurked over tiny dark eyes, though his nose was small and even more suspicious than his hair color, so well carved was it. His lips were small for his face but full, and at repose formed a kind of kiss. His chipmunk cheeks and Kirk Douglas dimpled chin were blue with five-o'clock shadow (and it wasn't even one o'clock).

Dempsey brought the radiant Fizer over, guiding him with a big hand on a shoulder that hadn't required the champ to lift that hand much at all to reach its destination.

"Here ya go, pally," Dempsey said to Fizer, and nodded to the booth where I was already seated.

Then Dempsey grinned and nodded and strode off, while Fizer settled into the padded booth like a kid finding just the right spot on Santa's lap. Poor Santa. The cartoonist's eyes sparkled as he looked around the now well-filled restaurant, checking to see if people had been watching.

"Well, kiddo," Fizer said, skipping hello, his voice as high-pitched as Dempsey's if not so squeaky, "what do you think of that? Did you see the way the champ himself walked me over here?"

The way he'd walked me and half the tourists in town to their seats.

"Yeah, Sam," I said, "impressive," and smiled, then sipped my Coke, wondering if the time to fall off the wagon hadn't just arrived.

He frowned, the thick black brows meeting, and shook a fat little finger at me. "You should keep that in mind, kiddo."

"Keep what in mind, Sam?"

"Respect. The kind of respect Sam Fizer's held in. Which makes a stark contrast, doesn't it?"

"Stark contrast to what, Sam?"

"The way you and your stepmother treat me. Most people know the Golden Goose deserves a pillow to sit on, not a kick in the keister."

I held up one hand like I was swearing in at court. "Come on, Sam. You know Maggie thinks the world of you. Me, too. *Mug* is still our top adventure strip."

"I'm glad you remember. . . . Waiter! Waiter!"

Fizer ordered the gefilte fish with boiled potato and mashed beets (buck fifty), despite which I damn near ordered the pork chop anyway; but then I remembered pork chops were hillbilly Tall Paul's favorite food, and not wanting to hit a sore spot, stuck with the fish cakes.

Fizer had a cocktail, a Rob Roy, as we waited. He was actually in a pretty good mood, smiling most of the time, big, white fake choppers gleaming in the midst of all that five-o'clock shadow. And he began with a concession of sorts.

"Look, kiddo," he said, and shrugged, and smiled like an understanding uncle, "I didn't just fall off the turnip truck. I know why you and Maggie have been ducking me for the past few months."

"We haven't been," I said.

We really hadn't. Not that we'd been seeking him out. Day-to-day editorial contact with talent like Fizer, as pertained to the strip itself (deadlines, minor rewrite requests, art corrections, et cetera), was neither my bailiwick nor Maggie's.

He waved that off, generously. "I understand, kiddo, I really do. You're embarrassed, Maggie is embarrassed, and rightfully so."

I said nothing, recognizing the words as English but not being able to make them add up to anything.

When he frowned, the dark little eyes disappeared under the caveman brow. "Maggie taking a role in that ingrate's so-called musical comedy . . ."

*Now* I got it. That "ingrate" was Hal Rapp, the former Fizer assistant who had been so bold as to become a success himself. Fizer rarely referred to Rapp by name.

". . . she was tempted, and anybody can be tempted, right,

kiddo? Let's face it, Maggie's getting on in years, after all. She's not the young sweetie pie anymore who can go out on a stage and get away with peeling off her knickers for applause."

I was so glad Maggie wasn't here.

He continued: "If she wants to get back on the stage at her age . . . and don't get me wrong, she's very nicely preserved . . . I can see where she's coming from. She can't afford to wait around forever for the perfect part to come along. So she's taken on a role in the ingrate's play, more power to her. Tell her Sam says mazel tov, and we'll let it go at that."

"Swell," I said.

The heavy beard made his face look dirty. "You *do* know my wife is in that stupid production, too?"

I did know—I'd never met Fizer's wife, a beautiful showgirl turned actress named Misty Winters, but anybody who followed the Broadway columns knew she'd bucked her husband to take the part of Bathless Bessie. And of course I'd heard all kinds of inside dope on the subject from Maggie.

Also I knew that Fizer had vacated their town house to move his studio and living quarters to a residential suite at the Waldorf Towers, uncomfortably close to his rival, Rapp.

"I thought she was your *ex*-wife," I said.

"No. We're just separated. Estranged, as they say. Just a little bump in the road. I love the child. Talented girl, you know. But it was an evil thing for that ingrate to do, even for him."

"Evil?"

His chuckle was mirthless. "Don't be naive, kiddo. You don't think Misty would have been cast in that role—a *speaking* role, a *singing* role, too. . . . I mean, as I say, I love the child, but she

59

was just a Copa girl when I found her, just so much window dressing."

What happened to "talented girl," I wondered?

He almost answered my unspoken question: "Not that she doesn't deserve a break, I mean, Broadway is tough, you need more than ability, you need luck and connections."

"And Hal Rapp was a sort of connection."

"Now you get it. Now you see. He had the director hire Misty just to rub my face in it. The ingrate thought it would anger me, that it would drive me crazy! Doesn't seem to dawn on him that Sam Fizer's a bigger man than that."

"So . . . Misty has your blessing, like Maggie does?"

The tiny eyes grew large. "No! My wife should know better than to play into the ingrate's hands."

"This isn't . . . why you're separated, is it, Sam?"

He twitched something that was neither smile nor frown. "She's angry with me because . . . because she knows I've been contemplating a lawsuit to halt the production."

This was news. "Really? You could stop *Tall Paul*?"

"That's right, kiddo." He grinned like a maharajah surveying his harem. "Wouldn't *that* frost my former assistant's shriveled matzohs, if I got an injunction slapped on his precious production?"

"On what grounds?"

His eyes flared; so did the well-carved nostrils. "The same grounds as always: plagiarism."

*Oh God*, I thought. *He's not singing* that *old song.* . . .

Fizer leaned forward, his expression that of a bulldog sniffing a hydrant. "You know who *really* created those hillbilly characters? Sam Fizer! In *Mug O'Malley*, a good *year* before that ingrate's 'new' strip appeared!"

I managed not to sigh. "I thought this had been resolved. . . ."

"I've spoken with lawyers over the years. And I could have filed suit any *number* of times . . . but as you know, ultimately, I've tried to be magnanimous about it. Somebody in my position always has little people trying to take advantage."

"But now that Rapp's insulted you by hiring your wife, knowing that he'd drive a wedge between you two, enough's enough?"

"No!" A pudgy hand pushed the air. "No, kiddo, that's not it at all. It's just a matter of what's right."

He paused to arrange his features in an approximation of concern for someone other than himself.

He continued: "You should probably warn Maggie that she ought not get her hopes up, about that musical ever opening at all on the Great White Way. Hate to disappoint her, and I hate to disappoint little Misty; but the day of reckoning will soon come for the smug son of a bitch who has made a fortune off of *my* characters, *my* ideas. . . ."

When Rapp had been Fizer's assistant on *Mug O'Malley*, in 1933, a story line about comic hillbillies had appeared—Mug and his manager Louie Welch had been traveling in the Ozarks when their car broke down, and they found themselves among a backwoods clan including a strapping lad called Little Luke. Luke had diminutive parents (Mam and Pap) and a curvy girlfriend called Sweetwater Sal and, as Fizer had frequently pointed out, the whole setup mirrored what would become Rapp's *Tall Paul*.

Fizer had pissed and moaned in public from the first week *Tall Paul* appeared nationally in a handful of papers; actually, his howls of indignation had probably helped inadvertently publicize the new strip.

And Rapp, when interviewed in 1934, took the position that he would take throughout the coming years: yes, the Little Luke sequence in *Mug O'Malley* was a trial run for *Tall Paul*—why shouldn't it be? Rapp insisted he'd written and drawn the continuity in question, ghosting for Fizer, who'd been off vacationing on the Riviera.

Since Fizer was legendarily touchy about his artistic limitations, and that his reputation as a cartoonist was largely based on the talents of his assistants, Rapp's words were salt in a very raw wound.

Fizer had indeed taken his case to a succession of lawyers over the years, and—as our luncheon conversation indicated—was still seeking redress, twenty years later. Sam insisted he'd written the Little Luke continuity, and done all the inked drawings and, anyway, the copyright was in his name and Rapp had been in his employ.

Still, the character names were different in *Tall Paul*, and comic hillbillies were blossoming all over the popular culture in the early '30s—on radio and in the movies and even the comics: cartoonist Billy De Beck's *Snuffy Smith* character was already a staple in the *Barney Google* strip when the Little Luke story appeared in Fizer's boxing feature.

"Do you know what the ingrate did last year?" Fizer asked.

"No," I lied.

"He wrote a so-called memoir about me for the *Atlantic* monthly! 'My Year Chained in the Monster's Cave,' he called it. *I* was the monster! *Sam Fizer*, who only *discovered* the ingrate. Have you ever heard the story, kiddo?"

I had, but didn't bother to say so.

"It was in Central Park South. I was on my way to my studio, sitting in the back of the Caddy, when I saw this creature limping along, with rolled-up bristol boards under his arm. I knew he was a cartoonist, and from his clothes I could see he was struggling. My heart went out to this young man, so I told the driver to pull over and said to the boy, 'Are those original cartoons under your arm?' And he said, 'Yes, sir.' And I said, 'Are you any good?' And he said, 'I was in the Associated Press stable, awhile, sir.' And I said, 'Want a crack at being my assistant? I'm Sam Fizer!' You should have seen his face light up! This was the depth of the Depression, remember. I paid him twenty-two dollars a week at first, and raised him to twenty-five and then twenty-seven fifty. I treated him like a son. He couldn't have asked for a better teacher or benefactor, a better *real* father . . . but who was it that said, 'How sharper than a serpent's tooth an ungrateful child?' "

"Papa Dionne?"

Our lunches came. No business was discussed, nor painful past history, as Fizer gave most of his attention to eating, though he would pause to smile and chat briefly with anybody famous or boxing-related who wandered by. With his rant about Rapp off his chest, Fizer was pleasant enough, and he could be a very likable and affable fella, when he wasn't focusing on some wrong, real or imagined, that had been done him.

We were waiting for Jack Dempsey's Famous Cheesecake, which was so very different from Lindy's Famous Cheesecake or the Stork Club's Famous Cheesecake (all stolen from Reuben's Famous Cheesecake), when Fizer said, "So, kiddo, I want you to know I take no offense, Maggie's Broadway turn."

I thought we'd established that.

"Good," I said.

"And if that's what you called this luncheon meeting for, we can consider the matter closed."

"Actually, it wasn't."

The tiny eyes under the heavy brows tightened. "Oh?"

I started with what I hoped would be the easier of the two matters I wanted to discuss. "These story lines, the, uh, anti-Commie stuff, in *Mug* this last year or so . . . it's been very exciting."

"Good, good! Glad you approve."

"But both Maggie and I, as well as Ben . . ." Ben Mathers was Starr's managing editor. ". . . think it's time you back off this political stuff, and get Mug back into the ring."

Fizer looked like a boxer who'd been sucker punched. He blinked a few times, then leaned in and said, almost whispering, "You want me to back off on the anti-Commie stuff? Are you *kidding*, kiddo?"

"No. Listen, you're a Democrat. A self-professed liberal. Everybody knows FDR personally praised you for having Mug enlist in the army well before Pearl Harbor, hell, well before the draft. The late president considered you a great patriot, Sam."

Yeah, I know. Laying it on pretty thick. But you deal with temperamental talent, you get used to puckering up where the trousers wear out first.

Fizer said, "I *am* a Democrat. And I like to think Sam Fizer holds liberal views. But I also consider myself a patriot, an *American*. Which is exactly why I can't understand why you would take anything but pride and pleasure out of my campaign against these damned Commies."

I shrugged. "Taking Mug behind the Iron Curtain for some spy stuff, in a story or two, that's fine, Sam. Doing continuities about traitors in the government, Commie congressmen and even army generals? That borders on McCarthyism."

He stiffened; swallowed. I was reminded of a frog on a lily pad suffering indigestion.

Regally, he said, "I happen to believe Senator McCarthy is a great man."

Okay. Enough ass-kissing.

"*I* happen to believe he's a fourteen-carat nincompoop," I said, "and so do about half of the citizens of this great country, and it's a growing number. Haven't you seen the public-opinion polls?"

A tiny sneer formed on a thick upper lip. "Why should I care what a bunch of idiots think in the face of an increasing national peril?"

"You should care because those idiots *used* to read *Mug O'Malley*. Sam, we've lost one hundred papers in the last eight months. We're bleeding clients."

His cheeks, beneath the five o'clock shadow, were reddening. "What are you suggesting I do?"

"Get Mug back in the ring. It's a boxing strip, for chrissake. Sam, we're sitting in Jack Dempsey's, and the champ himself obviously thinks the world of you."

Okay, I was puckering up again; you caught me.

I went on: "Right now the boxers and sportswriters and managers and a boxing commissioner or two sitting in these booths are thinking of you as ring royalty. Don't let 'em down."

"Sam Fizer *never* lets his readers down!"

"When McCarthy has one of his hearings, at the Senate, where are you?"

"What?"

"Where are you seated, Sam?"

"Why . . . nowhere. By the radio, maybe, in my studio."

"Right. And when there's a championship heavyweight bout at Madison Square Garden, where are you sitting?"

"Ringside."

"That's right. Think about it."

He got that sucker-punched look again. His jaw was slack. His eyes were wide. He was thinking.

Finally he said, "Well, kiddo . . . I wouldn't want to disappoint my readers. I guess it *has* been a while since Mug put on the ol' gloves. . . ."

I nodded emphatically. "Mug hasn't had a title defense since before the war. Maggie and I and Ben were talking, and we were hoping you'd work up a Rocky Marciano-type character for Mug to take on."

Fizer was nodding. "Okay. All right. I'll grant you that's not a bad idea. I stayed away from a Joe Louis–type boxer in the strip for obvious reasons."

Having Mug fight a colored opponent was a big no-no—if Mug had won, we'd have lost northern papers, and the southern papers wouldn't have run any such continuity at all.

"Good," I said. "You can have lots of fun with getting Mug back into shape, training camp stories, his missus worried about his health after so many years out of the ring, sportswriters saying he's over the hill. . . . Lots of possibilities."

"Don't oversell it, kiddo," Fizer said tightly. "I said yes, didn't I?"

The cheesecake came, and if it wasn't famous like the menu said, it deserved to be. Or maybe it was just the sweetness of knocking Sam's anti-Commie crap right out of his strip. . . .

Now came the real challenge—I'd got the pin back in the grenade, where shutting down these reactionary story lines was concerned; could I figure out which wire to cut, the red or the blue, to defuse the bomb that seemed sure to go off next?

"Listen, Sam," I said. Cheesecake was over and I was having a cup of coffee; Fizer was having another Rob Roy and smoking a cigarette in a holder. "Speaking of Hal Rapp . . ."

"Are we still on that unpleasant subject?"

That cigarette holder in his pudgy hand seemed ridiculously pretentious, but plenty of other guys in the comics business were doing the cigarette holder bit these days, *Batwing*'s Rod Krane and a certain Hal Rapp included. Was it a coincidence that all three of these top cartoonists did almost none of their own drawing? That even to smoke a ciggie they had to be assisted?

"I'm afraid so, Sam," I said. "Hal brought us a new strip. . . ."

Fizer grunted a sort of laugh. "*Lean Jean*, I suppose?"

"Yes . . ."

"I know all about it. Everybody in this business knows he's been working that thing up. Fool is stretching himself too thin, don't you think?"

I shrugged. "Mostly he'll just write it. I don't have to tell you about the importance of good writing. And he's got a first-rate artist lined up."

"Right—Lou Roberts. Very professional boy."

Fizer *did* know all about it.

I said, "I'm not sure why Hal brought it to us. I mean, King Features or the *Tribune* Syndicate would be sure to snap it up, but—"

He cut me off with a single laugh, exhaling smoke through the too-perfect nostrils in the otherwise less-than-perfect puss. "Don't be naive, kiddo—or are you just *pretending* to be? The ingrate came to you with his new strip for the same reason he had his director cast my wife in that stupid play—to rub my nose in it!"

And he touched a fingertip to his nose.

Immediately I thought of one of the most famous instances of Hal Rapp needling Fizer in *Tall Paul*—after Fizer had very obviously gone to a plastic surgeon to get his nose fixed, Rapp had written a horse-race continuity into the strip, dubbing a losing nag "Sam's Nose Bob."

Both cartoonists, for twenty years, had mercilessly tweaked each other's egos in their respective strips. Once a year, Fizer would run a Little Luke story line, each day accompanied by a box saying, "The *Original* Comic Strip Hillbillies," while Rapp would strike back, poking vicious fun at his old boss, including a sequence in which cartoonist Sammy Fissure hires Tall Paul to assist him on a big-time syndicated strip.

In the story, Fissure keeps Paul in a closet with no light on, and when Paul creates some hilarious new characters based on the folks back home in Catfish Holler, Fissure takes the credit, but generously buys his assistant a lightbulb.

"Let me give you some free advice, kiddo," Fizer said. The little dark eyes were glittering. "Stall a few weeks, before you sign onto this new strip."

"It's bound to take a few weeks, anyway—lawyers and so on. But why . . . ?"

"You may not want to be in business with that crooked, perverted son of a bitch, not in the near future, that is."

I leaned forward. "What are you talking about, Sam? This isn't that silliness about Rapp slipping dirty stuff into *Tall Paul*, is it?"

"I don't think the New York state legislature would agree with your definition of 'silliness,' kiddo."

"It's a sexy strip, Sam, but it's hardly pornographic. . . ."

His tiny eyes blazed under the dark brows. "Really? Why does the number sixty-nine appear so frequently? What about the phallic mushrooms around trees? Trees with suspiciously female knotholes?"

I didn't have a reply to that. I'd never really thought about suspiciously female knotholes before, though I might have finally just grasped my Freudian aversion to mushrooms.

"You know, Sam," I said, in as friendly a way as I could, "it's not really good for the comics business for you to go after another cartoonist like this. Is this what you 'have' on Rapp? Sixty-nine mushrooms and knotholes?"

Fizer was reddening again, and waved my question off like an annoying fly. He tried to stay jovial, but clearly wasn't happy with me. His full little lips were quivering as he said, "Just be careful who you get in bed with, is all. You tell that to *Maggie*, okay?"

"Is this or isn't this about Rapp sneaking filth into the funnies?"

But he was shaking his head. "This is a legal matter. I have to be discreet. I've already said more than I should. . . ."

I squinted at him, as if that might bring the conversation into focus. Maybe it wasn't Rapp's supposed smut sneaking. Maybe it was something else. . . .

"You're not *really* considering this plagiarism lawsuit?" I asked. "Sam, with all due respect, that'll be tossed out. Surely your own lawyers—"

"I'm just trying to give you fair warning, kiddo. We've done business for years, after all. The major was a real friend, and you're his son. You want to be *careful* where Rapp is concerned. A word to the wise, Jack. Word to the wise."

He removed the spent cigarette from its holder, deposited it in the JD-monogrammed glass ashtray, put the holder away, and slid out of the booth. He made a quick exit, not even stopping to schmooze with the boxing crowd in the booths he passed by, pausing up front only long enough to get his topcoat out of the check stand and nod, as if to an insignificant underling, to Jack Dempsey in his window booth.

I just sat there, remembering how Hal Rapp had said Sam Fizer wouldn't be a problem much longer, thinking that Fizer had just said pretty much the same thing about Rapp.

The moment we left the Halloween party, Maggie and I started arguing in the hallway outside Hal Rapp's suite and continued in the elevator going down and then in the hallway leading to Sam Fizer's suite, and guess who won?

I didn't think she should go anywhere near the crime scene, which this was even if we were dealing with a suicide, since killing yourself is a crime in the state of New York, though for some reason no successful suicides have ever been prosecuted.

Heading to Fizer's suite, as we followed the diminutive, trembling Murray Coe to the door, I was still insisting that if Maggie went in there, the cops would have to know about it, and if the cops knew about it, the papers would, meaning nasty and massive publicity fueled exponentially by her presence.

"You think so?" she asked.

"I know so," I said.

Murray Coe, Fizer's bald little assistant, had thick-lensed

glasses, not much chin, a red bow tie, a white shirt, dark slacks and a key to his boss's apartment, which he was using.

I was saying, "The papers love it when a world-famous striptease chanteuse shows up at a crime scene."

"I wasn't set to come in tonight," Coe muttered mile-a-minute in a mid-range nondescript voice, as he nervously worked the key in the lock, "but I had nothing else to do and thought I'd stop by and put in a few hours at the drawing board. Always a good idea to get ahead, deadlines always snapping at our heels, and I just came in on this . . . this *terrible* scene."

We hadn't asked for details yet, too busy arguing all the way here.

"Oh . . . okay, folks," he said, shivering, as if the hall were freezing and not on the warm side. "It . . . it's open."

Maggie said to me, "First of all, you only know the word 'exponentially' because of the crossword puzzles we syndicate, which is also why know you know 'chanteuse,' although you used it incorrectly . . . I don't *sing* . . . and—"

She was trying to edge in front of me, all 121 pounds fitted nicely into the red low-cut gown her character Libidia Von Stackpole wore in the musical, right down to the elbow-length pink gloves; but I stopped her with a warm hand on a cool shoulder. She gave me a clear-eyed, half-lidded look that would've frozen a cobra in midstrike.

"Hey," I said, gentle but firm. "Normally I'm a ladies-first kinda guy. But I'm going in ahead of you. No discussion. Got it?"

I didn't have a gun with me—my .45 Colt automatic, which the major had brought back from the First World War and bequeathed to me, was in a drawer between my socks and boxers, and anyway,

I didn't imagine I'd need firepower in this apartment . . . but I wished I'd had the damn thing, so I could have taken it out and made a point, maybe intimidated her a little.

Like a measly .45 automatic would have intimidated this dame. But for once she deferred to me, granting me a little nod.

Blinking, bespectacled Murray Coe—one of those guys in his thirties who looked like he was in his forties and probably had since his teens—was holding the door open for us, even gesturing in an "after you" manner more befitting a ballroom than a suite where somebody might be dead.

I instructed Maggie and Coe to wait in the hall, and I went through the deserted living room whose cookie-cutter resemblance to the Rapp digs above was, in this context, weirdly unsettling. The only difference was the color scheme, which was shades of green, not brown. A table lamp beside one of two facing couches near the fireplace provided the only light.

Throwing dark inky shadows Will Eisner would be proud of, I moved across the white mohair carpeting and, down by the windows on the city (curtains drawn), took a right into the bedroom.

Like Rapp, Fizer had set up the recessed area by the windows (also curtains drawn) as a mini-studio—two drafting tables with slanting drawing boards with file cabinets and such in between. Otherwise this remained a bedroom, with a double bed whose green satin spread was made, the bathroom door open, the light on. A very nondescript chamber, furnished in an anonymously modern way, with only one outstanding feature: the dead man seated at the first drafting table.

Sam Fizer, in rolled-up white shirtsleeves and no tie and brown slacks and in socks with no shoes, was slumped heavily against the slant of the drawing board with one hand, his left, dangling and a .38 blue-steel revolver on the carpet just below the still fingers. He might have been a kid resting on his desk in grade school, if that kid had a gunshot wound in his left temple.

His eyes were shut, and the blue of his five-o'clock shadow and the black of his slicked-back hair were stark against otherwise pale flesh. He looked at once big and small, like a grossly over-weight child. I touched his neck—no pulse, obviously, but the skin felt cool, not cold.

I was no expert, but I figured this had happened within half an hour. The smell of cordite was fresh enough to back that theory up. Cigarette smoke was mixed in, too, and a small table at Fizer's right had an ashtray with his cigarette holder angled in it among assorted spent butts; also on the stand was a tumbler with an inch or so of dark liquid (whiskey?), and various sharp-nosed pens and pencils and gum erasers and ink bottles and scraps of cloth splotched with black.

On the slanting drawing board, pinned there, were two *Mug O'Malley* daily strips on a single sheet of bristol board, the thick-tooth cotton-fiber drawing paper used by most cartoon-ists. The strips were completely drawn and inked, including the faces of Mug and Louie and the other characters, in that simple cartoony style Fizer imposed on the otherwise realistically drawn figures, courtesy of Murray Coe. The ghosts of underlying pen-cil drawings had been erased, as speckles of eraser on the paper attested.

Fizer's head rested just on the lower edge of the sheet of bris-tol, which was pinned rather high on the board, and some red blood spatter dotted the black-and-white drawings; but the bulk of the blood would be under the dead man's head. Off to the left of the sheet of bristol board were the perfectly inked words:

**GOODBYE,
MUG.
GOODBYE
EVERYBODY
LET ME GO OUT
UNDEFEATED.**

And below this was the thick, distinctive signature that had adorned so many *Mug O'Malley* comic strips over the years:

**SAM FIZER**

I went out where Maggie and a nervous Coe were waiting. I took her gently by the arm and walked her across the hall and spoke quietly to her. Coe, sensing I was after privacy, did us the courtesy of turning away.

"Sam's dead," I said. "At his drawing board."

Maggie's eyes flared. Nostrils, too. "Suicide?"

"Maybe. Listen . . . you don't have to go in there."

"I'm a big girl."

"Yeah, I know. I didn't figure somebody who shared a dressing room with Abbott and Costello backstage at Minsky's would be too squeamish. It's just . . . set foot in there, and you're not a quote in the story, you *are* the story."

Her eyes locked on to mine. "Jack, Sam is . . . or *was* . . .

Starr's star client. It will look *worse* if I don't go in there. I have a responsibility to go in there."

You know, I could have kept arguing, but I'd have been alone in the hall, so what good would it do?

Coe, who had led us here, now trailed after Maggie as she headed in. For as tight as that gown was across her fanny, she could move quick.

In the bedroom, she kept a respectful distance from the corpse at the drafting table—she really wasn't squeamish, but she knew enough not to disturb the evidence—and studied the tableau for all of thirty seconds before saying, "If that's a suicide, I weigh one-eighteen."

I came up beside her and we regarded our dead client. "Yeah, I know. Staged. Pretty badly, too."

Maggie, confirming something we already knew, raised her voice to speak to Coe, who was poised in the bedroom doorway, behind us. "He was right-handed, wasn't he?"

"Yes."

I looked back at the nervous little guy. "He wasn't secretly ambidextrous or anything, was he?"

"No."

I curled my finger at him. "Come over here."

He frowned; with all that bare forehead, it was a lot of frown. "Do I have to?"

"No. I could carry you over."

He sighed and joined me. I pointed at the signature under the comic strip lettering of the suicide note. "Is that really Fizer's work?"

"Seems to be."

"Who *usually* signed the strips?"

"He did." Coe swallowed, a protuberant Adam's apple bobbling on his long neck.

I grunted. "I always figured his assistants signed the strip for him. That's a pretty assured signature for a guy famous for not being worth a damn as an artist."

"It *is* self-assured," Coe admitted, eyes blinking a repeated SOS behind the thick glasses. "But Mr. Fizer wasn't as hopeless an artist as some people thought."

Maggie turned to us, an eyebrow arching. "No?"

"He was a pretty fair big-foot cartoonist," Coe said.

A "big-foot" cartoonist was an artist who drew in a humorous style, particularly that of the old-time strips like *Mutt and Jeff* and *The Katzenjammer Kids*.

Thinking back, I said, "Early days of *Mug* were done in a more cartoony style—that was Fizer's own work?"

Coe nodded; he was smiling, faintly, some affection for his late boss working its way through the nervousness. "That's why he took such pride in drawing and inking the faces of the main characters—even when he hired guys like me to draw the strip more realistically, after the public's tastes changed? Mr. Fizer insisted on putting in the original, cartoony faces himself. Whether it's a strip from '33 or one from last week, Mug always looked pretty much the same, his face, anyway."

"And Sam could do his own fancy signature?" I asked. "I hear Disney can't do his."

"Actually, Disney can," Coe said, the conversation settling his nerves some. "But they say Walt had to work at it a long time before he could pull it off."

"But that hand-lettered suicide message," I said, shaking my head. "Surely Sam couldn't have managed *that*."

"No, actually he could've—Mr. Fizer lettered the strip himself in the early days, and he always had assistants like me do the lettering in his own style."

That kind of thing wasn't unusual. Cartoonists working with assistants usually put together "style sheets" for the hired help: character designs, showing cast members in various views (front, three-quarter front, profile) and displaying assorted expressions. Sometimes these reference sheets included the alphabet in upper and lower case, indicating the desired look of the lettering for the strip.

Maggie studied Coe through narrowed lids. "You're saying Sam really could do his own comic strip signature? And could have lettered that suicide note?"

"Think back," Coe said, looking first at Maggie, then at me. "Almost all cartoonists do speeches and make public appearances, and part of that is doing big grease-pencil drawings of their characters, on big pads of paper on easels, for the audience, right?"

I nodded. That was very common.

"I saw Mr. Fizer do that a dozen or more times," Coe said. "Didn't you ever see him do that?"

I had, actually.

And Maggie was nodding, saying, "I remember the night Sam did the picture of Mug on the wall in our restaurant."

Recalling that myself, I said, "And he signed it with his own famous signature. . . ."

"But I can't say one hundred percent that that's his work," Coe admitted, nodding toward the drawing board where the dead cartoonist slumped near the hand-lettering and the flourish of signature. "*I* could have done that. Any of Sam's assistants could have—he's worked with half a dozen over the years."

I glanced at Maggie; her pretty face was frozen into a grave mask. But she gave me the barest nod that I had no trouble interpreting.

I said to Coe, "Go wait in the other room, would you, Murray?"

"Uh, sure." The little cartoonist swallowed again, Adam's apple bobbling. "Should we, uh . . . ? Nothing."

"What?"

". . . Should we call the police?"

"I'll handle that." I gestured toward the living room. "Just go take a seat out there, would you?"

Anybody who'd worked for Sam Fizer was used to being told what to do, and Murray Coe was no exception. He went out and, presumably, took a seat.

Maggie and I went over by a dresser near the bathroom and stood close enough to kiss or clunk heads. Instead we confabbed.

I hiked a single eyebrow. "So any assistant of Sam's could have lettered that note and done that signature. . . ."

"Don't say it."

"Like Hal Rapp, for instance?"

"I told you not to say it."

I nodded across the room toward the dead man. "What if Hal staged this slice of dark comedy?"

Now she hiked an eyebrow. "With a suite full of guests?"

"A suite full of guests one floor up. You know how easy it is to get lost at a cocktail party?"

"Even your own?"

"Sure. If he had this carefully planned enough, Hal could've popped down here, done the deed, and popped back upstairs in under ten minutes."

"*And* forged the suicide note?"

I shrugged. "For a skilled artist, that wouldn't have taken long."

Maggie frowned; not a wrinkle formed on that lovely brow, but you'd have to call what she was doing a frown, just the same. "Why would a smart guy like Hal Rapp be dumb enough to foul up this faked suicide? Surely he knew Fizer was right-handed."

"Yeah, but Maggie, you're forgetting something."

"I doubt it."

"*Rapp* is left-handed."

"Oh. That *had* slipped my mind."

"If this was something Hal planned, something that required him to work quickly in order for his Halloween shindig alibi to hold? As a left-hander himself, he just might make a dumb mistake like that."

"Maybe." The big green eyes fixed on me unblinkingly. "You're going to have to handle this."

"Handle this how?"

"Handle this like the top-notch detective you are."

I wished I could have found sarcasm in there somewhere, but I couldn't. "You're not serious. . . ."

"As serious as that stiff over there. Listen, think about where the Starr Syndicate sits right now."

I folded my arms. "Well, we're sitting prettier than Sam Fizer."

"Not much. We've just lost our star cartoonist—yes, *Mug O'-Malley* will continue, we'll hire little Murray Coe to draw the strip and . . . jot him down on your suspect list, would you, Jack?"

"Oh, I'll be sure to do that."

She continued on, as if this were an editorial discussion in her office and an apparently murdered man weren't slumped across the room. "As I was saying, we'll hire Murray to draw *Mug*, but the strip will exist under a black cloud, whether Sam killed himself or got murdered . . . and the only brain on the planet that can write *Mug* is over there with a hole in it."

"Yeah. Whoever shot Fizer put a bullet in our bank book, all right."

Okay, so neither one of us was Saint Francis of Assisi. But at a murder scene, a certain pragmatism comes into play, or else you bust out crying or do Daffy Ducks around the room.

"*Mug O'Malley* may not be as dead as his creator," Maggie said, "but he's on the critical list. So what could the Starr Syndicate really use to pick up the slack?"

"I don't know."

"Don't you, Jack?"

Actually I did. "Another top strip . . . like *Lean Jean*?"

"Or, better still, *Tall Paul*."

I grinned at her. "I like the way you think. Did anybody ever tell you you have a sweet face for a heartless bitch?"

"My third-grade teacher." Her head tilted, the green eyes narrowed. "Think about it, Jack—if we can clear Hal Rapp, we'll have the top cartoonist in America in our pocket, beholden to us in a big way."

"But what if Rapp *did* it? What if he killed Sam? Glorioski, Maggie, some people might just think there was bad blood between those two."

"Some people might."

"You know, Hal bragged to me that Fizer wouldn't be a problem much longer."

She shook her head, her expression as confident as it was cold. "I don't think Hal Rapp did this."

"Any evidence to back that up, besides wishful thinking?"

Her eyebrows went up and so did one corner of her red-lipsticked mouth. "How about the unlikelihood of a guy with one leg setting himself up for a marathon murder run? You've seen how Hal hobbles along. And if somebody had seen him in the hall, odds are a celebrity like Hal would be recognized. And even if he weren't, just how conspicuous is he with that wooden leg?"

She had a point. A couple of good points, and I don't mean that in a double-entendre way.

"We could just leave this to Chandler," I said. "He's a good enough cop."

Captain Pat Chandler of the Homicide Bureau was a friend, or anyway not an enemy.

"He might crack this," Maggie admitted. "Then Hal Rapp will be beholden to the Homicide Bureau. Maybe *they'd* like to syndicate *Tall Paul*."

I sighed. "Okay. I get it."

She raised a gloved finger. "But there is one thing you should do, where Captain Chandler's concerned."

"Which is?"

She nodded over toward her dead talent. "Call him before rigor starts to set in."

There was a better chance that the Yankees wouldn't be in the next World Series (they'd just won their fifth straight) than me finding Captain Chandler in his Tenth Precinct office on a Saturday night.

But the desk sergeant bounced me to Chandler's receptionist, who put me right through.

"What are you doing working nights?" I asked him. I was using a white phone in Fizer's white marble foyer.

"Homicide always works Halloween," the familiar baritone informed me.

"Why?"

"We always seem to catch more than our share of oddball killings, Halloween. Worse than a full moon. Why, Jack, do you need a fifth for that poker game of yours?"

"No, Captain, you were right the first time."

"What do you mean?"

"Got an oddball murder for you."

"You're not as funny as you think you are, Jack."

"No, I'm pretty sure I'm exactly as funny as I think I am. And I do have an oddball killing for you. At the Waldorf in a residential suite."

". . . You had one of those before."

"It's a big hotel. You still think I'm kidding, don't you, Captain?"

"Yeah. You moved straight to trick without asking for a treat."

I grinned into the phone. "Seeing you will be the treat. Got a famous corpse for you—Sam Fizer, the *Mug O'Malley* cartoonist."

He was rocking in his swivel chair: I could hear it creak over the wire. ". . . If you aren't pulling my leg, Jack, you're awfully calm for somebody calling in a murder."

"I said 'killing.' Might not be a murder. Might be a suicide. It'll take an expert like you to tell."

Now he started to sputter. "Don't touch anything! For God's sake—"

"A little credit, please, Captain. I was an MP in the war, remember? I'm a licensed private detective. You want the address, or would that squeeze all the fun out of it for a sleuth like you?"

He took the address.

Maggie and I got comfy on one of two pastel-green couches that faced each other over a glass coffee table beside the unlighted fireplace. Murray Coe sat opposite, hands folded in his lap, knees together, like a kid waiting to see the principal.

On the coffee table were National Cartoonists Society newsletters and annuals, as well as assorted copies of *Variety* and the *Hollywood Reporter*—all had cover stories pertaining to *Mug O'Malley* and his papa, and were hardly the latest periodicals: some dated to the mid-'30s, though others were as recent as this year.

On the mantel along a mirror over the fireplace were framed photos of Fizer with national figures—FDR, Bob Hope, Joe Louis—as well as Sam on the sets of various *Mug O'Malley* motion pictures. There'd been a big musical film in the '30s with Max Baer as Mug and Jimmy Durante as Louie the manager, then a series of shorts with Crash Corrigan as Mug and Shemp Howard as Louie, and most recently a long run of B movies starring James Gleason as Louie and, as Mug, a good-looking golf pro whose name escapes me.

Also on display were various honorary awards, mostly citizenship-type plaques and sports world honors, but also a bizarre statuette of comic figures seemingly wrestling, designed by cartoonist Rube Goldberg and named after him. This was the Oscar of the comics world: the Reuben award. One of the founders of the organization, Sam had won the very first Reuben, in 1944. Hal Rapp winning the next one, at the NCS awards banquet in 1945, must not have been Sam Fizer's happiest hour.

I said to Coe, "Sam seems to have brought a lot of his personal memorabilia over from the town house."

Coe nodded, his folded-hands-knees-together posture retained. "Yes. He was very angry with his wife—Misty Winters, the showgirl. He didn't trust her—thought she might ruin precious things, break picture frames and smash trophies and so on. But there's a lot more of this stuff in storage."

Maggie asked, "Isn't it odd that Sam Fizer happened to have the suite right below Hal Rapp's?"

"It's the other way around. This was my suite, paid for by Mr. Fizer, for several years. We both used it as a studio but I worked and slept here. I'm a bachelor, or I am since my wife divorced me five years ago."

"Sorry," I said.

"Hard on wives, living with a nationally syndicated cartoonist; anyway, living with the assistant to one is. I have my own suite down the hall now, smaller but very nice. Mr. Rapp's only been our neighbor for seven or eight months—he took that suite in anticipation of being in town for the musical, I understand."

Rapp's main studio was on Long Island, I knew, part of his palatial home; several assistants lived nearby. I hadn't realized the cartoonist's Manhattan move had been motivated by the upcoming musical—I just thought Tall Paul's pappy wanted to get closer to the action, since all Manhattanites knew that all the action anywhere was in New York.

Maggie asked Coe, "Why did you come running to Hal Rapp's apartment, of all places, when you found the body?"

"I . . . I don't know. I just thought Mr. Rapp, being a cartoonist, would know what to do."

I glanced at Maggie; Maggie glanced at me. Neither one of us thought much of that answer.

Uniformed men arrived, summoned by Chandler by radio, to guard the way in. The one in charge tried to get us to vacate the sofa and stand out in the hall, but I said I'd cleared it with the captain for us to camp out in the living room till he got there. It wasn't true, of course, but sufficed.

And Chandler didn't even give me a bad time about it. He even corralled his little army of technicians—medical examiner, photographer and lab boys—in the living room while he and I had a look at the corpse.

Chandler was a broad-shouldered six-footer with brownish blond hair and a narrow oval of a face complete with light blue eyes and cleft chin and a general ruggedly handsome quality that would have made him perfect for a TV or movie cop, except for the rumpled brown trench coat, baggy brown suit and darker brown fedora that no self-respecting wardrobe department would allow on screen.

His maroon tie was already loose around his collar—it was pushing eleven P.M., after all—which indicated it had been a rough day, or maybe a rough night. He had a kind of crush on Maggie—her pinups had got him through World War II—and for him not to snug his tie in place in anticipation of seeing her, well, that meant he was not at the top of his form. And he'd barely nodded to her, coming in.

His hands were on his hips as he surveyed the death scene: Fizer slumped at the slanting board of his drafting table; on either side of the corpse was the rest of his ministudio—at left, a sideways desk with the kind of drawers that large drawings could be stored in. At right stood the little stand for his ashtray and drink and such, then a three-door filing cabinet with various art supplies on top, bristol board, ink bottles, trays of pens and pencils. Next to that was the second drafting table and an empty, well-padded office-style chair on casters identical to the one Fizer occupied.

Of course the homicide captain's attention wasn't on the furniture, rather his eyes fixed upon the dead man whose hand dangled over the revolver on the carpet.

"Was Fizer a leftie?" Chandler asked.

"No. He hated the Communists."

Chandler closed his eyes. Then he opened them and said, "I mean, was he left-handed?"

"No."

"Sure of that, Jack?"

"Yeah."

He shook his head and let out the first of what would no doubt be many world-weary sighs. "First rule of staging a suicide—get the gun in the right hand."

"Unless the victim's a leftie."

"I meant 'correct' hand."

"I knew that. That was humor."

He gave me a sideways glare. "Appropriate in this setting, you think? Humor?"

" 'He was born with the gift of laughter and the sense that the world is mad.' "

"What?"

"Relevant quote from Sabatini, or maybe Stewart Granger. What do you make of that funny-pages suicide note?"

Chandler leaned in to look at Sam Fizer's last work of art, the two *Mug* strips speckled with blackening blood, under which was the hand-lettered suicide note with the cartoonist's flourish of a signature.

The captain looked back at me. "I'm supposed to believe he lettered that? And *signed* it like that?"

"Apparently."

Chandler came over and faced me. "I doubt our handwriting experts'll be able to confirm or deny that."

"I know they won't. Cursive handwriting has nothing in common with block lettering. And Fizer worked with half a dozen assistants over the years, any one of whom could have done the lettering *and* the signature."

His fedora was back on his head far enough to give his deeply furrowed brow plenty of room to breathe. "You say that like it's significant."

"Are you familiar with the Sam Fizer/Hal Rapp feud?"

Chandler shrugged. "Rapp's the *Tall Paul* artist, right? The comic with all the bosomy gals?"

I grinned at him, put a hand on his shoulder. "Aw, Captain. You are a detective in a million, and an art lover to boot."

He made a suggestion as physically impossible as it was unprintable.

"Listen," I said, "why don't you send your little crime scene elves in here to dust for fingerprints and look for clues and shine all the shoes? Meanwhile, let's find a quiet place where you can sit on my lap while I tell you a story. . . ."

So we moved to the kitchen, leaving the pipsqueak cartoonist and my gorgeous stepmother seated across the glass coffee table from each other in our late host's living room, one a study in nerves, the other in poise, while the platoon of police technicians headed in to the crime scene.

Captain Chandler and I sat at a gray Formica table in a medium-sized white-and-red kitchen and I gave him chapter and verse on Hal Rapp and Sam Fizer, from the day Fizer's Caddy stopped in Central Park and he offered an out-of-work cartoonist a job on through the *Tall Paul* musical and the hiring of Fizer's wife Misty to appear therein, wrapping up with the Halloween party one floor above.

Captain Chandler had been pretty subdued through all that, but when I started in on Rapp's Halloween gathering, its significance quickly dawned on him and the copper jumped to his feet like a hotfoot had just kicked in.

"You wait till *now* to tell me this?" he demanded, eyes wide, nostrils flaring like a rearing horse.

"Proper investigative technique demands a chronological accounting of events. Look it up."

"My chronological ass! Hal Rapp is the obvious suspect here, and you don't *mention* you and your stepmother were at his *party* when another possible suspect, this Murray Coe character, summons you to the *kill* scene? Christ, Jack!"

"Wouldn't have meant anything," I said casually, "till you had all the background. Context is everything in the detective game, right?"

"It's not a goddamn game, Jack, and goddamnit, you know damn well I should have sealed off that goddamned Rapp apartment as the first damn thing I did in this investigation! How many of those goddamn people have flown the damn coop by now, y'suppose?"

"I don't know," I said.

I can't promise you I caught all the "damns" and "goddamns" in that outburst, by the way; I've done my best.

"Like *hell* you don't know. . . ."

I gave him my most angelic smile. "You might want to send somebody up there and see if anybody's still around. And you might want to talk to Hal Rapp. If you don't mind me suggesting . . . if I'm not overstepping . . ."

He went out, trench coat flapping, and I just sat there, playing innocent, even though nobody was around to see.

Maybe ten seconds later, Maggie stuck her head in; more than her head, the uppermost, most exposed part of her. Very distracting neckline, that red gown.

She said, "The good captain ran out of here like a bull looking for a china shop."

"I just told him about the party upstairs."

"Oh." She smiled. She came in and sat down and folded her gloved hands. "You're a scamp, Jack."

"Also a rascal."

"You're trying to make it hard on your friend, the captain."

"No. Not hard. But if you want me to get to the solution of this before him, I can't make it too easy, either. He'll haul Hal in for questioning. And he'll track all of those guests down, but it'll take him and his squad the better part of a week to do it."

A pretty eyebrow arched. "He'll hold *us* all night for questioning, too."

"That's okay. Tomorrow's Sunday. You don't have rehearsal, do you?"

"No."

"We'll all sleep in. Busy week ahead. You've got a musical to open, and I've got a killer to catch."

Though Maggie and I were stuck in Sam Fizer's apartment long after Halloween had turned into the early hours of November first, we didn't really get much of a grilling.

Captain Pat Chandler had his hands full with the crime scene boys and rounding up a couple more plainclothes fellas to deal with the party up in Rapp's place. A good number of guests had hung around, it seemed, though Chandler didn't share a list of names with us or anything.

Apparently Hal Rapp himself had had the presence of mind to tell his guests that their own interests would be best served sticking around to talk to the authorities. Most of them had.

Maggie, Murray Coe and myself remained a floor below in Fizer's apartment and never got back upstairs to witness who had stayed around and how the cops were dealing with them. My guess is they gave everybody a quick interview and took names and addresses, but as many as forty guests had been in attendance, all dressed as Catfish Holler denizens and other comic strip characters, which meant it would have taken a while. And must have been quite a sight.

Comedian Charlie Mazurki alone, mustached, smoking a cigar, and dressed as mute comic-strip-kid Henry (right down to the bald pate), getting questioned by some poor dick hauled from who knew where in the middle of the night, would've been worth the trip upstairs.

But we were relegated to the living room sofas just outside the murder scene, and one at a time were questioned by Chandler himself in the kitchen.

The captain didn't spend much time with me, having already heard more from yours truly than he'd no doubt cared to; but for almost half an hour he indulged himself with Maggie, who must have laid the charm on, because in the midst of all the hassle, Chandler exited the kitchen just behind her with a goofy little grin on his kisser. Of course Maggie's neckline alone could have accomplished that.

While we were planted across the coffee table from a devastated-looking Murray Coe, I had nothing to do but sit there with the wheels turning, and along about two A.M., the wheels ground out something I should have thought of a long time before.

Sam Fizer had sold *Mug O'Malley* to the major back in '32 with a long-term contract for the cartoonist to produce the strip itself—ownership of a feature by its syndicator was standard for the industry, as Rapp's current situation with *Tall Paul* and the Unique Features Syndicate demonstrated.

Periodic renegotiations had given Mug O'Malley's creator the lion's share of licensing revenue and other benefits, but Starr and Fizer still split the net income from actual newspaper syndication fifty/fifty. And Starr held all copyrights and trademarks.

So Maggie and I had our own murder motive in this thing: the Starr Syndicate now owned the *Mug O'Malley* feature, with only a small percentage going to the estate from any revenue the feature henceforth generated.

It was three A.M. and then some when we were dismissed. Maggie, who as a showbiz gal was used to late hours, looked remarkably fresh, the only telltale evidence of the ordeal a few strands of the piled-up red hair gone astray. We'd come in a cab and went back the same way, both of us fairly shellshocked, neither saying a word.

Until we got to the Starr Building, that is, when Maggie said, "Stop up in the office for a minute."

I used my key at the street entrance and we stepped into an area far too large to be called a foyer but much too small to be called a lobby. The glass-frame door to the restaurant was dark, a few neon signs behind the bar still aglow, giving it a melancholy ambience. No elevator operator this time of night, so I took us up to the fourth floor, to the landing where I used another key, and soon we were in her office, where she hadn't set foot in some time, due to the musical.

To her credit, Maggie made no comment about the mess I'd made on her desk. She even played hostess, excusing herself to slip up into the kitchenette tucked away behind Bryce's desk in the reception area. I took the tufted wine-colored chair across from hers, just fine with not being in charge of the Starr Syndicate right now.

She was gone quite a while—I half fell asleep in the chair—and when she returned she was barefoot and bearing a small tray with two cups of steaming hot chocolate on them. Mine had a melting marshmallow, but Maggie hadn't indulged herself—the hot chocolate was bad enough for the battle she was waging against her rampant obesity.

"I spent some time alone in that living room," she said, handing me my cup, "with Murray Coe."

"Lucky you. Did you sign him yet?"

"I won't have to." She got behind her desk and rested her hot chocolate on a coaster, which she somehow located amidst the piles of paper. "The current contract we had with Fizer specifies that, should anything happen to Sam, Murray takes over the strip for the duration of the agreement."

I sat forward, almost spilling the hot liquid. "Under what terms?"

"Coe would split Fizer's take with the cartoonist, in the case of illness, or his estate, in the case of death, for the remainder of the contract, which runs till 1963."

"I never heard of anything like this," I said. "Why did we sign it? And by 'we,' I mean you."

"Why not?" she said, unpinning the tower of red hair and allowing it to tumble in a delightful mess onto her creamy shoulders. "Sam requested we do so, and he was our top story-strip talent. All it did, from our standpoint, was possibly extend our agreement with Fizer for a few years beyond his death."

"Well, that's a lot. We'd have owned *Mug* lock, stock and ink barrel."

"Yes, but we'd have had to hire Coe, anyway, and probably a

top writer. Maybe even a name from the sportswriting field, to try to lend the strip credibility. That would cost money. This agreement acknowledges that if a new writer has to be hired, any salary comes off the top."

"Why did Sam want this?"

She shrugged and red curls bounced off white shoulders. "He didn't say why, other than he wasn't getting any younger, and he wanted to make sure his 'baby' . . . that would be *Mug O'Malley* . . . stayed in good hands."

I grunted a laugh. "You may have done us a favor at that."

"How so?"

"You've removed our murder motive. If you hadn't signed that new contract, we *would* be the proud owners of *Mug O'Malley*, but for a minimal monthly royalty to the estate."

"There won't be much of an estate. Sam had no children. He had a soon-to-be ex-wife, and a couple of brothers back in Pennsylvania."

"We may be off the suspect list," I said, "but Murray Coe's up there pretty high, you ask me."

Her eyebrows lifted but the green eyes were cool. "Is he? He may be the only person on earth who really liked Sam Fizer. Seems Sam treated him like a son, and rewarded his loyalty with a steady paycheck."

"But not necessarily a decent one."

She shrugged again. "I don't know what Sam paid Murray. Sam was never known for his generosity, although the terms of the new *Mug O'Malley* contract might indicate otherwise."

I flipped a hand. "If that little assistant was getting a stipend for carrying the bulk of the work on the strip, but knew he'd get a *real* paycheck with Sam out of the way? Who *better* to bump off the boss?"

"It's possible. But I can't see that pipsqueak killing Sam Fizer. He had tears in his eyes as we spoke about Fizer, Jack. He seemed to love the guy like a father."

"Tell Oedipus," I said, immediately regretting the remark. With a "mother" who looked like Maggie, that was one myth you didn't want to dwell on much. . . .

She sipped her hot chocolate. "The reason I asked you to stop in the office, Jack . . . we need to talk to Hal Rapp, as soon as possible."

"By 'we,' I trust you mean 'me.' And by 'as soon as possible,' I sure as hell hope you don't mean right now . . ."

"No. Could still be a police presence over at the Waldorf Towers, as far as we know. But you *should* talk to him tomorrow. He'll likely be in on a Sunday afternoon, particularly after what went on today."

"All right. What do I talk to him about?"

"In particular, I want you to explore his relationship with Murray Coe."

I wasn't following. "Whose relationship?"

"Hal's. I didn't want to press the jumpy little creature with all those police around, but we both know it's odd that the first person Coe went running to, after finding Sam's body, was Sam's worst enemy."

"Yeah. Same thing occurred to me, but I wasn't ready to share it with Captain Chandler."

She nodded. "You need to convince Rapp we're his friends in

this affair. Tell him we're going to do everything we can to clear him of this."

"He *could* have done it, you know."

"I don't think so."

She drew in half a bushel of air and let it out and I'm sure it must have done interesting things to her décolletage, but I was fixed on those eyes, which were the color of emeralds and just as hard.

She said, "I believe you have two mysteries to solve, Jack— who really killed Sam Fizer is just the first."

"And the second?"

"Who framed Hal Rapp."

I thought Maggie was getting ahead of herself, but I was as usual behind the curve, or maybe curves, where she was concerned.

By the time I finally got to bed, dawn was a genuine threat, and when the phone on my nightstand trilled, noon was just a rumor. My hand knocked off the paperback (*Battle Cry* by Leon Uris) resting there, and somehow my fingers found the receiver and transported it to my ear, where Captain Pat Chandler's voice asked, "You up?"

"I seem to be. What time did you get to bed?"

"I haven't yet. Look . . . Jack. We got off the on wrong foot on this thing, last night."

Was I dreaming? Maybe I wasn't awake yet.

"Is that an apology?" I asked.

His voice took on an edge. "You're the one who should apologize, holding out on me like . . ." Then he stopped himself. "Can you get over here?"

"Where? The Bronx? Did your lovely wife set a plate for me at the table?" Mrs. Chandler was a blonde Maureen O'Hara; I kid you not. "Breakfast or lunch?"

". . . The precinct house, Jack. My God, you're hard to be nice to."

"You want something, Captain. What?"

"Cooperation. I spent the night interviewing comic strip characters, and all I can see is a four-color blur."

"Most cops who interview a bunch of half-naked Broadway chorus girls into the wee hours would've had a better time."

"Most cops don't have a wife as good-looking as mine."

"True. But how good-looking would her expression be if she knew you were interviewing half-naked Broadway chorus girls into the wee hours?"

"Let's just say she'd have fit right in with Halloween. Jack—please. I could use some help."

"Who is this, really? What have you done with Captain Chandler?"

A laugh and a sigh commingled. "Get your ass over here."

"So it *is* you."

"Here's the deal—you won't apologize to me and I won't apologize to you; but we will go forward in a new spirit of civic cooperation."

"Okay," I said.

"Should I send a car?"

"I have a ride. Anyway, I try not to be seen in public with cops. The uniformed variety are bad for my reputation, and the way plainclothes guys like you dress is also bad for my reputation. Ciao."

And I hung up on him, grinning to myself, fully awake and pleased to know Chandler was probably hanging his head over his desk, wishing he were dead, asking me for help.

The overcast day was threatening to turn crisp into cold as I walked to the garage on Forty-fourth where I kept my wheels; I was eating the apple that would have to pass for breakfast or lunch until time allowed. I'd left the trench coat at home, figuring the light brown Scottie tweed suit would keep me warm; I figured wrong, the brim of my dark brown fedora snugged down to fight a breeze off the Hudson River where somebody was trying to smuggle in winter.

I parked the little white Kaiser Darrin convertible (top up) a block down from the precinct house on West Twentieth Street, then strode briskly along underpopulated sidewalks to the six-story graystone with three prominent arches, going up a short flight of stairs under the middle one. I nodded to the sergeant at the judge's bench of a receiving desk, and headed up the creaking wooden stairs by a sign (with pointing arrow) that said, HOMICIDE BUREAU, 3RD FLOOR.

A new receptionist—a brunette in her midtwenties whose horn-rimmed glasses and severe white blouse and black skirt were trying to make her less a looker (with little success)—asked for my name, got it, recognized it and sent me right on in through the frosted-glass door saying CAPTAIN.

The office was big but drab, with cracked, water-stained industrial-green walls, wooden file cabinets on the periphery, windows with views on the city on one side and an alley on the other, and a big, scarred brown desk in the center, where Captain Chandler was the ringmaster of all this carefree fun.

Crime scene photos from Fizer's bedroom and witnesses statements and spiral notebooks and assorted diagrams and papers were scattered across the desk like puzzle pieces that refused to go together. Chandler, in shirtsleeves and the same loosened maroon tie as last night, sat with an expression so bleak, he might be the next suicide contender.

"Hi, Jack," I said to myself. "Thanks for giving up your Sunday afternoon. Pull up a chair. Get you anything? Coffee? A Coke, maybe? You are still on the wagon, right, Jack?"

His blue eyes were bloodshot as he looked up from the scattering of official paper. He smiled but it was pretty ghastly. "If you were any funnier, I'd have to strangle you."

I sat down in the wooden chair opposite him in his swivel number, tossing my fedora on the edge of the mess. "If I were any funnier, I'd charge you for it. And I'm pretty sure strangulation is illegal in this state. Even the governor prefers the hot seat."

"It's not suicide," he said.

"Wow, you *are* a detective." I started to get up. "Is that all?"

"Quit clowning, Jack. This is a hell of a mess. Famous people, a clumsily faked Dutch act, and more suspects than . . . than . . ."

"Want me to come up with something clever for you? How about, more suspects than you could shake a stick at, especially if you're a poor underpaid public servant who can't afford a stick and's been up for twenty hours or so?"

"Not funny. But accurate." He gestured to the pics and papers on his desk. "And there's one good suspect in particular . . . maybe a little *too* good. . . ."

I rested an ankle on a knee and folded my hands across my belly. "Hal Rapp, you mean? Why 'too' good?"

He grunted something that was almost a laugh. "Either Rapp's an idiot . . . and I find it hard to believe a man as successful in so tough and competitive a field could *be* an idiot . . . or somebody's fitted him for a hell of a frame."

I shrugged. "If you have suspects, including a good one, why the long face?"

And it was pretty damn long—normally Chandler was so handsome any self-respecting guy had to hate him; today his mug looked like a bad passport photo.

"For one thing," he said, rocking back, "we talked to lots of people at that party last night—just preliminary interviews, of course, and we'll follow up in the days to come . . . but I've already got a man working on a timeline, a chart—it'll be up on easel, next time you drop by."

"This room always did lack something—that sounds like just the touch. And maybe a bowl of wax fruit? . . . What's the timeline *of*?"

"Rapp's movements at his party. Like I said, we've taken preliminary statements from all the guests except for half a dozen who chose to leave Rapp's suite, despite his advice that they stay."

"But you have their names?"

He nodded. "Yes. We'll be talking to them today and tomorrow. Theater people, mostly. But already it's looking tough to come up with a time frame that gives Rapp enough leeway to get the deed done. Early this morning we used a stopwatch on our police artist, and—"

I frowned. "Why your police artist?"

He gestured with an open hand. "So I could have a trained artist go through the motions of penciling and inking that suicide note."

"Pretty smart."

"Don't sound so surprised." He leaned on his elbows on the desk and clasped his hands. "Our man fired a gun—we used a blank round—to see if any neighbors in the suites turned up, checking on the noise . . . They didn't—whether it was the thick Waldorf walls or simply New Yorkers writing off the sound as a car backfire or some other burp of the city, I can't say."

I was frowning. "What did your stopwatch tell you?"

"Fifteen minutes."

"Did you factor in Rapp's wooden leg?"

"What?" His face fell. "Oh hell . . . No. Hadn't thought of that."

"Well, you were distracted. Chorus girls and all. But I have to think you'd need to add a couple of minutes for that. The guy walks the way a rusty gate swings."

He nodded glumly.

"And have you considered how risky this would've been for Rapp? He's famous. He's a resident of that tower. People could have been coming in and out of their suites—Rapp's wasn't the *only* Halloween party in town. Why would he chance being recognized?"

Chandler shrugged. "Maybe the alibi his own party provided made it worth the risk. But we'll talk to everybody at that party in depth, and do our best to create a timeline, and see if we can demonstrate he had the chance."

I was shaking my head and working at making my smile not be a smirk. "Captain, I understand Rapp's a good suspect—hell, I was the one who clued you in on his feud with the victim. But Fizer wasn't universally beloved; there may even have been other potential suspects at that party."

His eyebrows went up. "I'm *sure* there were. For one thing, a certain guest last night, who played regularly in a poker game with Fizer, says the victim was in debt to local gamblers."

"*What* guest?"

"Charlie Mazurki. The TV funnyman? Although I frankly don't get his humor. You know, I shouldn't tell you that, but it's that spirit of cooperation I mentioned before, understand?"

"Sure. I'll keep it to myself that you don't get his humor. What gambling interests?"

Chandler shook his head. "That much Mazurki didn't know, or at least wouldn't say. But this wasn't nickel/dime/quarter poker, Jack, like that game of yours. Not even hundreds. *Thousands* changed hands at that table."

"What table?"

He pointed to his desk, as if the game had been held at the Tenth Precinct. "A table right in Fizer's suite," he said. "Been going on for years, even before Fizer moved to the Waldorf, when that suite was used as his studio and his assistant's living space."

I cocked my head. "Was the assistant in the game?"

"I don't know. I doubt it."

"Why?"

He shrugged a single shoulder. "Murray Coe made ten grand a

year working for Fizer. Not bad money—better than twice the average Joe's income these days, and certainly well above mine. But *not* the kind of dough it takes to play in a weekly high-stakes poker game."

"What night did they meet?"

"Sundays. A week ago today, or a week ago this evening, rather, was the last game."

I uncrossed my legs and sat forward. "Do you have a list of players?"

"Sure." He fished around among the papers, found his notebook, thumbed it open to the correct page and handed it across to me. The names were as follows:

Sam Fizer
Charlie Mazurki
Tony Carmichael
Ray Alexander
Mel Norman (guest)

"Ray Alexander is a big-time cartoonist," I said, "in case you didn't know."

"I *did* know—I wouldn't have, but Mazurki filled me in when I interviewed him. Alexander does that science-fiction strip, right?"

"The top one—*Crash Landon*."

"One of yours?"

"I wish—King Features has it."

"Do you know Alexander?"

I shrugged. "Just to nod to. Met him at a few NCS events."

"NCS?"

"National Cartoonists Society—Alexander's the current prez. It's a professional group that Sam Fizer helped form just after the war." I still had his notebook, studying the list of names of poker players. "Why is Mel Norman marked 'guest'?"

"Because he *was* one—there's a floating chair at the game, though Norman's been something of a regular of late. Played several times over the last few months. Norman was a guest at Rapp's party, too—he's on the list of the handful who scooted before we got there. Haven't connected with him yet, but we will, we will."

"You do know who Norman is?"

Chandler nodded, as I handed him back his notebook. "Hotshot Hollywood movie director, screenwriter, producer."

"And who says a cop can't be a patron of the arts? Norman's producing his first Broadway show, d'you know that? You may have heard of it. *Tall Paul*?"

"*That* Mazurki didn't mention," Chandler said with a frown, and made a note next to the original notes. "You figure that's significant?"

"Could well be. Fizer was thinking about *suing* Norman."

He was still frowning. "For what?"

"Plagiarism. That's the core of the Fizer/Rapp feud—Fizer claiming Rapp stole his hillbilly characters. Taking those characters into another medium was an excuse for Fizer to haul out the old charges, and make new trouble."

"Could Fizer have won?"

"No, but he could have stirred things up. Maybe even've got an injunction to block the opening of the show. A long shot, but Fizer was furious about Norman hiring Fizer's wife, Misty Winters, to appear in the play."

Chandler was nodding. "*Her* we talked to. She didn't seem too broken up about her husband's death. Maybe she was in shock."

"Or maybe she hated him—they were on their way to a divorce."

His eyebrows hiked. "Her idea or Fizer's?"

"Not sure. Possibly grew out of Misty accepting a role in the *Tall Paul* musical. My assumption is Rapp encouraged, maybe demanded, that Norman hire Misty."

"Why would Rapp do that?"

I laughed but there wasn't much humor in it. "To stick a finger in Fizer's eye. Just out of spite. The Hatfields and McCoys didn't need much of an excuse to fire a squirrel gun at each other, did they? And the upshot is, a match got tossed on the Fizer/Rapp gasoline—I mean, this time Fizer's *marriage* broke up as a result of Rapp's mischief."

Chandler offered up a rumpled grin. "That's why I need your help, Jack. You *know* these people, these situations, not to mention the stupid damn *comics* business, inside out. And Maggie's in the goddamn play!"

I was hoping he wasn't going to start up the "damn"/ "goddamn" barrage again; I didn't offend easily, but it was distracting.

Chandler gave me his best blue-eyed innocent look, and gestured to the list of poker players on the notebook sheet. "Is this Tony Carmichael a name you recognize?"

I studied him while trying not to seem to be. I *did* recognize the name; the question was, did the captain? And was he baiting me?

"No," I said.

Chandler grunted. "Sounds familiar. It'll come to me."

Maybe when he hadn't been up since last month, it would. Tony Carmichael was an alias for Tony Carmine, a gambler who took down high-stakes bets on championship boxing matches, big-purse horse races, the World Series and other high-profile sporting events. He was tied in with the top mobster in Manhattan, Frank Calabria.

Calabria was an old friend of the major's; they'd done various kinds of business together. Let's put it this way: Frank was my godfather. Problem here was, by not sharing this info with Captain Chandler, I was getting off to a bad start on this whole spirit of civic cooperation thing. . . .

Switching subjects, I asked, "Do the papers have the Fizer death yet?"

He shook his head. "We've been getting calls. Happened too late to make the Sunday editions. I'm supposed to issue a statement by . . . well, about half an hour from now. I've got a girl in public affairs working on it."

"What are you calling it? Murder?"

He raised his eyebrows, but then nodded. "It's certainly not a suicide. We're just getting started with the lab work, but we already have enough to rule out Fizer dying by his own hand; and we're well on our way to having enough to arrest Hal Rapp."

"I appreciate the overview. How about some specifics?"

His brow furrowed. "This is *not* for public consumption, Jack."

"No. It's strictly part of this share-the-wealth program you and I are instituting."

He let out what must surely have been his twenty-seventh

world-weary sigh of the day. "The gun was Fizer's—he bought it six months ago, and it was registered to him. He had a license to carry."

I sat up. "Why?"

"Stated reason was he carried large amounts of cash with him from time to time, and wanted the protection. I have no idea why he'd be hauling around greenbacks enough to warrant packing heat. Do you?"

I shook my head. "No idea."

But I *did* have one: if Sam Fizer was hanging around with the likes of Tony Carmine, the cartoonist could well have been indulging in high-stakes gambling—and not just a weekly poker game.

"That the gun belonged to Fizer himself," Chandler was saying, "is about the only thing consistent with suicide. Oh, and the .38 *was* fired at near-contact range, leaving a burn mark and gunpowder residue around the wound."

"How about the angle of the wound?"

A suicide-by-handgun wound is normally at an upward angle.

"The angle's acceptable," the captain admitted. "But everything else hits a very wrong note. First, no fingerprints on the gun. Apparently wiped clean."

"Jesus. Wouldn't even the sloppiest killer, faking a suicide, press the damn *weapon* into the victim's mitt?"

Chandler half smiled. "So you'd think. Then there's Fizer's left hand, and for that matter his right: no powder burns. We did a paraffin test right at the scene, Jack—Fizer did *not* fire that revolver."

"Something stinks, and it's not just cordite."

He regarded me with half-lidded eyes. "Did you happen to notice the tumbler of Scotch?"

"Yeah, I figured there was some kind of booze in that glass."

"Some kind, all right. The heavily-laced-with-a-sedative kind."

I frowned. "How strong?"

He was rocking in the chair again. "The lab boys say Fizer would have gone off to lullaby land with just one gulp—that strong."

My hands were on the edge of his desk. "Enough to *kill* Fizer? Was he dead *before* the gunshot?"

"We don't know," Chandler said cheerfully. "There'll be an autopsy performed this evening, or first thing tomorrow."

"No rush. Wait till Tuesday or Wednesday—he'll still be dead."

"Not everybody works on Sunday, Jack."

"No. God takes it off. You and I seem to be working."

Chandler grinned. "We do, don't we? And here's something *really* interesting—we *did* find some fingerprints . . ."

"But not on the gun."

"No. Not on the gun. On a pen. Something called a . . ." He thumbed back a page on the spiral pad and checked his notes. ". . . a Gillott number 170."

"A lot of cartoonists use that. But neither the nib nor the shaft would give you much of a fingerprint."

"No." His eyes met mine. "But we got a partial, and we have enough points of similarity to identify it as Hal Rapp's right forefinger."

"Hell you say." I sat back in the hard chair and regarded him suspiciously. "Why haven't you picked him up, then?"

He shrugged with two open hands. "So far it's all we've got. And he may have a perfectly good explanation for how that fingerprint got onto a pen of Fizer's. But, Jack, what bothers me is—this is *already* too pat."

"You've got the most blatantly faked suicide in history," I said, nodding, "with the deceased's worst enemy living a floor above."

"Motive and opportunity," Chandler said. "And all Rapp needed for means was knowing where Fizer kept his gun, and some kind of access to a sedative."

"Which would hardly be tough to pull off." I thought for a moment. "Wait . . . Maybe it's not quite so pat, Pat." I usually called him "Captain," but I couldn't resist. "What's the scenario this all adds up to?"

"What do you mean?"

"How does it all fit together? Like *this*, maybe? Rapp somehow gets into Fizer's apartment—presumably the front door was locked, right? And then Rapp, what? Waits till Fizer goes off to the john to slip him a Mickey in his Scotch?"

Chandler was frowning. "I don't think a jury would buy that."

"Not unless *they*'ve been in the Scotch, first. Or maybe Fizer went to the door and invited his archenemy in, and provided Rapp with the opportunity to somehow slip a sedative into his drink? Can you buy that? I can't."

Chandler was thinking hard, a deep furrow between his brows. "Maybe Rapp had got hold of a key, somehow . . . bribed somebody at the hotel, maybe . . . and went in when Fizer wasn't around, searched out where the gun was kept, and drugged Fizer's Scotch?"

"Why, was the whole bottle doped?"

"No," he admitted. "Just that tumblerful."

I shrugged. "I don't think you have enough to haul Rapp in for anything but questioning. Material witness, maybe."

World-weary sigh number twenty-eight. "You might be right at that. But we *can* rule out suicide."

"Yeah, but don't."

He gave me an RCA Victor dog look. "Don't?"

"Not officially. When you put out your police statement today, call it an 'apparent suicide.' Don't label it murder, don't even call it a 'suspicious death.' Make it 'apparent suicide.' Got it?"

"Why, Jack?"

"Let the killer think he's fooled you. Or if it was a phony suicide setup, meant to implicate Rapp, then make the killer think he or she has screwed up."

His head was tilted, his eyes skeptical. "You mean, make the killer think the police are just that *stupid*."

"Well, that would be swell, wouldn't it? What we're after is to give the killer a false sense of security. You're just out there asking questions because you have loose ends to tie up—suicide of a prominent person requires every *t* dotted and every *i* crossed."

"You got that backwards, Jack."

"See?" I got on my feet and tugged on my fedora. "I *told* you you were a detective."

# CHAPTER SIX

A standard investigatory technique is to arrive unannounced at a witness or suspect's residence for an interview. You catch them off guard, and it's not as easy for them to duck you.

But that wasn't my intention when I dropped by Hal Rapp's suite at the Waldorf-Astoria, late Sunday afternoon. After spending ninety minutes with Captain Chandler at the Homicide Bureau, I had worked up enough of an appetite to justify stopping by the hotel coffee shop for a late lunch. I placed my order, then stepped back into the lobby and used a house phone to try Rapp's suite.

Busy signal.

After my egg salad sandwich and chips and Coke, I went out and used the house phone again. Again a busy signal, which meant the cartoonist was either home on the phone and yakking to his lawyer or rabbi or somebody, or home with the phone off the hook, not wanting to be bothered.

Whether the cartoonist wanted to be bothered or not mattered to me not a whit, so I took a tower elevator to the twenty-fifth floor and knocked on Rapp's door.

No response.

I leaned my ear against the wood and thought I could hear Rapp's loud, distinctive nasal whine in there . . . and also a woman's voice.

But I couldn't be sure about the latter. The female tones were much softer (no surprise there), and I might be misinterpreting: maybe Rapp was talking on the phone with the radio or TV on in the background. That might be *Our Miss Brooks* or Faye Emerson I was hearing. . . .

So I knocked some more.

And I kept at it until I heard a night latch unlatching; then the door cracked open and Rapp peered out, exposing a single bleary bloodshot blue eye.

Though all I got was a slice of that familiar oval face, I could see enough to tell he was in rough shape—the dark hair mussed and hanging in ragged commas on his forehead, the mouth yawning open like one of the idiotic hillbillies in his strip. He hadn't shaved yet today and his cheeks were heavy and blue with a beard worthy of his late boss.

His forehead frowned and his mouth smiled. "Jaaaack?" he said, like a guy coming out of a coma, struggling to identify somebody hovering over his hospital bed.

"We need to talk," I said.

A smile managed to form. "No conversation in human history that started with *those* four words," he said, "was ever worth having."

"This is the exception. Maggie sent me. We want to help."

He winced; I might have been standing on his toes. "Couldn't it *wait*?"

"Till after Captain Chandler comes around later tonight, or tomorrow morning? Sure. Of course I just spent an hour and a half pumping him about the case, and you just might find some of what I learned helpful in dealing with his questions."

His eyes tightened; then he opened the door a fraction wider. "Case?"

"Say again?"

His brow was creased in thought and worry. "You said you talked to that *detective* . . . about the 'case.' *Is* this a 'case'?"

"It's a case, all right." I gave him a sunny smile. "Fizer was murdered, Hal. You want me to leave, so you can take a couple hours, and get back to me about who you think the Homicide Bureau's top suspect might be?"

The cartoonist turned very pale—deathly pale under the blue of his unshaven cheeks and chin, like the dead Fizer's face last night. I thought he might be getting sick.

And it's a wonder *I* didn't get sick: Rapp reeked of cigarettes—no booze on his breath, though. Like me, he wasn't a drinker.

"Maybe you should step in, Jack," he said with a weak smile.

"Maybe I should."

He ushered me into the suite, which looked a little like the day after a college fraternity had thrown a girl-chases-boy Batch'ul Catch'ul party. The hand-lettered cardboard signs were still pinned on walls and doors: INDOOR OUTHOUSE—ONE-HOLER; MINGO MOUNTAIN MOONSHINE THAT A WAY; CATFISH HOLLER POP.

69—and cocktail glasses and tumblers with the weak residue of booze and melted ice rested on various surfaces, usually (but not always) on napkins, while paper plates adorned by the remains of now-unappetizing appetizers resided similarly here and there, as did overflowing ashtrays. The odor was worthy of Tall Paul's resident pig-wallowing beauty, Bathless Bessie, that curvy lass who "fellers adores but thar nostrils abhors."

No radio was on, nor television; but neither was a female guest waiting in the living room that Rapp showed me into.

Looking vaguely debauched, Rapp was wearing a purple silk dressing gown, knotted at the waist, over yellow pajamas monogrammed with a fluid HR. Despite the pj's, he wore shoes and socks—maybe the artificial limb was unfriendly to slippers.

"Get you anything, Jack?" he said with a puppetlike gesture toward the kitchen. "Plenty to drink left from last night . . . oh, but you don't drink, either. Another damned *tee-totaler* like me. Say, I have some coffee made. . . ."

"No. No, thanks, Hal."

He seemed to be limping more exaggeratedly today, almost dragging the damn thing, and I wondered if his mood affected his gait. His spirits were noticeably low—he hadn't laughed once, although under the best of circumstances that laugh was as much nervous habit as an expression of glee, nor was he underlining his words as much.

With a sigh that had a smoker's rasp in it, he took a seat on the couch and gestured for me to sit across from him, the glass coffee table between us. That this arrangement eerily mirrored Maggie and me sitting across from Murray Coe last night, one floor down, was not lost on me.

I apologized for coming unannounced and explained that his phone had been busy; he acknowledged that he'd taken it off the hook. I removed my fedora and sat it next to me.

Using a shiny steel Zippo from a robe pocket to light up a cigarette, sans holder, he said, "I guess it's nice of you to want to help, Jack. But I don't really see how any of this is a *concern* of yours and Maggie's."

He tossed the Zippo, which clunked onto the glass beside a deck of Lucky Strikes and an overflowing ashtray, several butts in which bore lipstick stains. Also on the coffee table were two empty coffee cups, one on Rapp's side, the other on mine—and the one nearer to me had lipstick on its rim.

You're probably not a trained detective, so I'll clue you in that this almost certainly meant I had not heard *Our Miss Brooks* or Faye Emerson through the door from the hall.

But if I had, one of them was likely in Rapp's bedroom right now. . . .

"Maggie and I are very concerned about your welfare," I said. "But our motivation isn't entirely altruistic. The creator of our top story strip was murdered last night, which is a blow to our business."

Rapp nodded. He made a three-syllable word of his response: "Yeaaaah." Then his eyebrows went up and he said, "You people won't replace Sam *Fizer* easily."

I gaped at him. "Getting sentimental about your old enemy, Hal?"

He blew out a little vertical mushroom cloud of tobacco smoke; he was staring, but not at me. Not at anything, really. "Call it sentiment, Jack—I'm not very much keen on sentimentality."

"There's a difference?"

He grunted a laugh. "Ask Maggie. She's smart. She'll know."

I considered calling him a patronizing prick, but instead said, "Call it what you want, Hal—it still sounds funny, coming from you. And I don't mean ha ha ha."

He didn't respond right away—just sat there with a shell-shocked expression, staring past me, a hand-with-cigarette raised in a frozen gesture, a curl of smoke rising in a near question mark.

Then he sucked in enough air to send up the Goodyear blimp, exhaled it like the blimp was deflating and actually deigned to meet my eyes.

"Hard to believe, Jack, but Sam and me? We were close once. He taught me most of what I know about the comics business. No, not just the *business*, but the art of comic strips."

"Art? Sam Fizer?"

His voice had a faint tremor; he was looking past me again. "Sam Fizer was a better artist than anybody knew, and I'm sure that's part of why my goading got to him so. Having somebody who worked for you, as an assistant, go on to fame and fortune? If you're as insecure as Sam was, that's a tough pill to swallow."

I would almost have said Rapp was on the verge of shedding a tear or two for his old boss.

Almost.

Eyes meeting mine again, Rapp was saying, "See, Jack, back when I bolted *Mug* to start up *Paul*, I don't think the average person even *knew* that cartoonists had assistants—maybe they *still* don't, ha ha ha. But I was the first assistant to . . . well, graduate to the *big time*, like I did. A lot of interviews covered it, papers and radio alike, and after Sam made such a public fuss about me 'stealing' his hillbillies, well, ha ha ha, the secret was *out*. I was his *'ghost'* artist, in some accounts, which ironically enough wasn't really accurate."

I frowned, confused. "I thought you ghosted the first Little Luke sequence."

"Well, yes, I suppose I did. In the sense that I *wrote* it, and I *drew* it . . . but I still left the Mug and Louie faces blank for Sam to fill in, when he got back from his European vacation."

"Everybody says he insisted on drawing the faces."

Rapp nodded emphatically. "Sam was fetishistic about that— only *he* could draw Mug and Louie. And as for the story line, truth be told, the idea of the hillbillies was *mine*, all right . . . but the two of us kicked it around in a story conference before Sam got on that steamship."

A wide smile blossomed and Rapp's eyes disappeared into slits. The nasal quality had left his voice, and a melancholy tinged his tone.

"Funny thing, Jack . . . Sam liked to say he identified with Mug . . . a good-natured small-town innocent, an all-American hero with a heart of gold who believed in Mom and apple pie and fought his way to the top, honest as George Washington or Abe Lincoln. But it was Louie, the rascal of a boxing manager, willing to wheedle or weasel or do whatever it took to win, who was the *real* Sam Fizer."

About now my eyes were bigger than Little Orphan Annie's. "My God," I said. "I never expected to hear Sam Fizer's eulogy from Hal Rapp."

His eyes were moist but no tear slid out from those slits. "You don't understand, Jack. Even being in the business like you are, you can't comprehend the relationship that forms between a syndicated cartoonist and his top assistant. You spend hour upon hour together—you're in the trenches shoulder to shoulder, you battle deadlines, you chase ideas like goddamn butterflies, you rail against the demands of stupid editors. . . ."

He swallowed.

"Jack, I understand why you're staring at me like I'm *Jo Jo* the Dog-Faced Boy at the carnival. Believe it or not, as Mr. Ripley says—Sam Fizer was like a father to me, for two years at the start of my career, and I owe him everything. *Everything.* Who the hell do you think taught me the importance of story, Jack? That it was the *writing* that mattered in a strip? You can *always* find some idiot artist."

*Walking down through Central Park with cartoons rolled up under an arm . . .*

"If you felt that way," I said, "why the damn feud, all those years?"

He sucked in smoke, exhaled it, and said, "Well, Jack, ha ha ha, I'm a kid from the *slums.* You don't expect a kid from the *slums* to roll over when a *bully* kicks him."

"I guess not."

"He *attacked* me, Jack—the man I respected, the man I looked *up* to, the man I wanted one day to *be* like, *that man* told the press, told the *world,* that I *stole Tall Paul* from him. That I was a thieving *ingrate,* and I . . . I reciprocated. I reciprocated with the *truth* . . . but I reciprocated."

I half smiled. "The truth, Hal? Mostly you made fun of him— I mean, 'Sam's Nose Bob'?"

He grunted a non-laugh. "I knew Sam was hiding an inferiority complex beneath all that bluster, so I ridiculed him, lampooned his precious strip, poked holes in the overinflated balloon of his ego. He *sniped* at me, I *sniped* at him, and pretty soon we had ourselves a feud worthy of the Catfish Holler hills. And that feud, like *any* feud, well . . . it took on a life of its own."

"Here I always thought you hated him."

"Well, I *came* to hate him, I suppose. That's what the love turned into. I don't know if he ever loved me, you know, in that father-and-son way that grows up between a cartoonist and his right-hand man. . . . I had hoped that was why he *invited* me . . ." His expression curdled. ". . . Nothing."

"What?"

"Never mind."

I sat forward. "Invited you *what*, Hal?"

He sighed smoke. "It's not important."

"I think it might be. Spill."

His shrug was too expansive to serve its purpose, emphasizing the importance, not the smallness, of the matter at hand. "Sam invited me to his suite yesterday afternoon."

I goggled at him. "And you *went*?"

"Yes."

"Christ. Does anyone know?"

He waved a dismissive hand. "Well, Murray Coe was there. I don't believe I mentioned it to anybody."

"Did anybody see you in the hall, going in? Coming out?"

"I really don't recall, Jack. But they *could* have. Why? Is that important?"

"*Why?* You may have been seen going into the murdered man's suite, and you wonder why that's *important*?"

Absently Rapp flicked cigarette ash off his purple silk robe. "He wasn't murdered in the afternoon, was he?"

I rolled my eyes. "Why the hell did Fizer invite you down? Had he ever done that before?"

"No! It's the funniest thing. . . ."

Maybe it *was* the funniest thing; but I had a feeling I wouldn't bust out laughing when I heard about it. . . .

Rapp was saying, "Sam called me out of the blue and said, 'This has gone on long enough. It's stupid, Harold. We should talk.'"

Rapp's expression grew distant.

I nudged him with: "And he asked you to come downstairs for a meeting? What, of reconciliation?"

The dark eyebrows rose in a facial shrug. "That's what I *thought*. Jack, he hadn't called me 'Harold' in years—not since I was a kid working for him. His voice was . . . Sam could be kind. When he dropped all the Broadway big-shot bullshit, he was just another guy who'd started out as a little kid who dreamed of growing up and drawing comics for a living. All cartoonists have that in common, and, boy, ha ha ha, *we* sure did."

"So it was a patch-things-up meeting?"

He smirked, gesturing with cigarette-in-hand in that loose-limbed characteristic fashion of his. "I *thought* it would be. But after I *got* there, it only lasted a few minutes. He was at his drawing board—inking *faces*, of course. Murray was at the other drawing board, penciling figures."

"What, the door was open and you just walked in?"

"Of course not! Murray answered my knock and walked me in to see the 'great man' in his bedroom studio. He just sat there at his board, barely glancing back at me as we spoke."

"But you did speak."

"We spoke, all right. I said, 'Sam, maybe you're right, maybe this *has* gone on long enough. I'll lay off it if you will.' He just said, 'Drop Misty from the cast. It's an embarrassment to me. If you don't, I'll get an injunction slapped on your damn musical for plagiarism.' Or words to that effect."

"So he talked one game on the phone, and then when you got there . . . ?"

He gestured with cigarette-in-hand again. "Same old Sam—bitter, demanding. I don't know whether he *suckered* me down there, or I just, ha ha ha, read in what I *wanted* to, from what he said on the phone."

"He insisted Misty leave the *Tall Paul* cast—and that's all you talked about?"

Rapp's shrug was elaborate. "Yeah, uh, well, pretty much. We didn't talk for more than, oh, a minute or two. When I saw that nothing had changed in his attitude, I just got the hell out of there."

It was my turn to draw in a big breath, but when I did, I wished I hadn't, sucking in all that stale tobacco and after-party smell.

"Tell me, Hal—did Fizer drop his pen, and did you pick it up for him?"

"His pen? No!"

"Did the assistant drop a pen? Or did you maybe stand by a tray of pens and nervously finger them?"

He frowned. "What the hell are you *talking* about, Jack?"

"Captain Chandler says a pen with your fingerprints on it was found by the body."

His eyes popped. "What? Well, it's a goddamn *plant*, then! I don't remember touching *anything* in that apartment!"

"Think hard."

"I can think till *doomsday*, but I didn't touch a damn thing!" He leaned forward, shaking his head. "Look, it's suicide, it *has* to be suicide—Sam Fizer always had an overemotional streak a *mile* wide. He was one of these enormously *successful* guys who spends half his time envying other people, and the rest of it feeling *sorry* for himself. And for once, ha ha ha, he actually *had* a reason to feel sorry for himself."

"Which was?"

Rapp seemed momentarily flustered by the question, then said, "Well, uh, I just mean, *think* about it: his wife leaves him, and she's in my play, and his strip is failing, right?"

"No. It's still going strong."

He shifted on the couch. "Come on, Jack, it's fading, *you* know it and *I* know it! His wife had ditched him, and he wasn't on top of the strip world anymore, so the guy took the easy way out." His features darkened. "He was a *coward* at heart, the miserable son of a *bitch*."

Well, so much for the sentimental side of Hal Rapp.

"Hal," I said, raising a traffic-cop palm, "relax. Settle down and just listen."

"I'm listening."

"It was murder. No question."

"He left a *damn* note, Jack!"

"The suicide note was hand-lettered, strip-style, and signed with Fizer's comic strip flourish. . . ."

Rapp sneered, waving that off. "Hell, Sam could do his

trademark signature, no problem. That was one thing he *didn't* need help doing. He wasn't much of a letterer, I admit, but—"

"Any decent cartoonist, and certainly anybody who had ever assisted on the strip, could have lettered and signed that suicide note."

His eyebrows went up. "What about *handwriting* experts?"

"This kind of lettering is out of their purview. And that's just the start, Hal—Fizer had no powder burns on his hands, and the gun showed no fingerprints. Do you happen to know if Sam was right- or left-handed?"

"Right-handed. Me, I'm a southpaw."

"So I hear. Well, the gun was found next to Fizer's left hand, and the wound was in his left temple."

He squinted at me. "*That* can't be *right*. . . ."

"I saw it. Also, there was a drink by Fizer's drawing board that was doped with a sedative. Do you use sedatives, Hal?"

He looked stricken now. "I . . . I have prescription sleeping pills. I have bouts of insomnia, time to time, but, hell . . . thousands, *tens* of thousands in this town have sedatives within their reach. And I sure as hell didn't *touch* his damn glass! Did that cop say my fingerprints were on the *glass?*"

"No. Just on that pen."

"What kind of pen?"

"A Gillott 170."

His face lost all expression. ". . . I, uh, use those. Not the *only* pen I use, of course, but I do use 'em . . . but so do a *hundred* cartoonists! A *thousand* cartoonists!"

"How many of 'em live a floor above their biggest enemy in the business? How many of 'em were likely seen going into and/or coming out of said enemy's apartment, the afternoon of the night he was killed?"

Rapp was flicking glances my way as he mostly stared into space. "Has Coe told the cops about my meeting with Sam?"

"You telling me was the first I heard of it."

"Maybe he . . ." Rapp drew in smoke again. Let it slowly out, watching it dissipate.

"Maybe he *what*, Hal?"

"Nothing."

"Hal—you have to level with me. Come on, man! Maggie and I want to help you."

"Why?"

"Because we *need* a top strip, now that *Mug O'Malley* may soon be as belly up as his creator . . . and *Lean Jean* could be the ticket. And maybe, who knows, *Tall Paul*, too, if that works out."

His smile was lopsided. "So you're trying to get on my *good* side?"

"More like, trying to keep you out of the Death House." I turned over a hand. "Even if they let you draw in there, you'll eventually face a deadline that won't help the Starr Syndicate one little bit."

"You don't pull *punches*, do you, Jack?"

I shook my head. "I'm maybe a day, half a day, behind Captain Chandler on this. We caught a break with you having that party—the coppers have to wade through everybody in attendance, interview them in some depth, and that'll slow things down."

"Including my arrest?"

"Hard to say. That's why I want to crack this thing fast, before you *do* get slammed in stir . . . even if you eventually get out. Anyway, homicides tend to get solved in the first forty-eight hours or, often, not all."

"Should I talk to my attorney?"

"Haven't you already?"

"Yes. But he's saying I may need a criminal lawyer. What do you think?"

"I think you need Perry Mason."

That made him laugh, his familiar "ha ha ha." "Okay, Jack. I . . . I *appreciate* it. Looks like the Starr Syndicate having an in-house troubleshooter can come in handy for talent, from time to time."

"This is my first suicide/murder frame-up, but yeah."

His brow tensed. "Frame-up? You think I'm being *framed* for this?"

"If somebody planted that pen, what else would you call it? Now, before we got sidetracked, you'd just started to say that maybe Murray Coe *did* something . . . what?"

Rapp was staring into nothing again, his eyes wide and unblinking. Finally he said, "The kid . . . the kid may be *covering* for me."

Did all cartoonists consider their middle-aged assistants "kids," I wondered?

I asked, "Why would he do that?"

He gestured with cigarette-in-hand again and made trails of smoke. "We go way back. Murray was my assistant for a while, first couple years of *Tall Paul*, until Fizer hired him away."

This was news to me. "Fizer stole your assistant away from you? And that assistant was Murray Coe?"

Rapp nodded. "Just part of the, you know, back and forth backbiting between Sam and me."

I was shaking my head. "Why would Murray Coe cover for you, Hal, just because twenty years ago or so, he used to work as your assistant?"

"Well, we always got along. We stayed friendly over the years."

"You got along." I just looked at him. "He dumped you for Fizer, but you stayed friendly."

Rapp's eyes flared in the midst of a deeply frowning face. "Fizer offered him *twice* what I was paying, twice what I could *afford*! I didn't resent Murray taking a better position."

"Just out of curiosity, what were *you* paying Coe?"

Rapp frowned; thought back. "This was 1934 and 1935—depths of the Depression. I believe I paid him twenty-seven fifty a week."

Which was what *Mug O'Malley* assistant Hal Rapp had been paid by Fizer—the amount that Hal had cited in his *Atlantic* monthly article to demonstrate what a cheap monster his old boss had been, an article that failed to make the point that $27.50 a week in the Depression was good pay, if you were lucky enough to *have* a job.

Rapp was saying, "In '35, when Murray left me to work for Fizer, Sam paid him fifty bucks a week, a small fortune in those days. Must have *killed* the old skinflint . . . although he probably felt it was worth it, causing me an inconvenience."

"How big an inconvenience?"

"Murray is a great assistant. I always hoped to hire him back someday. Maybe that's why we stayed friendly."

"Is that why Murray came running to you, when he found Fizer's body? Because you'd stayed friendly?"

He blinked at me. "What?"

I served up a two-handed shrug. "Murray Coe finds his dead boss's body, and what does he do? Scream bloody murder at the top of his lungs? Phone the police? Call the concierge? No—he runs upstairs to his late employer's *worst enemy*. What's going on, Hal?"

"Who says anything is going on?"

"Murray Coe doesn't tell the cops that he saw you in Fizer's apartment the afternoon of the murder? After Fizer buys it, Murray comes to you, not the cops? What the *hell*, Hal?"

Rapp stubbed out the cigarette. He took the package of Lucky Strikes from the coffee table, removed a cigarette, tamped it down on the glass, then used the Zippo again. Took about a minute and a half.

"Had time to think, Hal?"

He blew smoke out his nostrils again, dragon-style. "Okay. Here's the deal. Murray's still assisting me."

"What?"

He gestured with a cigarette in hand and drew a smoky abstract picture in the air. "That was one of the reasons I took this suite. Just for the damn convenience of it. Murray is a workhorse—he's divorced, and he's got a lot of time on his hands, and for the last couple years, I been using him to ink my Sunday pages."

"Fizer *knew* this?"

Rapp's eyes widened. "No! *Hell* no! That's the thing—it was a secret. Murray has a room here at the Waldorf, just down from

Sam's suite, where he has his own little studio. See, Murray used to live in the bigger suite till Fizer moved out of his town house."

"Yeah, I know all about that."

Rapp shrugged. "Anyway, if Sam knew Murray was doing work for me on the side, Jesus, would that poor kid have been in hot water."

Scalding.

*If Fizer had found out Coe was betraying him by clandestinely assisting Rapp, what would happen to that sweetheart deal Fizer had signed with our syndicate, guaranteeing Coe's taking over* Mug O'Malley *after the creator's death?*

Rapp was eyeballing me. "You sure got less *talkative* all of sudden, Jack."

I nodded. "I don't think Coe's covering for you."

Rapp threw his hands in the air. "Well, *sure* he is! What else would you call it?"

"I'd call it covering for himself. He's almost as big a suspect as you are, Hal."

Rapp's jaw dropped. "Murray? How is *he* a suspect? He thought the world of Sam!"

"Yeah, while working for you behind Sam's back." I raised an eyebrow. "Suppose Fizer found out Coe was assisting you on the side, and threatened to fire his ass? Murray could have faked that suicide, knowing he'd inherit the strip."

"*That* little milquetoast?"

"Still waters can run deep . . . and *crazy*, sometimes." I shifted gears. "Listen, Hal, last night, when you were hosting—you didn't slip out or anything? To get more booze or ice or . . . ?"

"No. Of course not."

"Like I said, Chandler's going to try to account for your time at the party. That's good for you—it could take days for his people to talk to all the guests and develop a time line."

"What's this cop . . . looking for?"

"Hal, 'this cop' is looking for fifteen minutes or more where you can't be accounted for. Where none of your guests were standing chatting with you, or saw you chatting with anybody else."

"Oh."

"Tell me you were the perfect host, Hal—tell me you didn't duck into your bedroom studio to work on *Tall Paul* for half an hour, with the door locked behind you."

He smiled at me but it was one of those sick smiles that never portend anything positive. "No," he said, "but . . ."

"But? There's a 'but'?"

"I *did* go in my . . . Look, I *was* in my bedroom, for maybe twenty minutes, at one point."

I was sitting on the edge of the couch, like a kid in the last reel of a monster movie. "Alone?"

"No. With a guest."

"Oh. A *female* guest?"

The sick smile again. "Yes."

Relief flooded through me. "Well, hell, that's good! That's the perfect alibi."

From the bedroom door came a husky female voice: "Maybe not the *perfect* alibi."

There, stepping from Rapp's bedroom was a curvaceous,

black-haired, blue-eyed beauty with an ice-cream complexion, wearing the same short-skirted Bathless Bessie costume as the night before. You remember her, don't you?

Sam Fizer's widow?

Misty Winters.

The new widow was wearing black all right, although the Catfish Holler–style sheared-off skirt and low bodice and bare arms were not exactly typical widow's weeds. The fake dirt applied to her limbs by some Broadway makeup artist, to make Misty look appropriately Bathless Bessified for last night's Halloween party, she had washed off at some point. But her black hair was as tousled as the comic strip Bathless Bessie's always was, when sprawled seductively next to a hawg waller keeping company with her pals the pigs.

Other women might have been embarrassed, might have found something to put over themselves since this outfit covered what at best a bathing suit might; or at least their approach might have been shy, diffident, arms folded, head hanging, skulking over to where Rapp sat on his couch and I sat on mine.

But Misty hip-swayed over, unashamed, confident and displaying no signs of either embarrassment or grief. She chose not to sit beside either of us, pulling around a vaguely Egyptian-looking curved-back, cushioned chair and sitting between us, brazenly putting her bare feet (and red-painted toenails) up on the coffee table, the long shapely legs on display. Now she did in fact fold her arms, but not in a covering-herself-up manner, rather a matter-of-fact, even bored posture as she leaned back in the chair.

She gave me a disgusted smirk and arched a dark, well-shaped eyebrow. "It's *not* what it looks like, Jack."

Her Marilyn Monroe enunciation was wholly absent, though a husky femininity remained.

The purple-robed Rapp was covering his face with a hand, while the cigarette burning in his other hand was producing a gray snake of ash thinking about coiling itself onto the carpet.

"I'm not sure *what* this looks like, Ethel," I said, resurrecting the former Miss Schwartz's real name from her Bear Spring, Minnesota, days.

She shook a scolding finger at me. "Don't do that. Ethel is dead."

"So is your husband. Remember him?"

Something rose from her chest that wasn't exactly a laugh. "All too well."

"I want to congratulate you on how you're bearing up," I said cheerfully.

Rapp uncovered his face, caught the cigarette ash before it fell, tapping it into an already overflowing ashtray, and said, "Jack, Miss Winters is *right*—this really *isn't* what it looks like."

"Miss Winters," I said, "is really Mrs. Fizer, and you're lucky it was me who dropped by this afternoon, and not Captain Chandler. Not that he couldn't show up any second."

This got Misty's attention; she shot a glare at Rapp, then

softened her gaze when she turned it on me. "You don't think the cops are watching the hotel or anything, do you?"

"Naw. They're not that organized. Why, are you thinking about taking a powder?"

She frowned. "Are you for real with that tough guy talk? I thought they took *Sam Spade off* the radio."

"Put it theatrically, then: you want to exit stage right, or maybe stage left?"

"I want to exit, period."

"Okay. You have any other clothes with you?"

She nodded vaguely toward the bedroom. "Just a wrap. But it covers me up enough that I won't attract attention in the lobby."

This doll could attract attention in Death Valley at midnight, as Sam Spade might have said.

But I said, "You have a car?"

"No." Her attention went back to Rapp. "Call a cab for me, would you, Hal?"

I raised a hand, as if she were teacher, and said, "No need. I have wheels. Where are you headed?"

"Our town house on West Fifty-third."

"Our?"

"Sam's and mine," she said, with not a twinge of embarrassment or shame. "Actually, *mine* now, I suppose. Unless the son of a bitch changed his will on me when I wasn't looking."

Rapp gaped at her as if she were a freak of nature. Which maybe she was.

"For God's *sakes*, Misty," Rapp said, the flesh on his face drooping off the bone. "The man is dead. He wasn't a goddamned *saint*, but you were *married* to him. Have some respect."

She frowned at him. "What, are you trying to impress the gumshoe?" She turned back to me. "That's the right term, isn't it, Mr. Spade?"

" 'Shamus' would work, too. Though I'm not exactly Irish. If you want a lift, I'll give you one. Define that any way you like."

Both her eyebrows went up and those big dark blue eyes widened, reminding me how I'd wanted to dive into them the other day. Not now, not without a life jacket.

"Am I safe riding with you, Jack?"

"Am I safe riding with you, Misty?"

"I'll risk it if you will."

With no further fanfare, she dragged her feet off the coffee table, stood up, and hip-swayed back into the bedroom and came back swathed in a black mink coat that came down to her ankles. Some "wrap."

Her red-nailed hands gripping the fur lapels, she stopped next to Rapp, who looked up at her like Scrooge contemplating the Ghost of Christmas Future. "Do you trust me to fill Jack in about this? Because I'd like to get out of here, and right now, if there's any chance the cops'll show."

Rapp pawed at the air with his cigarette-in-hand. "Go, go *on*! We've covered it all, Jack and me."

"I was listening, and you haven't," she said flatly, if anything about her could be described as flat. "I'm telling *all*, Hal—any objection?"

"No." He gave me a grotesque grin. "I have no *secrets* from Jack."

Right.

She came over and stood next to where I sat taking all this in. "Listen, Jack, it really *isn't* what it looks like. Check under that couch."

I frowned up at her.

"Check under it, I said."

Used to doing what I was told by a strong woman, I checked: a pink fuzzy blanket was stuffed under there.

Mrs. Fizer pointed to the couch I was sitting on. "I slept right there, last night," she said. "Nothing's going on between Mr. Rapp and myself, not in the way you're thinking. After Sam's death, and considering the *nature* of Sam's death, well . . . we had some mutual concerns, and we talked them out last night, and some more today. . . . Right, Hal?"

The mortified cartoonist swallowed and nodded, but said nothing, which for somebody as talkative as Rapp was saying something.

I got to my feet, slapped my fedora on my noggin and said to my host, "We'll be talking later, Hal. Don't say a word to the coppers without your lawyer present. Got that?"

He nodded, his face saggy and grooved and about ten years older than yesterday.

"Shall we go, handsome?" Misty said cheerfully, smiling at me, holding out a mink-draped elbow; with her every move, the fur shimmered like a thumb riffling through money.

"Sure thing, beautiful," I said, taking the elbow.

And she *was* beautiful: she had no lipstick on, no makeup at all, and yet she was still 100 percent glamour girl. Amazing.

Frightening.

\* \* \*

On the way to West Fifty-third, Misty talked about nothing but my little white Kaiser Darrin convertible. She thought it was the cutest thing she ever did see. How fast would it go? One hundred miles per hour. How many miles per gallon did it get? Thirty. Was it a six cylinder or eight? Eight—V-8, like the vegetable juice. What was the body made of? Fiberglass.

She seemed genuinely interested, but I figured she was stalling. Mrs. Sam Fizer had hitched this ride on the promise of filling me in on what she and Rapp had been doing all night and all day, before I'd butted in—activities that I'd been assured by both parties were "not what they looked like." Which was why she had scurried to hide in the bedroom when I made my surprise appearance, I supposed. . . .

So, had her assurance she'd tell all been the bunk? And was Misty in mink planning to hop from my two-seater onto the sidewalk and up into her town house, leaving me at the curb with the same stupid expression on my puss that she created in most males on the planet?

I'd already made up my mind that this was a manipulative, selfish, dangerous little dame whose considerable charms would best be kept at arm's length. I was not about to be seduced by the likes of this nasty little piece of business. Not unless she gave it some real effort, anyway. . . .

Turned out that what got left at the curb was my convertible, as she led me up the eight steps into the old brownstone where she and Sam Fizer had once dwelled in connubial bliss, which if you were Sam married to Misty it probably *had* been, at least for a while, and if you were Misty married to Sam it probably hadn't *ever* been, unless connubial bliss was a synonym for "living hell."

I soon found myself sitting in a long, narrow room with a bookcase wall that was bare but for some stacked magazines on lower shelves, and other wine-colored walls that had bright square patches of assorted sizes where a vast array of framed items—from paintings to photographs—had once obviously hung. This had been Fizer's studio—I'd been here more than once—and it ran the length of the building, with windows at either end, curtained now, though the cold overcast day wasn't trying very hard to get in.

Fizer had stripped the room of his possessions, from books to drafting tables, leaving behind only a brown leather couch, which faced a fireplace built into the bookcase wall, a low-slung mahogany coffee table with a glass top (and nothing on it but some Philip Morris cigarettes and an ashtray) and here and there a few incidental chairs.

Misty had excused herself to freshen up. I heard water running and soon gathered she was either bathing or showering. A full half an hour later she entered this shell of her husband's studio wrapped up in a white terry-cloth robe that came down past her knees. Her hair was a nest of black moisture-pearled curls, making her a lovely Medusa, and she smelled great—soap plus a gentle spritz of Chanel No. 5. She'd taken time to touch her full mouth with scarlet lipstick, but otherwise she again wore no makeup.

She came bearing drinks—a glass of dark liquid on ice in one hand, and a wineglass of, well, wine in the other.

"Coke, right?" she said.

"Right."

"Permanently on the wagon."

"That's the plan."

"Good for you," she said. "But I need my daily dose of grapes." And she swirled the clear liquid in the glass.

"I thought you didn't drink, either."

"Wine isn't drinking. It's in the Bible."

"So is crucifixion."

She giggled at that and curled up next to me, sitting sideways with her legs tucked under her. This was cozy well beyond the scope of our relationship, which was limited to a couple of conversations, after all. Somehow I managed not to get indignant.

"Is the whole house like this?" I asked, nodding toward the bare bookshelves.

She had an earthy grin, and shared it with me. "You mean, like the movers were just here and left a few pieces behind? No, this one's the worst . . . but I like the couch, and the fireplace. My bedroom—we always kept separate bedrooms because Sam snored—is fully furnished. His bedroom is stripped, though there's a guest room that's as it was, and the dining room he left alone. But you saw that when you came in."

"Everything that said Sam Fizer, he took with him."

"Right. Awards and photographs and artwork and furniture from before we were married and . . . and why should I *stop* him?" She sipped wine. "I was married to him for three years and'd had more than enough of that fat little man and his big fat ego."

"You've really moved past your grief," I said, and sipped the Coke.

She stared blankly past me, as if Fizer were standing before her. "I didn't wish him dead. If I could blink and bring him back to life, I . . . probably would. But he's been a pain in the keister these past five or six months, and I'd be lying if I said I weren't relieved."

Her frankness revealed a self-centered, even cruel streak, not unusual in a woman going the showbiz path. But I found her candor almost as attractive as she was.

And she *was* attractive, though in an odd way. From a theater seat, she'd look pretty, even lovely; and I bet cameras just loved her. But close up, right next to her, her features took on a cartoonish aspect, just an edge of caricature about the angle of the thick, carefully plucked dark eyebrows, the long dark lashes, the big blue eyes, the pert nose, the lush yet angular mouth that Rapp himself might have drawn.

These attributes, and the ones from her neck down, had made her perfect for the *Tall Paul* musical, the personification of Bathless Bessie, despite her smelling like Chanel, not offal.

"Are we here to snuggle?" I asked her. Her terry-cloth-covered shoulder was against mine. "Or can I play Sam Spade again and ask you some questions?"

Her lips pursed in Marilyn-kiss manner. "Which would you rather do?"

I grinned at her. "I hardly believe my own ears, but I came here to play detective, not house."

She smirked fetchingly. "Not even doctor?"

"If you'd like a physical, I'll be glad to give you one. But sooner or later, you're going to be answering questions about why you and Hal Rapp, in the middle of his Halloween party, spent fifteen or twenty minutes in his bedroom last night. And about why, after hearing your husband had either killed himself or been killed, you decided to hang around at Hal's, spending the night there, and much of the next day."

She shrugged, not looking at me. "I told you—I *showed* you the damn blanket: I slept on the couch."

"You and your late husband slept in separate rooms, too. But I've got a hunch one of you tiptoed in to see the other, time to time."

She frowned. Sighed like an irritated child. "I take it back. You're *not* funny."

"Oh, but I'm a riot. I'm Olsen and Johnson and the Ritz Brothers wrapped together, with Milton Berle and Arnold Stang tossed in. But you know who *isn't* funny? Captain Chandler of the Homicide Bureau. And you know where you *won't* want to snuggle? In a cell at the Tombs."

She swallowed. She sat up, folded her arms, and did not snuggle. Again, she put her feet up on a coffee table, and displayed the admirable gams and the red-painted toenails and her casual insolence.

"Okay, party pooper," she said. "Ask your stupid questions."

"What kind of relationship do you have with Hal Rapp?"

She gave me a look like I'd just passed wind. "He's a *horrible* man, don't you know that? Just as bad or worse than my late husband."

"And yet you spent last night in his Waldorf suite."

She gestured vaguely about the room. "Yeah, and I spent three years in this dump with Sam Fizer. Haven't you put two and two together yet, Sinatra, and come up with why the lady is a tramp?"

I rearranged myself on the couch, sitting on one of my legs and looking right at her. I did admire her frankness. "What are you saying?"

She rearranged herself, too, sitting like an Indian now. Arms folded again, her manner businesslike, she said, "I have a little talent and I'm pretty enough and I have the kind of body most men would kill the Pope in Macy's front window to get next to."

"No argument."

She pointed to her terry-cloth-swathed breasts as if they were an exhibit. "This body may hold up another ten years, with the next ten not bad, but then after that? I'll be the best-looking grandma around, assuming I wind up married with kids, and my husband will be damn lucky, but how will I compare to the twenty-year-old actresses and singers and dancers who've come along, or even the thirty-year-old variety?"

I shook my head. "You have plenty of talent. You don't need to shortchange yourself—I've been around the theater and seen some rehearsals, and—"

She held up a red-nailed hand: *stop.* "I know my limitations. I had a chance to step out of the chorus line at the Copa and marry a celebrity. So I did. In the beginning Sam Fizer was sweet and charming and nice. Physically, repulsive, I grant you. But he had things I wanted, and I had things he wanted."

"What went wrong?"

She shrugged; the dark wet locks flicked water at me. "When we were first married, Sam said he'd help me on my showbiz career. He even got me a bit part in one of the *Mug O'Malley* B movies. And he and I did some radio shows together, got our pictures in the papers attending openings and big sporting events, celebrity-couple sort of thing. But then Sam started talking about me retiring from show business, and us starting a family. *That* wasn't what I signed on for."

"No?"

"No." She gestured to herself like a ringmaster. "I ask you— was *this* body designed for children?"

"I'll take the Fifth."

She shook her head firmly, flicking more droplets. "No kids for me, anyway not until I've made enough of a name for myself that I can afford the risk of being out of the limelight for a year per kiddie, not to mention the possibility that pregnancy would ruin my figure. My mother, back in Bear Springs, weighs two-twenty-five, and is two inches shorter than me. How do you think *she* looks in a terry-cloth robe?"

"I'll stick with the Fifth."

The big dark blue eyes were sparking. "My father is sixty-two and still working the farm, and eking out an existence, and I say, 'No thank you.' "

I took a sip of Coke, put the glass back on the table, let the moment pass.

Then I asked, "So where does Hal Rapp come in?"

Her eyes and nostrils flared. "Are you kidding? Surely you know his reputation."

"Humor me."

She leaned forward, grinning like a construction worker at a passing filly. "Jack, Hal is the biggest letch in a universe *filled* with letches. Does that *surprise* you? Haven't you seen his strip? Bosomy bare-legged babes half falling out of their blouses?"

"Yeah. I gathered he liked girls."

"Wow, Sam Spade has nothing on your deductive skills." Again she shook her head, and again water drops tickled me. "Hal has an out-of-control libido. Sam used his celebrity to bag one good-looking chorus girl . . . yours truly. But Hal? *He* uses his fame to take advantage of gullible girls, to convince well-stacked impressionable females that if they'd just be *nice* to him . . . I'll let you interpret 'nice' . . . he could help them get ahead in their careers."

"A funny-pages variation on the old casting couch."

She grunted a non-laugh. "Exactly. And when this *Tall Paul* musical came along, filled with young women enacting the fantasies of his own strip, Hal took full advantage."

"Full advantage of . . . you?"

She waved that off. "I slept with him three times over a period of a week, the week before I was cast in *Tall Paul*. He's younger and more attractive than Sam was, even with that wooden leg, and he can be funny, obviously, and charming."

"It was a brief affair, then?"

She goggled at me. "Affair? More like a *business* transaction. God knows how many other girls in the cast and the chorus he bamboozled into his bedroom. My guess is, if he'd carved notches in that wooden leg? He'd be hopping around by now."

I watched her sip her wine, then asked, "Did Sam know you'd slept with his worst enemy?"

"He confronted me about it, on the phone, and in person, tracking me down at Sardi's once, and outside the St. John Theatre, another time. Furious—spittle flying. But I denied it. And Hal denied it. But Sam knew Hal well enough to see through it— he knew how his old assistant operated."

"Must have driven your husband crazy."

She nodded emphatically. "I'm sure it did. But Sam should've kept his part of our bargain—he has friends on Broadway, he has friends in movies, in television; Sam could have got me a part in some play or film or show."

"And Hal, at least, made good on his promise."

Another emphatic nod. "That's right. I put out, and I got the part. Quid pro quo, Latin for you scratch my back . . . Don't look at me funny, Jack. I'm not ashamed of anything I've done. I've used the gifts God gave me to better myself. Pretty soon there won't be any Sam Fizers or Hal Rapps in my so-called love life— I'll be successful enough to sleep only with good-looking schmucks like you, who don't have anything to offer me in exchange but a good time."

A sadness in her eyes, in her general expression, had softened the caricature-ish quality of her features; for a moment I glimpsed the girl from Bear Springs.

"Okay," I said. "So much for past history. Let's move up the calendar—to last night. Why did you spend fifteen or twenty minutes alone with Rapp in his bedroom?"

Her eyes showed white all around. "Well, it wasn't a *tryst,* believe me! Rapp got his three nights of me, and that's *all* he gets."

"What was it, then?"

She took another sip of wine—a thoughtful one. "I'd had a call from Sam, first of the week. He told me he was getting ready to start official divorce proceedings. And I wasn't going to get a dime from him, no alimony, no nothing. He seemed confident, and I told him, 'I put in three *years* as Mrs. Sam Fizer, and I expect my damn combat pay!' . . . Seemed funny at that time. Little cruel, I guess, now that he's gone. . . ."

"Why was he confident he could wriggle out of alimony payments?"

The dark blue eyes went wild. "He was filing against *me*—divorcing *me* . . . and Sam said he'd be naming *Hal Rapp* as correspondent!"

"Ouch."

She wiggled a hand. "I said to Sam, 'You're bluffing,' and I thought he probably was—Hal and I had been *very* discreet, and our affair . . . well, like I said it wasn't really an affair. Barely lasted a week. But we'd been careful."

"So last night you sequestered Hal in his bedroom to warn him?"

"Yes—the party was my first chance to talk to Hal since Sam called about the divorce. I got him in there to ask him if he'd told anybody about it, done any manly bragging. He said no—he didn't kiss and tell."

"Who says chivalry isn't dead."

"But Hal *did* have another concern."

"Such as?"

She chose her words carefully: "Sam said, in passing, just gloating and being nasty? That he 'really had Hal now.' "

I squinted at her, like I was driving through fog. "In what sense?"

She opened a hand. "That's about all he said. I got the feeling Sam meant he had something incriminating on Hal—like maybe names of girls in the cast that he'd fooled around with, dates, photographs. Some of those girls are underage, you know.

Sixteen-, seventeen-year-olds whose parents signed permission slips so they could perform on Broadway."

"There's a reason they call 'em jailbait."

She nodded, saying, "On top of that, I wasn't the only married gal on Hal's list, I'm sure. The scandal would be *horribly* damaging."

She was right—as sexy as *Tall Paul* was, it coasted on its veneer of cornpone humor that, despite the underlying acid satire, gave the strip a home in family newspapers coast-to-coast. If Rapp were exposed as a raging satyr, despoiling innocent Broadway dancers (*was* there such a thing?), his fall would be as meteoric as his rise.

She was saying, "I told Hal what Sam had said, and Hal told me not to worry about that, that Sam couldn't have anything on Hal Rapp that Hal Rapp couldn't top where Sam Fizer was concerned."

"What did Hal mean?"

"He never explained. He just didn't seem too worried about anything Sam could do to him."

*I kept coming back to it: both Rapp and Fizer had insisted to me that the other man would soon no longer be a problem. . . .*

I said, "And this took fifteen or twenty minutes to discuss?"

"It did." She was frowning in thought. "We went back over the handful of times we'd been together, *where* we'd been together, *when* we'd been together, trying to figure out whether we might have been seen or in some way compromised. *You* try to think back about something you did five or six months ago, Jack, with any precision or clarity . . . and good luck!"

I shifted my position on the couch. "All right. So why stay overnight at Rapp's?"

She sighed. "After the police finished with all the questioning, God, it must have been three or four in the *morning* . . . I simply collapsed on that couch. Hal was actually very sweet. He brought me that blanket; got me some hot milk. I slept till about one o'clock this afternoon."

"But you didn't get up and just fold your blanket and go home."

She shook her head. "No. Hal and I went back over everything again—what had been a divorce-court matter before was something rather more serious now."

"Right. Murder."

"Or suicide."

"Murder, Misty. You were eavesdropping when Hal and I talked—you heard."

"I heard," she admitted.

"And once Sam was a murder victim, you and Hal had to start all over and compare notes again."

Her half a smirk had no humor in it. "I guess you could say that."

I gave her a serious, searching look. "You don't plan to lie to the *police*, do you? Deny that you and Hal were, however briefly, an item?"

Again she shook her head, emphatically. "No. We *did* make sure we would tell the same story, but . . . that story was true."

I arched an eyebrow at her. "I'm pretty familiar with those suites at the Waldorf."

"Yeah? So?"

"So I know that there's a door off the bedroom onto the hall— it's often used for maid service."

Her pretense that this was an insignificant point was crumbling. But she still managed: "Right . . . and?"

"And Hal could've slipped out that door, sent your husband to Comic Strip Heaven and slipped back in."

Her grin mocked me. "Don't be silly."

"You'd be his alibi. An *embarrassing* alibi, to be sure, but an alibi. You two could've cooked up the whole phony suicide. Sam and whatever it was he 'had' on Hal would be gone forever; and you would be a wealthy, very undivorced widow."

She was shaking her head slowly and firmly. "No. It wasn't that way. Hal *was* with me—he didn't leave that suite, not for even one second."

She was convincing; of course, Misty and Hal had had plenty of time last night, and today, to get their stories straight.

Standing, she said, "You mind if I get myself some more wine?"

"No. Not at all."

"You need that Coke freshened?"

"No. I'm fine."

She wasn't gone long; she curled up under herself next to me and sipped wine and appeared far more casual than was humanly possible in her situation.

I said, "A couple other things I need to ask you about."

"All right."

"What was Sam's working relationship like with Murray Coe?"

She shrugged. "It was friendly. Sam valued the little guy, and paid him well."

"So you don't think Murray would make a good suspect in the murder?"

"No." She laughed; she might have been just a touch tipsy. "Are you kidding? Sam was his meal ticket. And, you know, they really *did* get along, those two. Murray looks up to Sam. *Looked* up."

I didn't mention that any affection Sam had for his trusted, valued assistant might have faded had the cartoonist learned that Murray was also working for Rapp.

"Misty, can you think of anybody beside Rapp who might hate Sam enough to kill him? Or who would have some other kind of motive, financial or otherwise?"

"Not really," she said, shaking her head. She sipped at her wine, then shrugged. "Some people liked Sam, others didn't—he was a blowhard, and conceited, although secretly he felt inferior. Many was the night I held that big slob in my arms and soothed him, patted him like a damn baby. . . . Well. *That* was more than I meant to share!"

"What about these gamblers he owed money to?"

She frowned thoughtfully. "You know, I've heard about Sam's gambling, but it's all new to me. He never was a gambler to speak of, while we were married—far too cheap for that. But I heard from mutual friends that lately he was betting on prizefights and horse races, and even his weekly poker party got out of hand—high-roller stakes, not penny ante."

I leaned forward. "He used to bet penny ante?"

"Oh yes. This big-money gambling is something that was *never* a part of Sam's life when we lived together."

"When did it start, do you suppose?"

A funny little half smile formed on the full, scarlet mouth. "Well, *I* may be the root of this evil. . . ."

"How so?"

"From what I understand, Sam started this throw-caution-to-the-wind gambling not long after I left him."

"So you leaving him hit him hard?"

"Apparently. The last five or six months, he wasn't himself. Or maybe I should say he was too *much* himself—the feud with Hal, for instance, Sam went into high gear on that. Do you know about this campaign he started waging, against Hal and the supposed smut smuggled into *Tall Paul*?"

"Yes." I shrugged. "Of course, obviously the strip *is* sexy. And it seems like he might be sneaking little dirty private jokes in, here and there."

"Yeah!" She laughed. "All this 'sixty-nine' stuff. Schoolboy silliness."

"Right." I shifted on the couch. "But I don't think Hal ever really put, well, pornographic material in *Tall Paul*. How would it ever have got past the censors?"

She arched an eyebrow. "I asked Hal about this last night. Asked him if *that* was what Sam 'had' on him, the dirty stuff in *Tall Paul*."

"And what did he say?"

She sighed, shook her head. "Nothing, really. Just shrugged it off."

"Shrugged it off like it was nothing? Or like it was *something*, something he didn't want to talk about?"

"I really don't know." She sipped wine. "I was pretty worked up last night, worried about this divorce and Hal being named correspondent and all."

"Understandable. You know, Sam was threatening another plagiarism suit against *Tall Paul*, specifically the musical."

"I know!" Her smile said how ridiculous she thought this concept was. "Mel was actually pretty worried about it, though I don't know why."

Mel was Mel Norman, the director/producer of the musical— I hoped to be talking to him soon.

"*Tall Paul* is as much an American fixture now as *Mug O'Malley*," I said. "You'd think twenty years later would be a little late in the game to be claiming plagiarism."

"You'd think."

I studied her, not hiding it. The conversation had turned her into a human being—not a perfect one, by any means (you know—like me). But her features seemed real now—genuinely pretty, not cartoonish; and I had to wonder if she wouldn't have been happier staying in Bear Springs and marrying a druggist and starring in lots of community theater.

Then she leaned over and kissed me on the mouth—a wet, warm and very promising kiss. She drew back just a little and smiled wickedly, having left about half of that lipstick on my puss.

"Any more questions, Jack?"

"Uh . . . I can't think of any."

Maybe that Bear Springs druggist option wouldn't have panned out, at that.

She tilted her head and gazed at me; now I got why that war had been fought over Helen of Troy. "You *will* let me know, Jack, if anything comes up?"

"You'll be the first. Or anyway, the second."

She played with my hair. "You know, it's Sunday. You've been working awfully hard for a Sunday. What do you have planned for this evening?"

"Bible study class starts at seven."

"Does it? Here I was hoping you might take me out to eat. I know a nice little Italian place, walking distance. You wouldn't even have to put any miles on that cute little convertible of yours."

"Well . . . okay. Kinda early to eat, isn't it?"

She unbelted the robe and leaned in and kissed me again; this lasted twice as long as before and had four times the effect—approximately. I didn't have any wires hooked up to me or anything.

"Maybe we'll think of something to kill the time," she said, and got up from the couch, slipped out of the robe, letting it puddle at her red-toenailed feet, and just stood there and let me gawk at her and her hourglass figure, which I did, believe me I did, and then she exited, theatrically, hips swaying, all that well-toned dancer's flesh inviting me to follow her wherever she was going.

But you know me well enough by now to know I'm not so easily manipulated. This was a woman accustomed to using men for her own selfish devices, who probably didn't care for me as much as she did the milkman (lucky milkman) or paperboy (lucky paperboy!), and I hope you know what a man of my moral fiber would do in such a situation.

Don't you?

The St. John Theatre, between Broadway and Eighth Avenue, dated back to the late twenties, a typical Mainstem legiter with Moorish revival touches and a vertical sign above the marquee, which bore the familiar *Tall Paul* lettering right out of the Sunday funnies. Only one performer was billed above the title: Candy Cain, who played Paul's long-unrequited love, Sunflower Sue. Under the *Tall Paul* logo was one more credit: PRODUCED AND DIRECTED BY MEL NORMAN.

Monday morning, around ten thirty, I ambled down the slant of a side aisle looking for Maggie. Not a hard task: the house lights were on, and a few key players and other personnel could be spotted here and there in the fifteen-hundred-plus seater.

Down in the orchestra pit, the only musician currently in residence was banging anonymously away at a piano, as chorus girls and boys in the colorful rags of Catfish Holler residents were about midway through the Batch'ul Catch'ul Ballet against cutout backdrops of trees and cabins that were willfully reminiscent of Hal Rapp's artwork. I'd been to rehearsals enough to know where they were, in this fun, turkey-in-the-straw-type dance number that combined athletic balletics with sight gags right out of Buster Keaton.

Maggie had a couple of bits in the ballet—hip-swaying nonchalantly across the stage in red gown and a fur wrap, powdering her nose or filing her nails, an unconcerned blasé participant in the midst of the hillbilly hysteria of these girls-chase-boys proceedings. She and several other of the main characters, who similarly had walk-ons in the elaborate number, were sidelined while the choreographer worked out the kinks and the changes with the main dancers.

About a third of the way down the aisle and seated center row, was Maggie, again in the low-cut fire-engine red gown identified with her character, Libidia Von Stackpole, mistress of evil capitalist Admiral Bullfrog. In the musical, Libidia has been dispatched to Catfish Holler to catch and marry Tall Paul in the yearly "nuptulizing" chase for nefarious purposes too complicated to explain in the context of a mere murder mystery.

I settled in beside her. The piano kept tearing along on its Broadway-ized hillbilly way, and beautiful girls and beautiful boys, who didn't care about the beautiful girls, were leaping and pinwheeling and creeping and crawling and twirling and careening and much more, while their gifted young choreographer, Richard Childe, stalked the periphery of the proceedings like a hunter with a squirrel gun, waiting for just the right shot.

Periodically Childe would scream, "No!" or "Hell, no!" or "Jesus Christ, you people!" and other constructively critical comments, bringing the dancers and the pianist to rude standstills. He would then berate and gesticulate and demonstrate, then ambulate back to the sidelines while the dedicated kids had another try. It reminded me of boot camp with brighter colors. And girls.

While Maggie and I chatted, this sadomasochistic exercise in modern dance continued on; we both were used to it by now. We spoke sotto voce and occasionally had to pause when Childe was yelling.

"No orchestra yet?" I asked.

Maggie glanced sideways at me and gave me the tiny almost smile that was her hello. "Not till Wednesday. Richard's still fine-tuning."

"He's a tough little taskmaster."

"He'll win the Tony."

(She was right. He did.)

"You gonna have to get up there and strut across the stage?" I asked.

"Eventually. Why?"

I shrugged. "Hoping we can talk awhile, and catch up. I haven't see you since Saturday night."

Her red hair was piled up in its now-familiar tower; her eyes were on the stage. "Actually, that was Sunday morning."

I nodded. "Yeah, you're right."

Her hands—in the pink evening gloves—were folded in her lap. "Thought I might hear from you last night."

Making it sound as casual as I could, I said, "I got the chance to interview Misty Winters yesterday evening."

Another sideways glance, complete with a mildly arched eyebrow. "Interview?"

"Yeah."

Her unblinking green eyes drilled holes in my head. "Please tell me you didn't sleep with the widow of the murder victim."

I looked toward the stage as if choreography suddenly fascinated me. "That's a little personal, isn't it?"

"Very. Sleeping with the widow of the murder victim is about as personal as it gets." She gave me a smile that would have curdled rattlesnake milk. "The last murder you investigated, didn't you do the same?"

"I mean, if you're gonna keep score . . . Look, I talked to Rapp, too." I looked right at her, met the unblinking green eyes with my blinking dark blue ones. "And I promise I didn't sleep with the son of a bitch. See, that's where I ran into Misty Winters—at Rapp's place."

Another sideways look; another arched eyebrow.

"She stayed overnight at Rapp's," I said, "but claims she spent it on the couch. She just flopped there exhausted—cops didn't leave till the wee hours."

"Fill me in."

I did.

I gave her all the new info I'd garnered from Rapp, in some depth. I have a near-photographic memory, which is how I can write these detailed case accounts down for your edification and reading pleasure, with an assurance that you're getting the straight dope from a straight dope. That ability also allowed me to give Maggie all the detail she wanted, and she wanted it all.

She was half turned in her seat, her arms folded across the cupping bodice of that distracting gown. "Do you think Rapp did this thing?"

I made a face. "Stage a suicide? If he had, he'd have done it better. But I had to pry a lot of this stuff out of Hal—that Murray Coe's been secretly assisting *him*, too, for example—and at first Hal tried to hide that Misty was there. In fact, she came sashaying out of the bedroom under her own steam. Hal would never have told me she was there, otherwise."

She was doing that magical frown of hers that didn't wrinkle her brow. "So you figure Hal may still be holding out on us?"

"I do. Misty, on the other hand, was more forthcoming."

Maggie glanced toward the stage, where Misty was among the frenzied dancers, and deadpanned, "I'll bet she was."

I ignored that. I was sideways in my seat now, studying Maggie, whose facial expressions were usually about as illuminating as a mug shot of the Sphinx. This morning was no exception.

"So," I said, "what do you make of all this? Fizer inviting Rapp down to see him, hours before Fizer's death—how strange is that?"

"Strange enough." Now she frowned so hard, one tiny line asserted itself halfway down her forehead. "And this sudden streak of high-stakes gambling—that just doesn't seem characteristic of Sam."

I shrugged. "Hey, a guy who's gaga over a gal like Misty could do any number of nutty things."

She arched her other eyebrow; she was ambidextrous that way. "Your expert opinion?"

"Is my sex life troubling you? 'Cause I know you're real delicate where stuff like that goes, since you after all only started peeling for the raincoat crowd when you were what, fifteen?"

She returned her gaze to the stage, where Broadway hillbillies were leaping. "Sixteen, and I have about as much interest in your sex life as I do the sex life of a hermit crab."

I frowned. "What *is* the sex of a hermit crab?"

"You're the detective—check it out, after you solve this murder." She gazed at me again, or at least in my direction, her eyes narrowed. "I can't say I'm shocked to hear what Miss Winters said about Hal hounding the girls in the *Tall Paul* chorus."

"He even put his hand on your leg, as I recall."

"A lot of men have . . . or have tried to, anyway." She offered a bare-shouldered shrug. "I've always known Hal was a horny toad. But if he's seduced underage girls in the cast, and Fizer had proof of that, well . . . he's finished. *Nobody* would syndicate him, us included."

I frowned, making plenty of wrinkles. "Well, I'm gathering that Fizer really had something on Rapp. And I gotta say, Maggie, that's what bothers me most."

"What is?"

"Both Fizer and Rapp seemed dead certain that each had the other one snookered. What did Fizer have on Rapp—this sleazy sexual behavior, possibly with teenage girls? And what did Rapp have on Fizer, other than maybe a plan to kill the SOB and fake a suicide?"

She mulled that. Then she asked, "When did you last talk to Captain Chandler?"

"Not since Sunday. How much of this stuff should I tell him?"

She mulled some more; up on stage, Childe was screaming and jumping up and down—I wasn't sure if he was showing them a new step or having a tantrum.

Finally she said, "You have no responsibility to share with

Captain Chandler anything that Hal told you . . . or, for that matter, anything Misty Winters told you. He's already interviewed them once, and he'll undoubtedly interview them again. Let him do his job. Besides, you work for me, not him."

"Agreed."

Her eyes locked with mine. "But do call Chandler and make one request."

"Which is?"

"If they've already done their postmortem on Rapp, which they probably have, looking at his stomach contents, to check for that sedative-style Mickey Finn? Strongly advise our friend the captain to have the coroner's office perform a full autopsy."

I cocked my head, as if I wasn't sure I'd heard this right. "Well, they'll autopsy him, routinely . . ."

The green eyes flared. "I don't *want* a routine autopsy—left to their own devices, Captain Chandler and the coroner will cut open Sam Fizer just enough, and in only the limited number of places, where it will benefit their take on the case. Which is to say, that Fizer was doped and murdered."

My expression was probably dumber than Tall Paul's. "Well, Fizer *was* doped and murdered . . . wasn't he?"

"Almost certainly."

"Then why . . . ?"

Her smile barely qualified as one. "Call it a hunch. But tell Chandler in no uncertain terms to have the coroner do a thorough job of it."

I shrugged. "Okay. Listen, is Mel Norman around? He's next on my interview list."

Mel Norman was the director, co-writer and producer of the

musical; he usually stepped out of the theater whenever he turned the reins over to choreographer Childe.

"He's around," Maggie confirmed. "I'm surprised you didn't stumble over him coming through the lobby—he's usually pacing out there, smoking, or is inside the box office using the phone to check on half a dozen Hollywood projects."

From the stage came Childe's voice: *"All right, Miss Starr! We need you to wiggle your lovely fanny across the stage for us!"*

She stood, smoothed the gown with her pink-gloved hands and said, "The fine arts call."

As I edged out of the row of seats, with her following me, I said, "You know, that gown you're spilling out of, that's the only thing I've seen you in for days and days. It makes a good costume for you. You should stick with it, like Wonder Guy and his colored long johns, and a fireman and his hat."

She goosed me and I jumped almost as high as those kids on the stage. Then she turned her back to me and she and her magnificent rear end headed down the aisle, and I'm sure she was confident I hadn't seen her smiling.

In the lobby I indeed found Mel Norman. The diminutive impresario was sitting on the red-and-black-striped carpeted balcony steps next to a big glass display case where a *Tall Paul* poster loomed, an incredible Hal Rapp drawing of virtually every character in the Catfish Holler universe chasing after poor Paul, with voluptuous Sunflower Sue closing in. If I cleared Rapp of this, I'd ask for the original to hang in my bachelor pad.

Norman was a slender little guy in a yellow sportshirt with a pink sweater knotted around his neck, gray slacks and Italian loafers with pink socks. His face was round, his eyes small and blue (but made bigger by thick-lensed, dark-rimmed glasses), his brown hair cut short to the scalp to minimize incipient baldness, and he had retained a deep Hollywood tan here in the wilds of Manhattan.

He was smoking a cigarette. Two dead butts were squashed on the floor not far from where he sat on about the fourth step of the balcony stairs.

"Mr. Norman?" I asked.

He looked at me the way you do an insect that lights on you. "Yes?"

"We've met. I'm Jack Starr? Maggie's—"

"Stepson! Yes, and partner in the syndicate, right!" He started to rise.

I held up a palm. "Don't get up, sir."

He obeyed, beaming at me, all friendly now. "I'm nobody's 'sir,' Jack. Call me Mel. Your stepmother's amazing, a real trouper. My God, she's beautiful, and how old is she, anyway?"

I grinned. "Why don't you ask her? That's possibly her favorite question. Mind if I join you?"

"Not at all."

The steps were plenty wide for two backsides.

He reached for a package of Chesterfields in his breast pocket. "Care for a smoke, Jack?"

"No thanks, Mel. I quit those when I got off the sauce. For me, the two went together and I couldn't ditch just one."

He gave me an astounded look. "You don't smoke? You don't drink? What *do* you do?"

"I'm considering taking up girls," I admitted. I nodded toward the theater. "And this show is full of possibilities."

The round face split into a grin that displayed a gleaming grand's worth of dental caps. "I always try to give the people what they like—nobody in show business ever went broke serving up hunky boys and busty girls."

"Amen." We could hear the muffled voice of Childe screaming from inside the theater. "You know, I really like your movies."

His smile turned shy, almost embarrassed. "Well, thanks."

"I think both Bob Hope and Danny Kaye make their best pictures when you're writing and directing."

He chuckled, drew in on the cigarette and sent smoke out his nostrils. "I'm only willing to listen to this kind of thing for another four or five hours, Jack. But, uh . . . I really *am* sufficiently buttered up. What's on your mind?"

"It's the Fizer murder."

He frowned, and he had plenty of forehead to do it with. "Isn't that a suicide? That's what the papers say—'apparent suicide.'"

And they indeed said that: Captain Chandler had taken my advice on handling the press.

"Well, it isn't suicide," I said. "This isn't for public consumption, Mel, but Sam Fizer was almost certainly murdered. And Hal Rapp is the suspect the cops are looking at hardest."

He blanched. "Oh, Christ. *Just* what we need. That'll *kill* us! Our box office will—"

"Die? You mean, like Sam Fizer, Mel? I thought he was a friend of yours. But you seem to be over it."

Now he reddened, from white to red in a heartbeat; if he could turn blue, he'd hit the whole patriotic spectrum.

"You're right, Jack," he said feebly. "I'm a typical low-life Hollywood schmuck, thinking only of me and my bank account, and a friend getting himself killed doesn't even get my attention. . . . I'm not proud of it, Jack. It's that *town*."

"Hollywood?"

He nodded emphatically, sighing smoke. "It *is* the rat race you hear it is."

I gestured to the *Tall Paul* poster nearby. "But this is Broadway. You've finally made it to Broadway, Mel."

He was looking up at the poster like King Arthur seeing a vision of the Holy Grail. "I have, and that's always been my dream. So you'll have to excuse me for being so insensitive about Sam's passing."

"That's okay." I shrugged. "I figure you didn't like Sam much."

"Well . . . actually . . . I didn't."

"But you played poker with him, regularly."

He nodded. "I have been, last four or five months, whenever I've been in town, which has been quite a bit, putting this show together."

"High-stakes game, I understand?"

He rolled his eyes. "Highest I've ever been in! Brother, it got rough. You should see the way Candy's husband, Charlie, bets. My God, he's a lunatic! I've seen him bet five grand on an ace high. Hell, I've seen him *call* on an ace high!"

"Who else was in that game?"

I knew, of course, but I was just checking to see if Mel Norman would level with me. Or maybe he'd add a name to the list.

"I don't know who sat in my seat when I wasn't available," he said. "But Charlie Mazurki, as I say, was a regular; so was Ray Alexander, the cartoonist who does *Crash Landon*, classy guy, very suave, droll as hell; and this kind of scary underworld character, Tony Carmichael—looks like he stepped out of *Guys and Dolls*, only not so good-natured and bighearted as Nicely-Nicely and Sky Masterson."

"How did you do in the game?"

Behind the thick lenses, his eyes grew even larger. "Over the course of the months, broke even, and felt lucky to. Both Carmichael and Alexander were winners, Carmichael more so. Charlie Mazurki is a terrible, stupid gambler; he'd chase a losing streak to hell and back. He was so bad he lost to Fizer! And *Fizer* lost big. Real big. He owed probably, oh, man, I can't even guess . . . *fifty grand* to Carmichael?"

I let out a slow whistle. "Last time I played poker, I lost five bucks and was depressed for ten days."

Norman shifted on the balcony step. "Yeah, I have to admit, I was uncomfortable in that game."

"Then why were you in it?"

"Why? Well . . . I don't know. Something to do while I was in town, I guess."

Now *there* was a great reason.

"Come on, Mel," I said, with a familiarity I didn't begin to deserve. "Why did you play poker with Sam Fizer? My understanding is that he was a thorn in your side—that he was threatening to shut down your musical with an injunction, claiming plagiarism on the *Tall Paul* characters."

His expression darkened; he stared numbly across the lobby toward the box office. ". . . That would never have gone anywhere. It would never have held up in court."

"No, but that injunction might have happened; and in any

event, the publicity would be lousy. Mel! Why were you hanging around with Fizer, a man who was threatening to sue your ass?"

He drew in smoke. Let it out. Said, "Jack, we had history, Fizer and me."

"What kind of history?"

He swung his head around and met my gaze with an earnestness a Hollywood guy shouldn't have been able to muster. "Jack, Sam's frustration with the *Tall Paul* musical . . . and he would've been frustrated about that, in any case, Hal Rapp having a Broadway show? . . . Well, that frustration was multiplied by a couple of other factors."

"Like Rapp getting you to cast Misty Winters."

His eyebrows rose above the dark-rimmed glasses. "Misty is a talented girl! She's going to break out as a star with this production, you wait and see, Jack, and—"

I patted the air with a traffic-cop palm. "Yeah, okay, fine, I agree. But she slept with Hal, and Hal pressured you to hire her, Mel. Let's move on."

He didn't argue. I'd deflated him somewhat. His voice cracked a little as he said, "It was more than just Misty Winters. You see, about five years ago I took an option on *Mug O'Malley*, to make it into a musical."

Now my eyebrows went up. "This I didn't know."

"We never went public. Sam may have been concerned about possible royalties due to the Starr Syndicate, and so never mentioned it to you . . . but I in fact held an option for a year, and tried to develop a book and songs and, well, the *Mug* musical just didn't come together."

"Which isn't unusual, right?"

"Not at all." He gestured to the looming poster. "Hell, I'm not the first to try to make a show out of *Tall Paul*, either—Rodgers and Hammerstein gave it their best shot, and so did Lerner and Loewe . . . and got nowhere! Anyway, I dropped the option on *Mug O'Malley*, and then, a few years later, I started working on *Tall Paul*. And Sam really blew."

"And began threatening to sue."

Norman nodded. "That's right. Of course, Sam knew it was just nuisance stuff; but nuisance suits can be costly, they can even shut down a show."

"So when Sam invited you, you played poker with him."

Another nod. "That's right. Just trying to rebuild our friendship."

I studied the director. "What was Sam up to, Mel?"

After another big sigh of smoke, Norman said, "He was working on me to fire Misty. Whether he wanted to get back at her, or hoped to get back *with* her, it was still just that simple—if I would fire Misty, Sam would drop any lawsuit. He actually never *filed*, you know."

"And you, what? Strung him along?"

A bunch of nods now. "That's right. I had this fantasy that Sam would lose big to me, like he had with Carmichael, and I'd hold all this IOU paper on him, and use that to get him off my back. But it was a fantasy. I won off Sam, but nothing to write home about."

In the theater, Childe was screaming.

"Listen," I said to Norman, leaning in confidentially, "do you know anything, have you *heard* anything, about Hal getting overly frisky with your female cast members, specifically these younger chorus girls?"

Norman smirked. "Well, let's just say for a guy with a wooden leg, Hal gets around."

"Did Fizer mention anything about 'having something' on Rapp? Like maybe he had private-eye photos and statements indicating Rapp might be looking at charges of sex with a minor? Mann Act kind of stuff?"

This appalled Norman, who had turned white again. "My God, you really *do* want to ruin my day, don't you, Jack?"

"Nope, Mel, I'm your new best friend. I'm the guy trying to keep the lid on." I put a hand on his shoulder, or on the draped pink sweater, anyway. "If you know something on this subject, spill—it'll strictly be between us underage girls."

Norman took a couple nervous puffs, let them out and said, "I know of four or five dancers he's had . . . flings with. I don't know of any who aren't eighteen or over, though. And Fizer never told me, or implied in any way, that he might have that kind of smear ready for Rapp."

"Okay." I gave him a changeup pitch. "You were at Hal's Halloween party, right?"

"Yes. I came as, uh, Dennis the Menace." He grinned. "Right down to the slingshot."

"Were you with anybody?"

"No. I came alone. My wife's out in Hollywood, and, believe it or not, I don't run around on her in public."

That left private, but I let it pass.

"So, then, Mel—you mingled at the party?"

"You could say that."

"And if you'd slipped out, maybe nobody would have noticed. That possible?"

His eyes popped behind the lenses. "Christ, are you saying . . . I'm a *suspect*?"

"Yeah," I said, as if that were no big deal. "You had reason to wish Fizer dead. You have plenty of company, but I won't be the last detective you'll talk to about this."

He was squirming. "I already talked to that Captain Chandler, after the party!"

"That was just the newsreel and cartoon. The feature attraction will show sometime today, you can bet."

Shaking his head, he tossed his spent cigarette to the floor and let it sizzle there on the painted cement. "Oh hell. Will this hit the papers?"

"The cops are playing it close to the vest. It *will* hit the papers, but with any luck, I'll have this thing solved before then."

He looked at me with renewed interest. "*You're* solving this?"

"That's the plan."

"Why you?"

"Self-preservation. Fizer was the Starr Syndicate's top story-strip cartoonist, and we're negotiating with Rapp to do a new strip with us. I'm hoping to clear Rapp, and if Fizer turns out just a tragic victim of murder, that would be nice."

"Would be *nice*?" The little eyes behind the glasses were huge. "My God, Jack—you're worse than the Hollywood crowd."

"It's a rat race on Broadway, too, Mel. It's just—here, it's *real* rats."

I thanked him for the time, stopped to stamp out his discarded cigarette and strolled back into the theater. Seated right in back was a character who'd leapt her curvaceous way right out of a comic strip, specifically *Tall Paul*.

Namely, Sunflower Sue.

Actress Candy Cain, in her pink-with-purple-polka-dots low-neck blouse and her sawed-off black skirt and bare feet (actually in pink bunny slippers right now), was sitting rather glumly in the back row.

The Batch'ul Catch'ul Ballet was still in rehearsal up on stage, with choreographer Childe continuing to crack the whip, and the piano starting and stopping its hillbilly stomp according to Childe's whims.

"Miss Cain?" I asked, leaning in.

The peaches-and-cream, blue-eyed blonde turned and gave me a pleasant if cool glance. "Yes?"

"We were introduced, but you may not remember me . . ."

Her smile was guarded but warmer than her glance, anyway. "You're Maggie's stepson—Jack. Sure. I remember."

"You mind if I come sit with you for a few moments?"

"No. Not at all."

I settled in next to her.

Candace Cain had been married to Charlie Mazurki since they teamed up on radio and television in Philadelphia around 1950. Mazurki had a surrealistic sense of humor that Candy's corn-fed innocence played off of nicely. In her own right, she was a gifted singer and comedienne, one of the best female impressionists (her Marilyn Monroe takeoff was an *Ed Sullivan Show* favorite), and when she wasn't appearing on her talented husband's various wacky TV shows, she traveled with a successful nightclub act.

Appearing in a Broadway show was a financial comedown for her, but Miss Cain had made her first notable non-Charlie-Mazurki-related success as an ingenue in a Broadway musical a few years ago, costarring with Rosalind Russell, and now she was top-billed in one.

Candy was about five-six and nicely curvy with lovely legs and lots of platinum hair; for rehearsal she wasn't in full makeup and her pleasantly pretty face seemed very youthful. But then she was probably only about twenty-five.

"You're very good in this show," I said. I knew from Maggie that Candy was not happy with her part; but she really was perfect as the wide-eyed innocent, Sunflower Sue.

"Hardest thing I ever did," she said with good-natured disgust. "I have to stand there clasping my hands and saying, 'I loves you, Tall Paul. I loves you, Tall Paul,' until I think my eyes will cross."

"It's a fun, funny show, and you're great in it."

Her expression was gently amused. "You're sweet. But I'm a married woman."

"I know you are. I'm not making a pass. I just think you're swell. Would 'gee whilikers' be the appropriate thing to add at this point?"

She laughed and it was a nice, musical laugh. "Sorry. Didn't mean to assume the worst of you. But it seems like ever since this thing started, I've spent half my time trying to make a silk purse out of my sow's ear of a part, and the rest of it fending off stupid passes from overgrown boys who should know better."

"Like Hal Rapp, maybe?"

Her expression was a frown with a smile stuck in its midst. "How the hell did you know that?"

I shrugged. "He put his hand on Maggie's thigh."

"Who could blame him? Your stepmother's a real doll."

"Yes, but Rapp's lucky he still has all his fingers. She respects him as a talent, I guess, and cut him some slack."

Candy watched the stage, idly. "I suppose I did the same. You know, I thought the Great Hal Rapp would ride in at the last moment and revise this script and take out some of this country-fried slapstick and put in the sharp satire and biting wit that the newspaper strip is famous for. But, no—all *he* wants to do is seduce young women."

"Well, everybody needs a hobby. How bold did he get with you . . . if I'm not too bold asking?"

She shrugged; her shoulders were every bit as nice as Maggie's. "We went out for dinner—Sardi's, of course. Charlie was out in Hollywood, doing a bit part in a service comedy. Here I am a married woman, former Sunday school teacher from Ohio, and Rapp's putting the most amateurish moves on me, making the most adolescent pass. You know, I really admired him, and his work! I went after this part, lobbied for it, because I was such a fan of his darn strip!"

"You must've been furious."

She shrugged again. "I wasn't. Just disappointed. But if my husband knew?" She rolled her big blue eyes. "It would've been *Hal Rapp* who lost his life the other night, not Sam Fizer."

"Could Charlie have found out Hal got too friendly?"

"Not from me he wouldn't! And I've been discreet about it."

I didn't point out that I was pretty much a perfect stranger and she'd just told me the whole sordid story.

"Speaking of Sam Fizer," I said, "are you aware that his death was a murder, not a suicide, like the papers say?"

She nodded. "I chatted with Maggie about it this morning,

MAX ALLAN COLLINS

a little bit. You know, Charlie and Sam were friends. Played poker together."

"So I hear. Do you know if your husband owed Sam any money?"

She sighed, clearly frustrated. "Charlie could have. My husband makes a lot of money, Jack. He just signed the first million-dollar contract in the history of television. But he gambles like a drunken sailor drinks. It's a . . . sickness. It's the only thing we've ever fought about."

"But did Charlie owe *Sam* any money?"

"I have no idea. Charlie is very secretive about his gambling."

I shifted in the seat. "Candy, I need to talk to Charlie. Do you know where I could find him?"

"What time is it?"

I checked my watch. "Ten forty-five."

"Well, his morning show over at NBC started at ten thirty. He's on till eleven thirty. Why don't you go catch him over there?"

182

The RCA Building at Rockefeller Center was known as the Slab, thanks to its big broad, flat north and south facades, and its ability to be massive and thin all at once. The seventy-floor structure was home to the National Broadcasting Company, whose soundproofed, air-conditioned quarters included twenty-seven broadcast studios (for both radio and televison), assorted offices and other facilities that consumed most of ten floors.

Home to *Mid-morning Mazurki*, 6B was the second-biggest of the studios. By the time I got there, the studio audience was streaming out, guided by pages wearing uniforms suitable for a Victor Herbert operetta. I had no trouble moving through the exiting audience and past the bleachers into the studio itself, a high-ceilinged chamber with a lighting grid above and big boxy cameras on dollies below, as well as microphones on booms and lights on stands and milling guys in suits wielding clipboards, plus all sorts of technical people in the kind of jumpsuits you see on airfields, right down to the headphones.

Just past this chaos was a strikingly simple set on a platform up off the floor maybe six inches: a desk at left and several chairs at right in front of a curtain on which was pinned a big Hirschfeld caricature of the cigar-smoking comedian, who happened to be sitting at that desk, in the flesh, shuffling a deck of cards.

Nobody asked who I was; I was in a suit and tie—having checked my trench coat and hat in the lobby—and looked like I knew what I was doing, which I did: I was intruding upon the star of *Mid-morning Mazurki*, whose sleep-eyed countenance somehow seemed simultaneously amused and doleful.

The hot lights were off and the room was cool as I walked onto the set and right up to Mazurki at the desk, like he was a loan officer at a bank and I was some poor schmuck who needed a down payment for a Buick.

He glanced up and a sleepy smile formed under the thick, wide mustache; a cigar shorter than a pool cue was confidently angled downward from full, sensuous lips. Its richly fragrant scent permeated the air.

"I know you," he said, in a melodious and oddly soothing baritone, and then he returned to shuffling the cards, which looked small in his big hands.

I pulled up one of the guest chairs, or actually a modern approximation of a chair made out of polished steel and lightly padded wood with nubby orange upholstery.

The large-framed Mazurki wore a black sportscoat, a white shirt and a black tie; he might have been a mortician, or maybe a paid pallbearer—in any case, this was an unlikely wardrobe for a wacky comedian.

But then Mazurki was an unlikely comedian. His satiric, surrealistic sense of humor had brought him out of local radio in Philly to the big time of New York and national radio and TV.

Consensus was the guy was an eccentric genius—one of the few reasons buying a TV set was a good idea. In a broadcast landscape where most humor was rehashed vaudeville and Catskills schtick, Mazurki had a hipster sensibility given to great verbal humor, with an offbeat intellectual edge—from prissy poet Bruce Birdthrob of the impossibly thick Coke-bottle glasses, to ridiculous lederhosen-sporting German disc jockey Ludvig Von Schnitzel, Mazurki did the kind of sly, wry humor that made a smart viewer feel you were in on the joke.

On top of that, Mazurki was a master of silent comedy, perhaps the best since the days of Chaplin and Harold Lloyd. On Charlie's show you might see gorillas in tutus dancing to *Swan Lake*, or witness an overenthusiastic used-car salesman slap the hood of a car and cause it to fall to pieces.

"I know how you did the bit with the guy eating his lunch," I said.

"Hmmm," Mazurki said, as he dealt himself a hand of solitaire. There was plenty of room on the desk, which had only a glass ashtray, a big, bulky microphone whose wires disappeared down a desktop hole and a stack of note cards.

"You were sitting at a tilted table on a tilted chair," I said, "with the camera adjusted to an angle that made everything seem on the level."

"I like that," he said, actually looking up at me, a child's smile blossoming under the mustache. We might have been old friends. "On the level. That's a good way to put it."

"Then when you began taking items from your lunch box, they all rolled down and off the table, olives, an orange, an apple, a pear. And when you poured milk from your thermos, it shot off at angle, missing the cup you held."

He laughed softly. "None of the reviewers figured that one out. Good job. Would you like a cigar? These are wonderful cigars, you know."

"No thanks. But one thing I can't work out—how the hell did you manage blowing smoke from a stogie in that underwater gag?"

He put a black jack on a red queen, shrugging a little. "That wasn't smoke. It was another milk gag."

I snapped my fingers. "You filled your mouth with milk before you went under!" And it looked like smoke when he expelled it.

He beamed at me, the cigar angling upward. "What did you say your name was?"

"I didn't, but it's Jack Starr. You think this format will work?"

He took a drag on the cigar, exhaled a small dark cloud of smoke. One eyebrow lazily raised itself, like an old man doing a push-up. "Talking to guests? Maybe. It's cheap and easy. NBC likes cheap and easy. Anyway, I can still do my crazy sketches, and I get to fill in for Sid Caesar next summer."

"That's more your speed, Charlie. All right I call you 'Charlie'?"

He was studying the cards, the cigar drooping. "It must be. It's my name."

"Why aren't you heading for your dressing room? Show's over."

"Oh." He gave me a lazy smile, putting a red six on a black seven. "I'm waiting for the stagehands."

"The stagehands?"

"Yeah. When they finish up, we always play a few rounds of poker. Small stakes. Dime, quarter, half-dollar."

"A few rounds?"

He shrugged and studied the possibilities the cards were offering him. "Nobody's in this studio again till three. We'll be out of there by then."

"And nobody minds you tying up the staff like that?"

The smile grew as wide as the mustache. "Oh, no. I'm a star. They like me around here . . . for now. The ratings will have their own opinion, but . . . have we met, Jack?"

"No."

He frowned at me genially; he had the distracted air of an absentminded professor. "And yet I *know* you."

"You've met my stepmother, Maggie Starr."

His cigar went erect. "Now there's a wicked stepmother any boy could love."

I shifted in the uncomfortable would-be chair. "You might have seen me at Hal Rapp's Halloween party, the other night."

His eyes left the cards to study me, disappearing into slits under eyebrows that were small replicas of the mustache. "You weren't in costume. I went to some trouble, you know." He gestured to his full head of Brylcreemed black hair. "Think it's easy stuffing all this under a bald cap?"

"I was in costume, sort of," I said. "I came as a detective. But I cheated a little, because I am one."

Black four on a red five. "With the city?"

"With the Starr Syndicate. My official title is vice president, but I'm really the in-house troubleshooter. If our talent gets in a jam, faces a lawsuit or whatever, I do my best to keep 'em out of trouble."

"So, then I take it *Sam Fizer* was on your talent roster."

"That's right."

His expression took on a rumpled sympathy. "I guess that shouldn't be held against you."

"It shouldn't?"

"No." He gestured with open hands, the remainder of the card deck in one of the massive mitts. "How can you anticipate suicide? Sam always seemed cheerful enough."

"It wasn't suicide, Charlie. The papers *say* it was, but they've been fed a line. That was murder, which is why the cops kept you and your wife and everybody else at the party until damn near sunup."

He looked past me, appearing even more distracted than usual. ". . . I might know why."

"Why what?"

His eyes shifted to mine; no smile, no expression at all, really, a betrayal of the serious human being behind the mask of distraction.

"Why Sam killed himself," he said. "We played poker every week, Sam and I and some other stellar citizens. He's been losing, really losing. I think he owed a gentleman named Carmichael at least fifty thousand, maybe more. And I use the term 'gentleman' loosely, in the men's room door parlance."

"Tony Carmichael is Tony Carmine, Charlie. And Tony Carmine is part of the Calabria mob."

"I met Frank Calabria, once," Mazurki said absently, still working at solitaire, my Carmichael/Carmine info apparently no revelation. "He stopped by the dressing room after my wife's opening night at the Copa. Very charming. Dresses well."

"How charming is Carmichael?"

His half smile was wider than most full ones; again the cigar angled skyward. "Not that charming. I'll play poker with just about anybody, but I have to wonder where Sam Fizer bumped into that specimen."

"Tony Carmine is a big-league bookie—one of his specialties is championship fights. That's no doubt how Sam met him—Sam took the boxing aspect of *Mug O'Malley* seriously, you know."

Mazurki nodded, eyes on the cards. "I knew Sam, casually, for years. Loud but harmless. These last five or six months, he's not shown much restraint with his gambling. I'm no one to judge—I lost ten thousand playing gin last week—but Sam never bet that kind of money until lately."

"Not until he and his wife went bust over her playing Bathless Bessie in *Tall Paul*."

He glanced up, both black eyebrows lifting. "Is *that* why they split? Interesting. But if Sam *had* killed himself, these gambling debts might be the reason."

I shook my head. "Sam Fizer was a wealthy man. He made a small fortune off his strip over the years."

He beamed at me, the sleepy eyes providing an ironic edge. "I'm sure he did. Look at me, Jack. I signed a million-dollar contract with the network two months ago, and I'm up to my eyeballs in debt. The cards hate me lately, but I don't give up on a love affair that easily. Still, it can give a man . . . pause."

"How can you sign a million-dollar contract and be broke?"

"I didn't say I was broke. This is a five-year contract and they don't hand it all to you in a laundry basket in cash. And I have a business manager who has his own ideas about where my money should go, and an ex-wife with her own point of view, and a present wife also with her own ideas. Uncle Sam has been making noise about wanting *his* share, too, greedy bugger. It can get . . . tricky. For example, I eat at Sardi's at least three times a week. Very expensive. Do you know why I continue eating there, at such prices?"

"I couldn't guess."

He shrugged elaborately. "If I stop, they'll expect me to pay my bill. I owe them seven thousand and change."

"How can you live like that?"

"How could I live any *other* way? The cards will warm up to me, Jack. Plenty of time—I'll live forever. I have the formula."

"Which is?"

"All it takes is three steam baths a day, lots of good brandy, twenty superior cigars and working all night. You should try it, boy."

"I'm on the wagon, so your health regimen doesn't suit me."

"Pity."

"How much did you owe Sam Fizer?"

Both eyebrows went up as he gave me the endless smile again under that infinite mustache. "Twenty-five thousand. Interesting thing is . . . I know Sam could have used it, to help pay off Mr. Carmichael, if nothing else. But Sam never pushed. Never called me about it, never took me aside at his poker party to suggest I pay up before betting any further. He couldn't have been nicer."

"That sounds unlikely."

"Doesn't it?"

I leaned forward. "I have an idea for a comedy sketch, Charlie. It's a spoof of murder mysteries. Can I try it out on you? If you want it, it's no charge."

"Shoot."

"Stop me if you've heard it. . . . There's this comedian who has a beautiful actress wife. An obnoxious cartoonist puts the make on the comedian's actress wife. She's as faithful as she is beautiful, the actress wife, so she sends the cartoonist packing, but doesn't tell her comedian husband, who's known to be jealous and to have a real temper bubbling below his placid surface."

Solitaire had lost his attention. "This isn't so funny."

"We aren't at the punch line yet, Charlie. As it happens, the cartoonist has an archenemy . . . a comic strip term, archenemy, but it fits . . . and that archenemy is *also* a cartoonist, who we'll call Cartoonist Number Two. As chance would have it, the comedian owes Cartoonist Number Two a lot of money. So the comedian, a very tricky, clever guy, almost a magician the way he stages things, comes up with a stunt. . . . The comedian murders Cartoonist Number Two, staging an obviously phony suicide, framing Cartoonist Number One."

"Two birds," Mazurki said, nodding, "one stone."

"What do you think? Any potential?"

He tapped the big cigar into the glass tray. "Not for comedy. You should try Jack Webb. He's in Hollywood. Planes are leaving regularly."

"Did you know Rapp put the make on your wife, Charlie?"

His face took on a stony blankness now. "I did. I heard about it."

"She doesn't think you know."

"But I do."

"And you did nothing about it? Why would you attend Rapp's Halloween party, if he'd tried that kind of garbage with Candy?"

His expression warmed up; he couldn't have looked more genial. "Because that low-life one-legged son of a bitch is the creator of *Tall Paul*, and my wife is starring in the musical based on *Tall Paul*, meaning said son of a bitch was throwing the party with the cast as special guests. For appearance's sake, to lend some support to my wife, I attended. As Henry, the boy mute. Since I was required to *stay* mute about the situation, that seemed in keeping."

"And you just let Rapp get away with it."

He chuckled; he had lost this round of solitaire, and was gathering the cards for another shuffle. "Jack, you've seen my wife. She's a living doll. If I really took time out to thrash, much less murder, every man who makes a pass at her, I wouldn't have time left to do the important things, like doing television shows and appearing in movies and playing cards and making passes at Candace myself, which I'm glad to say she considers a compliment, coming as they do from her husband."

It did seem a stretch—bad temper or not, Charlie Mazurki was a grown-up who swam regularly in the murky waters of both Manhattan and Hollywood, and the notion that he would frame a guy for murder over making a clumsy pass at Candy Cain seemed thin at best.

And a guy running up the kind of stupid debts Charlie was, killing Sam Fizer to get out of a mere twenty-five grand worth of IOUs? Ridiculous.

"I don't think you did it," I said, rising. "But be ready for

Captain Chandler of Homicide to come back around, with another load of questions."

"Thanks for the tip."

"You mind if I make a comment, apropos of not much?"

His cigar had gone out; he was relighting it. "Why not?"

"You're not that funny off camera."

He released smoke through a big grin. "No one's paying me to be."

I went back to the office but had the elevator boy (who was in his fifties) stop at the third floor, and the landing off of which my apartment was. Half a Lindy's corned beef/pastrami and Swiss on rye was waiting in my fridge, as well as half a serving of cole slaw and another half of potato salad.

I was in the process of washing all of that down with a Coke when the phone rang in my bedroom. The apartment was laid out boxcar fashion, kitchen in back, bedroom after that, living room beyond. The bedroom had warm yellow walls and Heywood-Wakefield furnishings plus some framed ersatz Picasso prints I picked up in the Village. A small desk served as a second office area, and that's where the phone was.

When I saw the white flickering light that meant it was the house line, I sat and picked up the receiver. Then my right ear was treated to Bryce's arch tones, still tinged with resentment: "Do you expect me to hold down the fort alone?"

"That's what holding down the fort usually means," I reminded him. He was Maggie's assistant, not mine, and I didn't pay him and I didn't have to put up with him.

"You have half a dozen calls this morning. Are you coming in?"

"Give 'em to me," I said, and he sighed as if I'd tried to borrow a C-note, and I jotted the names down and sometimes a précis of the message. Four of the callers were Starr Syndicate business that could keep.

Two weren't.

"When did Captain Chandler call?" I asked.

"Late morning."

"And this call from Tony Carmine?"

"That just came in. He's rude. He called me 'honey.'"

"Maybe he meant it in a nice way."

"He didn't."

So I called Captain Chandler's office and he was in, the receptionist connecting us immediately.

"If there was any doubt before," the Homicide captain said, "there's isn't now: it was murder."

"You got the postmortem results?"

"Fizer had a belly full of sedatives."

"I guess that's fitting. A lot of people had a belly full of Fizer. So he was unconscious when he was killed?"

"Like they say, he didn't know what hit him."

"Look, Captain, I don't know what Maggie's up to, but she said you people need to do a full autopsy."

"'You people'? I work for you now?"

"That's the way it goes in a democracy where working stiffs pay taxes and civil servants do our bidding."

"Yeah, well, swell, only what do you think the postmortem was, if not an autopsy?"

"I think some coroner's assistant cut open Sam's stomach,

checked its contents and, having worked up an appetite, went to lunch."

A long pause.

Then he said, "Well, why not? Cause of death was obvious, gunshot to the left temple."

"I'm just saying, Maggie wants you to request a full autopsy. From toenails to bald spot."

"Why?"

"I don't know. She's mysterious sometimes. She's a beautiful woman, and all beautiful women are enigmatic."

"I don't have much trouble figuring my wife out. When she closes one eye and stares at me with the other, I know damn well I'm in for it."

"Are you doubting Maggie? Do you want me to tell her you told her to go jump in a lake? Captain, I know you're sweet on her."

"Jack, I'm a happily married man."

"I must be mistaken, then, that you turn into a tub of goo when Maggie's on the scene."

"Don't talk like that."

"Why? If your wife hears, will she shut one eye? Listen, I'm a detective, you're a detective, but Maggie? She has intuition."

"Is that right?"

"By intuition I mean, she's smarter than me, and we both know I'm smarter than you, so add that up and get back to me."

Another long pause.

"I'll call the coroner," he said. "What have you got for me? You've been running around talking to our potential suspects, haven't you?"

"Yeah."

And I threw him a couple of bones, stuff he'd find out for himself, anyway, if he hadn't already—that Fizer threatened to name Rapp as a correspondent in the divorce proceedings against Misty; and that Charlie Mazurki was into Sam Fizer for twenty-five grand. Let him work for the rest.

So we bid each other wary good-byes, and I looked at the other message I'd scribbled down: *"Tony Carmine wants to see you ASAP."* There was a third-floor office number at the *"Brill Bldg."*

I leaned over to open the bottom drawer on the left-hand side of my desk. I reached in and took out the old .45 Colt the major had brought home from his war; it resided in the brown-leather shoulder holster I'd bought myself right after my war.

Rarely did I wear the rig. But I got up, slipped off the jacket of my light brown Botany 500 worsted, gently rested it over the chair, and arranged the straps until it was as close to comfortable as possible, the big gun under my left shoulder. How did women put up with brassieres, anyway?

Like a kid playing cowboy, I drew the pistol a couple times; first try, it caught on the leather, but second and third and in particular fourth time went fine and fast.

When a guy like Tony Carmine asked you to come around, you had to be a good Boy Scout.

Prepared.

The golden front entry of the Brill Building was rather grand, but the brick exterior of its fifteen stories or so were as drab as the interior was smoke-grimed; even the elevators seemed to cough, when they weren't wheezing and creaking.

And yet the Brill Building was the nerve center of two enter-
tainment industries: prizefighters and their managers and the assorted helpers and hooligans of the boxing game made this
unlikely, unpretentious structure their stronghold; but they
shared it with Tin Pan Alley, the music publishers and songwriters
and arrangers and piano players who created much of America's
popular music. The unlikely convergence of these two worlds,
thanks to the proximity of Madison Square Garden and the
theater district, was reflected in the two restaurants at street level—
Jack Dempsey's, where you've already been, that palace for pugs;
and the Turf, a musician's hangout, where we won't be going.

Tony Carmine had an office halfway down an industrial-green
hallway of frosted-glass doors and frosted-glass-and-wood walls,
behind which pianos pounded out potential hits (and probable
flops). Singers, male and female, solo and group, were often going
at it behind the frosted glass, providing a kind of shifting musical
tapestry as I passed.

Carmine's door bore only a number, no name (neither
Carmine nor Carmichael), and I knocked on the wood frame, rattling it.

I could hear a chair scrape the wooden floor and then footsteps; the door opened and Tony Carmine smiled at me with the
sincerity of a guy showing hot jewelry at a pawn shop.

"You must be Jack Starr," he said in a nasal grating mid-range
voice that was odds-on favorite for least musical on this floor.

He was a small man, pale enough to call into question his
ever having set foot in daylight; he wore a white shirt with a red
bow tie and red black-edged suspenders and black slacks. His
black hair was slicked back, his eyes were small and close-set

and ratlike, his nose prominent and ratlike, with a Clark Gable mustache over a small, ratlike mouth.

He reminded me of a rat.

"Yeah," I said. "We haven't met, but I've seen you around. We have mutual friends."

"I know we do." He made a gracious gesture with a tiny, perfectly manicured hand. "Step into my humble abode."

Of course it wasn't an abode, it was an office, but pointing that out would have been rude; and, anyway, it was fairly humble.

The side and rear walls were covered in green soundproof tiles, meaning this had been set up for musical tenants, and you could see the shadow on the floor where an upright piano had been. A big blond desk faced the door with a table against the wall behind it with stacks of this and that—newspapers, magazines, photos, and correspondence.

He had a window whose blinds were shut, and the one unsoundproofed wall, behind him, was decorated with framed photographs of professional fighters, some famous, some not. A red sofa was off to the left, and a couple of wooden chairs were against the walls here and there; a coat tree in one corner was home to his bloodred sportscoat and a wide-brimmed white Borsalino with a black band.

I took off my fedora and sat it beside me; my suitcoat was unbuttoned, the .45 a reassuring weight under my left arm. "What is it you do out of this office, Tony?"

I knew full well the guy was a glorified bookie; but what were all the photos of fighters about?

"I represent boxers," he said, settling behind the desk. He was so small I could only think of a grade-school kid sneaking a moment in the teacher's chair while she'd stepped out.

He was saying, "Not in the ring, I'm no manager—it's the public appearance stuff, opening supermarkets, signing autographs at car shows and so on. . . . Sit, Jack, sit. It's generous of you to respond to my phone call, us being more or less strangers."

Just to be difficult, the seat I took was the sofa, which meant he had to swivel sideways and talk across the office to me. That wasn't a big deal, as the room was hardly spacious; but I liked needling him a little.

His chair was a leather-upholstered number and he rocked in it as we talked; his socks showed—they were red with black stripes. He reminded me of Eagle-Eye Spiegel, the little zoot-suited character in *Tall Paul* who could freeze you in your tracks with his hypnotic double whammy.

"You're wondering why I asked you up here," he said.

"Yeah, particularly since I wanted to talk to you, anyway."

He gestured with two hands as he rocked back. "Well, you're my guest—you go first. Say, there's coffee and soda down the hall—would you like anything?"

"No, I'm fine." I shifted and the fake leather under me squeaked. "I'm looking into the Sam Fizer murder."

Skinny eyebrows rose. "Murder? I thought Sam took *himself* out."

"The papers would make you think that. But it was a put-up job—gun in the wrong hand, no powder burns on his hand, gut full of sedatives."

Carmine grunted a laugh. "Amateurs. Well, you can't think *I* had anything to do with it."

"Why can't I?"

His smile was white, possibly purchased. "Well, Jack, he owed me money. You don't kill a guy owes you money. Seventy-five thousand in poker debts, from our weekly game—I was in a weekly game at Sam's, over at the Waldorf. Or did you know that?"

I nodded. "There's more?"

His eyes flared; nostrils, too. "Plenty. One hundred grand on the Marciano/LaStarza match."

"Ouch." I'd been at the Polo Grounds for that. Pretty brutal— the ref stopped the fight in the eleventh, first six rounds having been a fight, the final five a slaughter.

He rocked back, kept rocking. "Which is why I asked you here, Jack."

"I bet on Marciano."

"The smart money *did*, obviously. But Sam was a lot of things, a famous cartoonist, and a great guy, really . . . but smart about where he bet his money, he wasn't."

"Which has what to do with me?"

His smile expanded beyond the confines of the skinny mustache; his hands were tented together, as he rocked and rocked. "How I understand it, when a big-time cartoonist drops unfortunately dead, the syndicate that distributes it more or less . . . inherits it. Keeps it going, and rakes in the dough."

"Something like that."

He shrugged elaborately. "Well, I think it's only *fair* that the Starr Syndicate, as the heirs of *Mug O'Malley*, clean up this gambling debt. It's a hundred and seventy-five thousand . . . but I am graciously willing to settle for one-fifty."

"Are you?"

A tiny shrug now. "You see, I can't go to his estate for relief, 'cause after all these are illegal gambling debts. But a technicality like that shouldn't stand in the way of what's right and what's fair."

I had to laugh. "And what's right and what's fair is that we pay off Sam's gambling debts?"

"I'm knocking off twenty-five grand, ain't I?"

I leaned back on the sofa, folded my arms. "You know, Tony, I was thinking you weren't much of a suspect in this thing. Now I'm not so sure."

The tiny eyes popped. "Suspect?"

"If you're dumb enough to think that the Starr Syndicate would pay up where Sam Fizer himself wouldn't, well . . . maybe you're also dumb enough to stage the clumsiest phony suicide in history."

His smile, like his eyes, was tiny—and nasty. "You're a big guy, Jack, physically, I mean."

I shrugged. "Little over six feet. Two hundred pounds, maybe. Nothing the freak shows on Broadway would be interested in. Why, Tony?"

He rocked. Rocked. "Well, I'm thinking you're looking at me, and figuring, where does this little pipsqueak get off threatening a big lug like me?"

"*Are* you threatening me?"

He jerked a thumb at the wall behind him. "You see these photos, Jack?"

"That's a lot of ugly wallpaper, Tony. Why surround yourself with so much cauliflower?"

He turned a hand as he continued to rock. "Y'see, not all of my fighters get the work on the side they need, you know, to support their own habits and hobbies and such like. Some of 'em don't have as much luck in the ring as others of them, but they all got two things in common."

"Which are?"

"Which are, they can always use a little cash on the side; and that there's not one of them that couldn't pound you into a puddle of what used to be you. Two at a time, they make two puddles out of you. Or more."

I just grinned at him.

"What are you smiling about, Jack?"

I got on my feet. "Could I use your phone, Tony?"

He frowned. "What? To call the police? Don't be a jackass, Jack."

"Not to call the police. It's a call you'll be glad I made."

He studied me, nose twitching. Did I mention he reminded me of a rat?

"Go ahead," Tony said. "Just don't get too cute, Jack."

"Usually I get just cute enough, Tony."

Then I stood at his desk, where I swung the phone around and dialed a number I knew by heart. No answer. Then I dialed another number I knew by heart.

"Joey?" I said. "This is Jack Starr. Is he in?"

He was in.

"Frank," I said. "Sorry to bother you, but I'm over at the Brill Building talking to a comical character who thinks the Starr Syndicate should pay Sam Fizer's gambling debts."

Frank Calabria said, "Put that little weasel on."

One man's rat was another man's weasel.

I handed the receiver toward him.

He took it.

"Hello?" Carmine's complexion had started out pale; now it was arctic. His little eyes bulged like buttons on a fat man's vest; his tiny mouth was trembling and the nostrils of his big nose opened and closed and opened and closed. "Frank, I'm *sorry*, I had no way of *knowing*. . . . Frank, I *swear* I didn't know. . . . Complete pass, he gets a *complete* pass! . . . Thank you, Frank. God bless you, Frank."

Tony swallowed and hung up the phone carefully, as if it might bite him otherwise. He looked up at me like a newly naturalized Latvian-American contemplating Mount Rushmore.

"Frank says you're an old pal," Tony said timidly.

I went back to the sofa and flopped there. "Yeah. He and my father, the major, were in business together. Frank still has a tiny piece of the Starr Syndicate."

"Oh, hell . . . I didn't know." He swallowed again. "You mean, by putting the arm on you I was . . ."

"Putting the arm on Frank Calabria."

He shuddered.

I waved it off. "But don't worry about it. It's not like he'll send a guy around to shoot you."

The knock that came to the door could not have been more perfectly timed by Hitchcock. It made Carmine jump, and that would have been funny as hell if I hadn't jumped a little, too.

Carmine got out of his chair and headed toward the door, where a second series of knocks insisted on attention. He paused and said to me, "I got an appointment. You better go."

But I was still seated, reaching for my fedora, when Carmine opened the door, said, "Yes?" and all I saw was the snout of the silenced automatic come into view as somebody in the hall pointed it at Tony Carmine's belly and fired twice, two coughlike reports that crumpled the little man, dropping him to his office floor in a shivering fetal position.

I couldn't help it; my first thought was: *Jesus, Frank, that was fast.*

But my second thought was to get out the .45 and try to catch whoever had done this.

**I**f you're wondering why I didn't call for an ambulance or at least notify the police, what with my diminutive host sprawled on the floor just inside his office door with his white shirt turning as red as his suspenders, well, I was a cop once myself. An MP. I'd seen people gut-shot, and I knew he was a goner.

Tony Carmine had minutes at most left, when I stepped over him to go out into the corridor, .45 in hand, still enough of a cop to put pursuit of the killer ahead of calling in the kill.

And there he was, down at the end of the hall, a big guy, over six feet, in a black fedora and a black woolen topcoat that flapped as he ran, his trousers and shoes black, too, Death trading in its flowing black robe and scythe for street clothes and a silenced automatic. He went through the fire exit door, leaving an empty narrow hall for me to barrel down.

With that sound-suppressed weapon, the shots hadn't been heard by anybody but Tony and me and the shooter, although had the guy just blasted away with that rod unsilenced, who can say anybody would have noticed on a floor where a different concert was in session behind every smoked-glass door, fingers banging away at pianos, machine-gunning ivories and sharps and flats . . .

Luckily I didn't bump into anybody coming out an office, and when I burst through the fire exit door onto the landing, I quickly shut it behind me to minimize the pop music cacophony of the Brill Building's third floor.

Right now I was listening not for singing or piano playing but percussion, the snare drumming of feet on wooden steps in the echo chamber of the stairwell. And I heard those racing footsteps all right, but I had to squint and really perk up my ears to tell whether the hollow cadence was coming from above or below.

Logic said the shooter would head down, with the street only a few floors below; but my ears said he'd gone up, maybe hoping to confuse the issue and reach an upper floor and either duck into an office or an elevator before anyone was the wiser. These thoughts were accompanying me as my own feet rattled up the screaky stairs, and I at first didn't catch it when the footfalls I was following ceased.

I got to the fifth-floor landing, damn glad I was no longer a smoker, and paused for a split second to listen when a flash of black like the wings of a dark giant bird came from above, as the son of a bitch dove from the half landing where he'd waited to surprise me.

The wings were that flapping topcoat, unbuttoned to make getting at his gun easier I suppose, and I was lucky he'd tucked the thing away because maybe then he'd have done more than just jump on me, taking me down hard on the wooden landing, my right hand popping open to send my .45 rattling down the stairs on its own way, God knew where.

The momentum took the two of us down, too, and we instinctively clutched each other as we rode down the stairs, him on top of me, like a kid on a sled navigating a particularly bumpy hill.

The steps played my spine like a xylophone but made no music at all, unless you counted the curses and grunts I was spitting out; the guy making a Radio Flyer out of me kept silent. In the blur of topcoat and fedora, snugged so low it stayed on his skull despite the leap and the fall, a black-and-red scarf tied over his lower face like the pulp magazine's Shadow, I got no real look at him, had no idea if I knew this guy or not.

And when we finally hit the next landing, halfway between floors, he crawled off me and was scrambling to make a getaway; I was a bug on its back but I somehow managed to catch him by an ankle and yank his leg out from under him and dropped him hard on his side onto the landing floor.

I was on my feet maybe half a second before he got to his, and socked him in the scarf, or maybe the nose under the scarf, and he reeled back but in a flash responded with a forearm aimed for my throat that I blocked with a forearm of my own. He swung a hard fist into my side, and I clenched in response, inadvertently giving him time to bring up a knee whose precious target I twisted to protect, getting caught in the hip bone instead. My balance already in question, he shoved me into the wall and my back caught just the edge of the railing and it felt like a knife had been jammed into me. I winced and he was flying down the stairs again, topcoat flapping.

That was when I spotted the .45 against the wall three steps below. I retrieved it and clamored after him, yelling, "Stop or I'll shoot!" Not original, but you do better under the circumstances. . . .

He jumped from two-thirds down the flight onto the second-floor landing and, in midair, in a move worthy of his Shadow-like appearance, pulled the silenced automatic from his waistband and pointed it up toward me and fired.

With no grace at all, I ducked, as the bullet chewed up wood on the step just above me, and I returned fire.

The bullet caught him in the left shoulder, just as he was alighting, and slammed him against the railing and the wall; but as I came charging down at him like the wrath of God, he swung his gun-in-hand my way, and when I dove out of the slug's path, the cough-like report followed by more splintering of wood, I lost my balance and went bumping down the stairs on my butt as he disappeared down the half flight to where a door onto the alley awaited.

Blood drops on the stairs to that door and then trailing down the alley toward the street were unintentional breadcrumbs he was leaving along his path, but they did me no good out on the sidewalk, Broadway bustling, my quarry just another hat and top-coat lost in the busy parade.

Maybe I would have run along after him, but two factors worked against me. First, I looked like a wild-eyed, disheveled maniac who'd emerged from an alley with a .45 in his hand. And second, I felt like some poor bastard who had just fallen down a bunch of steps, the hard way, although I'm not convinced there's an easy way. Both were apt descriptions of me on that late afternoon.

That was the exciting part.

I'm going to spare you the rest of that day, except in condensed form. I called Captain Chandler, who came over personally with crime scene boys and assorted other plainclothes men, and it only took till about eight P.M. for them to ask their questions, walk me through what I'd seen and done, and take a formal statement. Thankfully I was not taken into custody, although my .45 was. One guy with a clipboard was doing diagrams so elaborate, I thought about signing him to the Starr Syndicate for a strip.

Captain Chandler and I were out front of the Brill in the cool, crisp evening air sharing the unwarmth of the neon glow when he asked, "Say, you need a doctor or anything?"

"Thanks for asking. It's only been, what? Four hours since some thug threw me down a couple flights of stairs and used me as a punching bag. But I appreciate the thought."

He was lighting up a cigarette, its orange blush illuminating his face under the brim of the fedora. "I can drive you over to Bellevue if you like. On the city's dime."

"Right. I let you take me to Bellevue and the next thing I know, I'll be fitted for a jacket that buttons up in the back. You want to do something for me, buy me a chunk of cheesecake."

I lied before, when I said you wouldn't be going to the Turf. Because that's exactly where Captain Chandler and I shared a booth as we each enjoyed a piece of the famous cheesecake invented by Arnold Reuben, owner of the joint. I was having another of my rare cups of coffee, because Coca-Cola and cheesecake don't mix.

Chandler, his fedora on a hook alongside our booth, was saying, "I don't think your description of the guy's going to do much good."

I forked some cheesecake. "Can't you put an all points bulletin out on black topcoats and red-and-black plaid scarfs? Then call me in for the lineup?"

The Homicide captain ignored my sarcasm; he was so distracted, he'd already abandoned his cheesecake halfway through—best in New York, best in the world.

"We'll find the guy," he said. "I've already put word out to all the hospital emergency wards."

"But he'll go to some underworld sawbones, won't he?"

Chandler shrugged. "Depends. If he's a mob guy, some Murder Inc. hired hand, he'll avoid the kind of doctor who reports gunshot wounds. But I don't think that's the case here."

"You don't?"

He shook his head with certainty. "You're up to your belt buckle in the Sam Fizer murder; and Tony Carmine was an associate of Fizer's. I'm not much for coincidences, Jack—this is the second murder in the same case, and it changes everything."

I didn't figure he'd thought this through right. And later I would tell Maggie as much, and why I thought so, and she would agree. But I didn't see any reason to help Chandler at the moment. The cheesecake was a nice gesture, but that went toward the hours of my time he and his crew had burned up in the Brill Building.

Chandler sipped coffee; his brow was furrowed. "The guy in the topcoat and scarf, Jack—who could he have been in this case?"

"I don't know if I follow."

"Let me put it this way—based on his general size and shape, could the killer have been any of the Fizer suspects or witnesses you've talked to?"

I swallowed cheesecake, thinking the Statue of Liberty should come down and one of Arnold Reuben should go up. "I kind of doubt it was Misty Winters; wrestling with her would've been more fun. And I don't think it was Murray Coe, unless he was standing on somebody's shoulders under that topcoat. If it was Hal Rapp, he's gotten damn good with that wooden leg."

"Be serious."

I shrugged a single shoulder; that's all it was worth. "Really could've only been one guy in this affair—your favorite TV comedian and mine, Charlie Mazurki."

"He's not my favorite. He doesn't make me laugh."

"Well, his stuff is really only for the cognoscenti." From the look on Chandler's puss, I could just picture him going home and trying to find that in the dictionary, to see if I'd insulted him. "Charlie's a big man, and could give me a bad time like that guy in the stairwell did."

"*Was* it Mazurki?"

"I wouldn't rule him out. Check on him. See if he's got an alibi, because that's what detectives do, I'm told."

And that was as much help as I was in the mood to give the captain. I had my own ideas about what might be going on, plus I had the rest of my cheesecake to eat.

Ray Alexander, the creator of the phenomenally successful science-fiction strip *Crash Landon*, resided in a penthouse apartment on upper Fifth Avenue, overlooking Central Park. It was the kind of place where the living-room carpet was a twenty-by-thirty garden-pattern Kashan, the framed paintings on the walls were by Cézanne, Monet and Renoir, and the baby grand was whiter than Pepsodent.

The day after I'd composed my symphony to bruises and bumped bones at the Brill Building, I wrangled an invitation to join Alexander for a meeting I'd been trying to arrange since yesterday morning. Actually, Bryce had been trying to arrange it, but Alexander had been reluctant to give Maggie's assistant any time for me, saying he was behind deadline and a "syndicate man" like Jack Starr would surely understand.

Late this morning, I'd called the cartoonist myself and made it clear that Maggie and I were working on behalf of Hal Rapp, with his approval and cooperation. This had finally cleared the way.

I was moving slow. I had slept in, having dosed up on over-the-counter sleeping pills. And today my bloodstream was about 90 percent aspirin and 10 percent corpuscles. Nothing seemed broken, but I was getting around with the speed, agility and grace of a Civil War survivor.

Right now Ray Alexander and I were sitting on his sunporch with afternoon rays streaming in the many windows; one corner of this enclosed terrace was taken up by his drafting board and attendant furnishings and materials, and the rest was potted evergreens and bamboo sofas and lounge chairs, appropriately padded.

We were in a couple of wicker chairs, angled to suit conversation, and between us was a glimmering green view of the park and a small wicker table that provided a home for his ashtray and a chilled pitcher of martinis.

Alexander—a big, rangy character in a blue untucked sportshirt with lighter blue collar, chinos and slippers—was sipping a martini. When I'd politely turned down the gin, he provided me with a Coke in a tumbler of ice. (I've been asked if the frequent mentions of Coca-Cola in these recorded cases have resulted in my receiving any free product. The answer, thus far, is no. But I can be reached at the Starr Syndicate in New York, if Coke is interested. We're listed.)

As he'd ushered me in, past the white piano and through glass doors onto the sunporch, Alexander had noticed I was staggering like Frankenstein's monster, and I'd told him that in the course of the Fizer investigation I'd recently witnessed a murder and slugged it out, up and down several flights of stairs, with the murderer himself.

At first he thought I was kidding, and somewhere in there I mentioned I hadn't hurt this bad since the day after a football match back in prep school. Turned out he'd played football and been to prep school, too, and we were suddenly comrades. Well, buddies. With Senator McCarthy around, being a comrade these days was dangerous.

Alexander was yet another of these cigarette-holder-wielding cartoonists; but somehow he didn't look ridiculous or pretentious doing it. In his early forties, he had those ruggedly handsome good looks you hear so much about but seldom see, deeply tanned, with dark curly hair, sky-blue eyes and, like the late Tony Carmine, a Clark Gable mustache. No one would have mistaken Ray Alexander for a rat, however.

"I have to admit," Raymond said, his voice deep and mellow, "when the papers said Sam committed suicide, I had no trouble buying it."

"Really? A guy with an overblown ego like Sam Fizer? Who's more unlikely to take his own life than a guy like that?"

His expression turned odd, his mouth freezing into a small, stilted smile. "Certainly Sam was a little guy with a big ego. But he was also volatile, overemotional. That's why suicide seemed a reasonable out for him."

I sipped my Coke, encouraging the leisurely atmosphere. "I think there's no question Sam hid a lot of insecurity behind that bombast."

I gestured to a *Crash Landon* Sunday-page original that leaned against the wall next to his drawing board—a beautifully rendered page with swooping spaceships and bold men and beautiful women, done in Alexander's distinctive style known as dry brush and more appealing, to me at least, than the museum's worth of paintings in his living room.

I said to him, "You're the best artist in the business, Mr. Alexander. Imagine what it would be like to be as famous a cartoonist as Sam Fizer and know in your heart you're lousy?"

The smile unfroze and the mustache twitched. "Well, you're kind to say I'm the best in the business. There's a guy named Hal Foster who might put up an argument." He saluted me with his martini. "And make it 'Ray,' would you, Jack?"

"Sure."

He filled his big chest with air and let it out in a matter-of-fact sigh. "Anyway, why are we even *discussing* suicide? Sam *must* have been murdered if, as you say, there's been a second killing. Who's the new victim? My God, I hope it's not somebody else I know!"

I dropped the bomb I'd been nurturing: "Actually it is, Ray. A friend of yours. Or at least an acquaintance."

He frowned. "What the hell?"

"Tony Carmine. It was in the papers this morning, but didn't get much play. Page seven or deeper."

"I didn't see it." The cartoonist didn't seem very heartbroken to hear about the loss of Carmine. "Not much press play, you say, Jack? Why not, you suppose?"

"The cops are putting a lid on any connection Carmine's shooting might have to the Fizer murder . . . which is, remember—as far as the press is concerned—still a suicide."

The sky-blue eyes were cool. "Understood."

"Carmine ran with a tough crowd," I said. "A guy who takes bets on that scale, and who has an army of ex-pugs to collect for him, doesn't win popularity contests. You can't expect the press to express much surprise when somebody pumps a couple slugs into his breadbasket."

Alexander chuckled, then seemed immediately embarrassed. "Sorry," he said. "Don't mean to laugh over such a tragic circumstance. But you really *do* talk that way, don't you?"

"What way?"

"Like *Martin Kane, Private Eye* on television, or Mike Hammer in the paperbacks." He shifted in the wicker chair, and it whined. "You know, I put in my notice with King Features last week. I'm turning *Crash* over to an assistant."

That surprised me just a little more than that guy knocking on Carmine's door and killing him. "Why, Ray? You're on top of the world with *Crash*."

"I'm following Milton's lead." He meant Milton Caniff, creator of *Terry and the Pirates* and, more recently, *Steve Canyon*.

"Oh. You're putting together a *new* strip—something you can own yourself."

He nodded, sipped his martini. Gestured with the cigarette-in-holder. "King Features owns *Crash*. I was just a kid, in my twenties, when I signed away the farm to them. Anyway, this space-opera stuff is boring my behind off."

"Well, if you have a new property, Maggie and I would love to see it. You'd like the terms we'd offer."

As it happened, we'd just lost our top story-strip man. . . .

"I was considering maybe a western strip," he mused, "but you've got me thinking."

"In what way?"

"Maybe a detective strip. People like private eyes these days."

"Sounds good." Actually, it didn't. The private-eye fad had never crossed over to comics, and anyway didn't look like anything that could last. But Starr would take on any strip a star like Ray Alexander wanted to show us.

"Listen," he said, pouring himself a second martini from the pitcher, "I need to know why you're so convinced Sam didn't kill himself. I'm willing to answer any of your questions, but first I want some background."

So I gave it to him. Frankly, I gave him more than I'd ever given Captain Chandler; I instinctively trusted this guy, who had an urbane, sophisticated nature that merged in an unlikely way with a man's man quality, possibly due to his serving in the Pacific as a marine captain. Anyway, when Alexander realized his friend

Hal Rapp had been framed for Sam's murder, he got interested, and helpful.

"Hal is no angel," Alexander said. "He's a randy SOB and it'll get him in trouble someday. But he's basically a good guy, and he sure as hell is no killer."

I sat forward in the wicker chair and it protested. "You were part of that weekly card game at Fizer's, Ray. A lot of money was changing hands; a lot of IOUs, too. Could somebody in that game have wanted Sam dead?"

The blue eyes twinkled with amusement. "Do you gamble, Jack?"

"A little. I have a weekly poker game with some friends."

"High stakes?"

"Dizzying. You can lose five bucks if the stars align against you."

He shrugged the broad shoulders. "Well, I like to gamble. It's not a sickness or an obsession with me, but I've always liked cards, and I need the stakes to be high enough to give it a little spice. A little risk."

"Risk, huh? I hear you drive a sports car."

He grinned. "I own *four* sports cars. And do you think when I'm out in the country, driving one of them, I obey the speed limit?"

"I would guess that a guy doesn't buy a sports car to drive the speed limit. . . . I have a little Kaiser Darrin, myself."

"Those are cute. You'll have to come for a spin in my Mercedes 300 SL."

Properly put in my place, I said, "You were saying . . . about gambling?"

"Oh. Well, yes. The kind of money . . . the kind of IOUs . . . that changed hands at Sam's poker table, no question it could engender hard feelings. Tens of thousands were involved, over time. A man like Tony Carmichael . . . Carmine, as you call him . . . could put the squeeze on, if you didn't pay up. That may be why Sam invited him, and why I didn't object—you know, I don't normally hang out with gangsters, Jack."

"I'm not following, Ray. Sam invited Carmine to be part of the game *because* Tony was dangerous?"

He gestured with the cigarette-holder-in-hand and traced an abstract pattern in smoke. "Yes. That was the fun. The risk. The ride. Anyway, Sam Fizer was rolling in dough. He invested well over the years, and in general he was frugal, when he wasn't throwing money around to impress people. And I don't have to tell *you* that the strip paid well."

"I get all that. But what's your point?"

"My point is, Carmine or anybody else in that game, who Sam might have owed money to, had a motive to *keep* him alive, not kill him."

I agreed with that, but didn't say so. "This gambling obsession, as you put it—this was new to Sam."

Alexander nodded. "I believe it was. Last five or six months."

"He seems to have gone off the deep end, after he and his wife Misty broke up."

"That could be it."

"Ray, you're starting to clam up on me again."

"Am I?"

"What am I getting *close* to, that you don't want to share?"

"Nothing." He sipped the martini. "Ask me whatever you

like." He drew on his cigarette-in-holder. Blew out smoke. "I'm happy to help out where Hal is concerned."

"The thing is," I said, "I had conversations with both Hal and Sam, shortly before Sam's death. Hal seemed positive that Sam Fizer wouldn't be a problem to him, much longer . . . but he didn't specify *why* . . ."

Alexander appeared cool, unless you noticed his eyes had gone unblinking and hard. And I noticed.

I went on: "But the funny thing is, Sam said the same damn thing to me about Rapp—I came away thinking Fizer had something on *Rapp*, something that would destroy him, professionally, maybe even personally."

"Interesting," he said, as if I'd just shared the least interesting thing imaginable.

"The only thing I can come up with, and I don't have anything solid, is Hal's propensity toward . . . as you put it . . . randiness. He's put the make on every pretty girl in the *Tall Paul* cast, from my stepmother and Candy Cain to the underage chorus cuties whose charms could land you behind bars."

"That's not it," Alexander said, with casual finality.

I just looked at him.

He smiled at me.

And I looked at him some more.

Finally his smile wilted. "Wait here," he said.

The big man rose from the wicker chair and strode from the sunporch with a speed and purpose quite at odds with the relaxed nature he'd displayed till now. I wondered if he was going out to count the Renoirs and Cézannes and so on. My Coke was watery, the ice half melted, but I steeled myself and drank it anyway. Alexander wasn't the only man's man around this joint.

When he returned, perhaps two minutes later, he carried in both hands—like a country preacher protecting a Bible—a 9-inch-by-12-inch black leather pouch. He sat on the edge of the wicker chair and unzipped the pouch and removed a fat manila folder. The pouch he rested beside him on the floor, against the chair; the folder he began to thumb through.

"Jack," he said, in a businesslike voice entirely new to this conversation, "you're aware of Sam's efforts to embarrass Hal with these accusations of sticking smut into *Tall Paul*."

"Yeah." I shrugged. "Saying *Tall Paul* is a sexy strip is like accusing you of putting spaceships in *Crash Landon*. Or should I say phallic symbols?"

I thought that would get a smile out of him. It didn't.

"Take a look at these," Alexander said, and handed me a small stack of slick sheets of paper.

"Syndicate proofs," I said, thumbing through.

Six daily strips printed on a long glossy sheet, a week's worth as sent to subscribing newspapers—this was what they printed the strips from in their individual papers.

As I swiftly scanned the art, I said, "Full of the supposed offensive mushrooms and knotholes, I see, and occasional appearances of the dread number 'sixty-nine.'"

"Over the last five or six months," Alexander said, "Fizer was going around to newspaper editors and showing them examples of the offensive material Rapp is supposedly sneaking into his strip."

"This stuff?" I asked, holding up the proof sheets.

Ducking that, Alexander, his face somber, raised a hand.

"Understand that these were private meetings between a very prominent cartoonist and newspaper editors all across the country."

I nodded. "Not just phone calls, or things Sam said if he happened to bump into one of these editors, socially or on a promotional jaunt. This was a . . . campaign?"

Alexander was nodding, too. "Definitely a campaign. In addition, Fizer submitted his examples of Rapp 'pornography' to the New York state legislature's inquiry into the relationship between juvenile delinquency and comics."

"I have heard about that. I guess I wasn't aware of the extent of Fizer's efforts to embarrass Rapp, but—"

"And," Alexander cut in, "there's a similar inquiry on the docket in Washington—a senate witch hunt into our business. The kind they televise, coast-to-coast."

I grunted a dismissive laugh. "Well, the do-gooders are mostly concerned about comic *books*, not syndicated strips, right?"

Raymond's expression was grave; the Fifth Avenue bon vivant was gone and the marine captain was there in his stead. "We strip people get tarred with the same brush. Jack, you are aware that I'm president of the National Cartoonists Society?"

"Sure. Starr Syndicate has a company membership."

The blue eyes were steely now. "And you can imagine that, in this atmosphere of fear generated by Senator McCarthy and his followers, the last thing the comics field needs right now is this kind of bad publicity."

"Sure. So I guess the NCS wasn't getting ready to vote Fizer a public service award?"

He let out a weary, frustrated sigh. "Over the years, every president of the NCS has written both Rapp and Fizer requesting that they abandon their embarrassing, childish public feud. Our last president, Milton Caniff, a close friend of Hal's, made a personal appeal to Hal, after that article in the *Atlantic* appeared that called Fizer a monster. And Hal finally agreed to back off."

"Didn't anybody talk to Fizer?"

"Of course they did, myself included. I made it clear to Sam that he was giving not just Hal Rapp a black eye, but comics in general. And that for the good of our field, he needed to back off."

"His response?"

"His response was that the field would be better served by the exposure, and removal, of this 'sick pervert.'"

I gestured with the syndicate proof sheets. "And *this* was his evidence?"

"Unfortunately . . . no."

And Alexander thumbed through the manila folder again and handed me a second stack of paper sheets, not syndicate proofs, rather photostats and blowups of individual *Tall Paul* panels. They were bleary and the drawing was, in places, crude, as was the subject matter. Those earthy mushrooms and knotholes were less symbolic and more overt; a male character, talking to a female one, leaned close with a large nose that was not exactly a nose. The wish-granting critter, the Shlomozel, was carried by Paul in a manner that made it unmistakably suggestive of a male member.

These were *Tall Paul* drawings that had poorly drawn or redrawn elements that inserted truly troubling elements into the original drawings.

I took a few moments to compare the syndicate proofs I'd first been handed with this second stack of blurry photostats. The panels as they'd appeared in newspapers had been blatantly doctored after the fact, fairly amateurishly, to look offensive. Others were outright forgeries. Bad ones.

"Fizer did this?" I asked.

Raymond nodded. "Hal Rapp hired his own documents experts, including an ex-FBI man, and submitted the evidence you're looking at, to the executive committee of the NCS."

And now I knew what Fizer "had" on Rapp, or thought he did; and what Rapp really *did* have on Fizer.

"This is fraud," I said. "Fizer could face criminal and civil charges over this."

And the Starr Syndicate's top story strip would be finished. Not that this occurred to me immediately. All right, it did.

"Hal was gracious," Alexander said, "considering—all he asked was for the NCS to deal with Fizer."

"How did you do that?"

Alexander looked past me, his expression rather glazed. "Last Wednesday night, Sam was called here for a meeting. We met right here on this sunporch, and Milton and other top cartoonists were present. We showed Sam the evidence, he offered no defense, and we expelled him."

"You kicked him out of the NCS?"

"Yes." The rugged cartoonist had the expressionless expression of a judge passing a death sentence. "The first time in the history of the organization."

The irony was bittersweet, except for the sweet part: the former assistant had been assisted, even ghosted, by his old boss, whose clumsy touch had been evident.

I asked, "Did you tell Sam you'd go public with this garbage?"

"We told him that would be Hal Rapp's call, not ours."

"How did he react?"

"Quietly. Hardly uttered a word. Turned fish-belly white on us. Just sort of . . . stumbled out of here."

I indicated the material he'd handed me. "Could I borrow these?"

"No. I've spoken with Milton and the others, and it's the executive committee's decision not to have this material made public. We see no reason to embarrass a deceased member of the society."

I wasn't sure you could embarrass a dead guy, but I said, "Fizer wasn't a member, anymore."

"Technically true . . . although for many years, he was—he'd been a founding member, in fact. And he was obviously a sick, troubled man, doing these forgeries, mounting this sad vendetta against his former assistant, who happens to be one of our top cartoonists now. We decided not to sully Sam's memory with this . . . this embarrassing lapse in a career that was otherwise one of the great success stories in our field."

"Plus, it wouldn't do Rapp's reputation any good—that he exposed Sam and pushed him into suicide."

Alexander frowned. "That's a little harsh, Jack."

"Yeah, but accurate, except for one thing: Fizer was murdered, remember. So you, Ray, and the rest of the executive board of your society need to regroup, and quick—you need to share what you know about this sad situation with Captain Chandler of the Homicide Bureau."

His frown deepened. "Is that really necessary?"

"Oh, no—it's strictly optional. Only, you big-shot cartoonists won't care much for the morning light that comes in your new studio windows after you're arrested as material witnesses. The bars play hell with it."

". . . Captain Chandler, you say?"

"Yeah. Why don't I call him, and we'll ask him over?"

Maggie had the evening off from rehearsal, as a freshly written song for Sunflower Sue was in the process of getting inserted into the show, and that—and other musical numbers—was tonight's focus.

So I found her in the gym beyond the office; she was in black leotards riding a stationary bike, hair still pinned up Libidia Von Stackpole–style but face free of makeup.

The room was carpeted in tumbling mats and arrayed with all the latest exercise equipment, to help her work off that excess flab she was carrying round (all two or three pounds of it), plus a punching bag for me to take out my frustrations on.

Except I was in no mood or shape to punch the bag. I was still aching from my stairwell fight, and just standing in that gym, thinking about exercise, made me ache more. She pedaled and I sat in the nearby rowing machine, not rowing, and gave her the lowdown on what I'd learned at Ray Alexander's. Her face gave nothing away, remaining as blank as a bisque baby's throughout my account, as she listened and pedaled and listened and pedaled.

The last thing I shared with her was the conversation with Captain Chandler I'd had on the phone at Alexander's, when I called him to come over to the cartoonist's Fifth Avenue penthouse. Chandler had shared several interesting tidbits with me, including the results of the full autopsy performed on Fizer.

Finally I said, "That's the whole boat," which struck me as clever, since I was sitting in that rowing machine. But Maggie was tough to amuse even with a good joke. And right now she had stopped pedaling.

"I guess we both know what really happened here," she said.

"I guess we do. Did you know before or after Captain Chandler's report?"

"Before."

"Well, then, it's just barely possible you're smarter than me. I needed that last puzzle piece."

She climbed off the bike, picked up her towel from the tumbling-mat floor and patted off pearls of perspiration from her improbably young-looking face.

"I guess I've known all along," she said. "I just didn't have any evidence."

"Do we have any now?"

She offered up a glum smirk. "Not really. Nothing that would hold up. Do you think Chandler has anything we don't?"

"No," I said, climbing out of the rowing machine. "What do you suggest?"

"We have full dress rehearsal tomorrow night," she said absently. "That means I have the afternoon off."

"And?"

She shrugged. "That should be time enough to put on our own little show."

"Okay, Judy," I said. "I'll be Mickey . . . just as long as you provide the barn."

HAVE **YOU** FIGURED OUT WHO KILLED **SAM FIZER?** JACK AND I KNOW **ONE** THING FOR SURE...

"... A **RIGHT-HANDED** MAN DOESN'T SHOOT HIMSELF IN THE LEFT TEMPLE, ESPECIALLY WHEN HE'S UNCONSCIOUS FROM A **DOPED** DRINK."

"MAGGIE'S **RIGHT**—THIS IS NO SIMPLE SUICIDE. YOU HAVE **PLENTY** OF CANDIDATES FOR THE MURDERER, STARTING WITH GRIEVING WIDOW **MISTY WINTERS**...

"...AND DON'T FORGET **CANDY CAIN!** SHE SAYS HAL RAPP GOT FRISKY, BUT DID HE GET EVEN **MORE** OUT OF LINE?

"AND DID 'SUNFLOWER SUE' FRAME THE LECHEROUS RAPP TO GET RID OF SAM FIZER, WHO HER HUSBAND, **CHARLIE MAZURKI** OWED MONEY TO? OR WAS IT CLEVER FUNNYMAN CHARLIE HIMSELF?"

"A POSSIBILITY, JACK - BUT DON'T RULE OUT THE EQUALLY CLEVER **HAL RAPP.** HE MIGHT'VE RIGGED A SLOPPY FRAME-UP AGAINST HIMSELF, KNOWING IT WOULD FALL TO PIECES... "

"MAGGIE, ISN'T IT POSSIBLE **ANOTHER** PLAYER IN FIZER'S POKER GAME DIDN'T LEVEL WITH US ENTIRELY? ... CRASH LANDON'S CO-PILOT **RAY ALEXANDER,** MAYBE?"

"JACK, YOU'LL NEVER FIGURE THIS OUT UNTIL YOU UNDERSTAND WHY STINGY SAM FIZER STARTED THROWING **MONEY** AROUND, THE LAST SIX MONTHS OF HIS LIFE...

"...AND IT WASN'T JUST BECAUSE MISTY WINTERS DUMPED HIM TO TAKE PART IN THE **TALL PAUL** MUSICAL, EITHER."

"YOU MAY BE THE **BOSS**, MAGGIE, BUT I'M THE **DETECTIVE** IN THE FAMILY. AND WE HAVEN'T EXHAUSTED ALL THE SUSPECTS...."

"... STARTING WITH FIZER'S LOYAL ASSISTANT, **MURRAY COE**, WHO INHERITED **MUG O'MALLEY**, AND PRODUCER/DIRECTOR **MEL NORMAN**, WHO WAS THREATENED BY FIZER WITH A LAWSUIT..."

"AND WINDING UP WITH THE UNKNOWN PARTY WHO CASHED IN **TONY CARMINE'S** MARKERS, THE HARD WAY.   OR WAS THE MASKED ASSASSIN ONE OF OUR **OTHER** SUSPECTS?"

The next afternoon found Maggie holding down her desk during business hours for the first time since she'd accepted her role in the *Tall Paul* musical. She had traded in her low-cut scarlet gown for a man-tailored gray suit with black braid trim and a collarless white blouse; her red hair, however, fell to her shoulders, providing a nicely feminine contrast to the executive fashion.

She had restrained herself and tidied my mess on the desk only so much as to stack and straighten: she knew I'd be in that chair again soon enough, although once the play opened she intended to hold down two jobs, syndicate magnate by day and Broadway siren by night.

The lighting in the large, narrow windowless office was subdued, supplemented by a green-shaded banker's lamp on the massive cherrywood desk. Maggie didn't like harsh light, not wishing to subject her eyes to it or her carefully maintained beauty. Ironically her elaborate makeup—false eyelashes, freckle-disguising face powder, scarlet mouth, phony beauty mark (war paint, I called it)—only made her look older, if still ten years short of her age. Behind her on the wall loomed the ghost of her younger self, that massive pastel portrait of her in a clinging pink-feathered getup, circa 1941.

In a dark blue Botany 500 suit with a darker blue tie and a lighter blue shirt, I was every bit the syndicate VP, comfortably arranged across the desk from her in the wine-colored tufted-leather chair, angled somewhat so I could maintain eye contact with whomever might sit in the visitor's chair on my left.

We'd already had one meeting this afternoon, having to do with syndicate business, and were waiting for our two o'clock. It was ten after.

"Maybe he's not going to show," I said, slouching in the chair, hands tented, right leg crossed over left knee, foot dancing nervously in midair.

She pointed at my wiggling Florsheim. "Stop that. . . . He'll be here. He wants to get the terms on the new contract settled just as badly as we do."

She was right. At twenty after two, man-in-black Bryce ushered diminutive, unassuming Murray Coe into Maggie's chamber. He approached with literal hat in hand, a bald, bespectacled man in an off-the-rack dark brown suit with a blue bow tie, a prominent Adam's apple bobbing under his excuse for a chin.

"Sorry I'm late," Murray Coe said, flashing a nervous smile at Maggie and then at me. He settled into the dark wood, dark leather padded chair, the hat—a narrow-brimmed felt number—still in his hands. He reminded me of a child taking a place at the grown-up's table, his feet barely reaching the floor. "Actually, I've been here since ten till two."

"Yeah?" I said. "Get lost on the elevator?"

That got another nervous smile out of him, which was more than it was worth. "I stopped at the editorial office, downstairs. Ben and I got to talking about whether I should work up a memorial strip to Sam."

Maggie said, "I think that would be a good idea."

Murray nodded, his smile turning brave now. "I do, too. I was thinking . . . Mug and Louie and the rest of the cast at Sam's graveside, with Mug and Louie wiping away tears, and in the sky, in a cloud? Sam smiling and saying, 'So long, gang! Keep up the good fight!' . . . You think that's too . . . too corny?"

The little assistant had tears in his eyes.

"No," Maggie said, her smile gentle, supportive. "It's in keeping with the strip."

I said, "You bet. Sam always had a sentimental streak a mile wide."

"Didn't he, though?" Murray said, a little embarrassed, shrugging, turning the hat in his hands like a wheel. "Anyway, I do apologize for being late. I should've called from downstairs and let you know I was in the building."

"Don't give it another thought," Maggie said. "Thanks for coming—I know you're drowning in deadlines. But we need to talk some business. We'd like you to sign an agreement with Starr for you to take over *Mug*."

His eyebrows rose above his glasses. "Well, isn't that more or less automatic? Sam showed me his will, and how it was all set up—"

"We'll make the contract consistent with Sam's will, and his wishes," she said. "Actually, we intend to improve on those terms, somewhat. That's part of what we want to discuss this afternoon."

He damn near glowed; he was sitting on the edge of the chair now, hat still turning nervously in his hands. "Really? Well, that's very generous of you, Miss Starr."

She gave him a smile both beautiful and businesslike. "I admit to a certain element of self-interest, Murray . . . and do please call me Maggie. I feel like we've been through quite a lot together, after that long night with the police at the Fizer suite."

"I suppose we have." He frowned curiously. "But what do you mean, self-interest?"

She gestured with a graceful hand. "The unusual circumstances of Sam's death make delays and inconveniences inevitable. There's not even been a funeral date set as yet, because the police are holding on to the body as evidence. There may well be a struggle between Sam's widow, Misty Winters, and his two surviving brothers; the probate of the will, and the unavoidable red tape, mean that settling Sam Fizer's affairs will take many months."

"I suppose that's true."

She shrugged. "We simply can't afford to sit around for all those months, waiting for legal ducks to be lined in rows. The Starr Syndicate is in the business of delivering its features in a timely fashion to its subscribers. How far ahead were you and Sam, on *Mug*, at the time of his death?"

"Three months on the Sunday pages, two months on dailies. And Sam left enough script behind for me to stay in production for another month before a new writer is hired."

Maggie arched an eyebrow. "Do you think you could handle the writing yourself, Murray?"

An astonished grin blossomed above the lack of chin. "Actually, I do. I was going to ask you if I might submit a sample story line and several weeks of script. . . . I took the liberty of bringing them along."

He set his hat in his lap and reached a hand in his suitcoat and withdrew a folded manila envelope from the inside pocket. Gingerly, almost embarrassed, he placed the folded envelope on Maggie's desk, smoothing it out with two hands, like a student with high hopes turning in an assignment that lots of extra effort had gone into.

"I look forward to looking at this, Murray," she said, and took the envelope and placed it atop one of the neat new piles she'd made out of my sloppy old ones.

I said, "Have you ever done any writing on the strip before? Or was your assisting strictly on the art?"

He swung eagerly toward me. "Oh, I helped Mr. Fizer work out lots of the plots over the last decade or so. I admit I haven't done any of the dialogue, and Sam had a real flare for that . . . but I think I worked with him long enough for it to, you know, seep in."

"After all," Maggie said, "you did the lettering, so every line of dialogue Sam wrote, you'd have studied, in a way."

He nodded. "That's right."

She gestured with two hands. "Well, Murray, we're anxious to give you full rein on *Mug*. Everyone knows you've essentially ghosted the artwork for many years, and Jack and I and everybody in editorial feel the strip couldn't be in better hands. We'll keep Sam's name on it, of course, for the first year."

He nodded some more. "Of course. We can retain it permanently if you like. I could just add a little 'M. Coe' beneath Sam's signature block . . ."

She shook her head. "I don't think that will be necessary, Murray. At any rate it's a trifle . . . ghoulish. Sam's death isn't exactly a secret; the public will grasp that we need to move on, and a year from now your name can be the sole byline."

"Understood."

Her expression a combined frown and smile, Maggie said, "There is *one* delicate issue that, uh . . . Jack, perhaps you'd best take it from here."

Coe turned to me, his thick-lensed glasses magnifying his eyes, turning cartoonist into cartoon.

"Murray," I said, "we're going to have to include a clause that releases us from the contract, in its every particular, should what you did ever come out."

The big eyes under glass blinked. "What . . . ? What I . . . *did?*"

I nodded, my manner nonchalant. "You see, Murray, we know all about the role you played in Sam's death."

He sat up sudden and straight, a jack-in-the-box effect. "Role! I didn't play any *role* in—"

"Of course you did." I sat forward and grinned at him obnoxiously. "You played the role you *always* played—Sam Fizer's assistant." Then I sat back and shrugged. "And we get it—we understand. We're not sitting in judgment."

He was trembling now; it would have been funny if it hadn't been so sad. "You're . . . you're mistaken. . . . You're *seriously* mistaken. . . ."

I grinned some more. "Murray! We don't *care* about what you did. We neither approve nor disapprove. For us it's strictly business. But we have to be protected should the police stumble onto the truth . . . not that I think that dimwitted dick Chandler ever will."

Coe was shaking his head, his manner desperate, the hat sliding onto the floor without him noticing. "Please . . . I don't know *what* you think I did, but I *didn't*. You're making an *awful* mistake, and putting me in a *terrible* position."

I turned from him to Maggie. "Maybe you'd better take over for a while."

She nodded crisply, then she gave him a direct, firm look. "Murray, I don't share Jack's disdain for the police. I believe they may well put the pieces together, here; and they have already come up with a certain amount of evidence that confirms what I've suspected from the start."

"What . . . *what* did you suspect from the start?"

"That Sam Fizer *did* commit suicide," she said firmly. "And that you helped him."

He turned white as a ghost. But then he was a ghost, wasn't he?

"Sam's behavior these last six months or so had been very uncharacteristic," Maggie said. "Oh, he was outwardly his usual self-centered self. But his reckless behavior indicated something in his life had gone terribly wrong."

Rather timidly, Coe said, "Something *had*—he and his wife broke up. Everyone knows that."

She smiled and shook her head, the red locks bouncing on the shoulders of the severe gray suit. "That's the *excuse* everyone has for Sam's reckless behavior—but why would a marriage breaking up explain his sudden love affair with high-stakes gambling? Or explain why his longtime feud with Hal Rapp had escalated to dizzying new highs? Or perhaps I should say lows."

He was shaking his head insistently. "Sam was mad at Hal because of Misty, because Hal had slept with her before casting her in that musical."

Maggie shrugged. "I'm sure that was part of it. But Jack met with Ray Alexander yesterday, and saw the doctored and forged strips that Sam created to try to ruin Rapp. I'm assuming *you* didn't doctor those strips *for* Sam?"

"No!"

I said, "Murray didn't do those forgeries, Maggie. They were too crude—only Fizer himself could have."

"Right," she said, as if she should have known. "So why such harebrained behavior? I could think of only one possibility: illness. Impending fatal illness. So through Jack I asked the police to request a full autopsy, and the coroner . . . taking a closer look, second time around . . . found cancer."

"Sam's organs," I said, "were riddled with the stuff."

Coe shivered and swallowed. "Please. Some respect, please. I knew Sam was dying, but he never spoke of suicide. That's just . . . just *crazy*, a vital man like Sam. Anyway, the evidence doesn't support suicide. And besides, wasn't there a *second* murder? Didn't someone kill that Carmichael character, from Sam's poker game?"

"That's right," I said. "Only it had nothing to do with Sam's death. . . . Or actually, it did, but in an indirect way."

"I . . . I don't follow . . ."

"Tony Carmichael, alias Tony Carmine, was a big-time gambler, and he had overextended himself, in part due to debts incurred in that poker game that weren't getting paid off. Someone above him made an executive decision to remove him, taking care of a problem while making an example."

Coe was shaking his head again, but slowly now, and the eyes were staring, not blinking. "How could you *know* this?"

I grunted a laugh. "To give the devil his due, Captain Chandler got a lead to a defrocked underworld doctor with links to gamblers—you see, I wounded the guy when we had our little stairwell scuffle at the Brill Building. The coppers watched the doc's place and nabbed the guy."

Maggie said, "But Jack knew from the start that the second murder was almost certainly unconnected to Sam's suicide."

Nodding, I said, "Nobody in this case has any underworld connections except Tony himself. And maybe me, a little. Anyway, Tony's killing was a professional job—shooter used a silencer on an automatic, not the kind of thing that, say, a cartoonist or a comedian would have access to, much less use."

"So," Maggie said, "we're back to the suicide."

He about fell off the chair. "But it *wasn't* a suicide! You were there, both of you! You *saw* the evidence."

Maggie smiled patiently. "We saw the faked evidence, designed to implicate Hal Rapp in murder, and to take the onus of suicide off Sam Fizer."

"If Sam committed suicide," Coe demanded indignantly, "how did he manage it? That police captain told me Sam had been drugged! Sam was asleep when that gun was fired!"

"You should know," I said. "You fired it."

He seemed to shrink back into the chair. If he'd been any whiter, he'd have been dead.

"Sam Fizer was a terrible boss to Hal Rapp, those many years ago," I said. "But Sam learned his lesson, and he was always good to you. He paid you well, and treated you like a son, and he even set up his will to guarantee that you would continue the strip."

"That . . . that much is true."

"But when Sam's forgeries and doctored strips were exposed to his own peers—when instead of Hal Rapp being disgraced for sticking smut into the funnies, *Sam Fizer* faced disgrace for trying to smear a colleague, well, the only way out for a proud, insecure guy like Sam was suicide. He'd been kicked out of the cartoonist organization he'd helped form; in a matter of days, his shame would be on every front page in the country, coming out of every radio, jumping out from every television. He couldn't face that."

Maggie said, "Sam was dying anyway—by hastening that process, he would avoid the public humiliation. Perhaps his old colleagues would even see fit to bury what he'd done with him, so he didn't have to go out a disgraced man."

"And then Sam, that clever comic-strip plotter," I said, "came up with a scheme. He would make his exit in a dramatic fashion, in a way that made him a victim, and not just any victim: a murder victim. And the murderer? Hal Rapp, natch."

Coe looked from Maggie to me and back again, as if one of us had to be reasonable. "This is really . . . it's not *fair*. It's just a bunch of preposterous presumptions pulled out of thin air."

Maybe so, but he didn't make a move to leave.

"I have a hunch," I said, "that Sam Fizer knew damn well you were 'secretly' assisting Hal Rapp on *Tall Paul*. You were a spy for Sam, weren't you? Keeping an eye on his nemesis? And then, when Sam came up with this ingenious scheme to turn his own suicide into a murder committed by his worst enemy, you—the only person with access to both suites—were in a perfect position to lift that pen, with Rapp's fingerprints, and plant it in Fizer's studio."

He swallowed.

"It was a two-man job," I said. "Sam invited Rapp over that afternoon to help set him up—so you could tell the police you saw Rapp in there, hours before the murder. And I have no doubt that Fizer signed his own suicide note. But Rapp told us that Fizer wasn't much of a letterer—*you* were the one who assured us and the police that Fizer could do his own lettering. Truth is, he wasn't up to the job. You even had to assist on the suicide note. Where did the sedatives come from?"

"I . . . I use sleeping pills, sometimes," he said. He looked even smaller now, lost in the chair.

"So Sam went to sleep there at his drawing board," Maggie said, "and somehow you found the terrible courage to use the gun that Sam had bought. . . . He bought it six months ago, right after he learned he was dying and began contemplating the deed you eventually helped him with."

"You must've worn a glove," I said, double-teaming him, "and disposed of it before going upstairs to Rapp's to announce the suicide you'd 'found.' Or maybe you didn't wear a glove—I don't imagine these thickheaded cops thought to do a paraffin test on you."

"I . . . I wore a glove."

Maggie gazed at him with genuine sympathy. "It must have been horrible."

Coe stared at Maggie, but was looking through her. "It was.

Horrible. Hardest thing I ever did. But Sam didn't feel it. He was asleep. It put an end to his pain, and he'd grown *so* miserable. . . . Sam really loved that stupid woman, that floozy Misty. She broke his heart, right after he'd found out he was dying. He didn't tell her, of course, because then she'd have stayed around and pretended to love him just to get his money. She has a big surprise coming when she sees his will—she's out, she's gone, the horrible witch."

Maggie leaned forward and asked, "Murray, why would you help frame Hal Rapp? Hadn't Hal always been good to you? You were working for him, on the side, after all?"

For a moment he sat expressionless. Then that nondescript face of his twisted into a mask of contempt. "He's a *monster*. . . . Rapp's an utter monster, don't you *know* that? When I was first working for him, he got fresh with my wife. *More* than just. . . . fresh. He was my boss, and she demanded I confront him about it, and I just couldn't. . . . It was the Depression, I needed the money, *we* needed the money. My marriage lasted for a long while after that, but it was never the same. My wife still loved me, I think, even the day she left me. But she'd stopped respecting me, long ago. *That's* what Hal Rapp took from me."

There was warmth in Maggie's voice: "You were just helping Sam. Assisting him, like you always had, loyally."

"Yes." He stared blankly straight ahead. "I would never hurt him. He was like a father to me."

There was no warmth in my voice: "You said that before, Murray. Trouble is, Sam didn't squeeze the trigger, you did. You were right the first time—it *was* a murder. And you committed it."

Eyes, full of rage and denial and pain, flared big behind the exaggeration of the thick lenses. "But it was *Sam's* idea! It was *his* plan!"

"I thought you guys worked the stories out together," I said, but now I was starting to feel sorry for the little bastard myself. "For Christ's sake, how much more do you need?"

Coe looked at me, confused. "What?"

But I wasn't talking to him.

Captain Chandler and Sergeant Jeffords, a colored plain-clothes officer, came in through the connecting space between the office and the gym, where Chandler had been listening as a tape recorder picked up the conversations from a microphone planted on Maggie's desk between those neatly stacked piles.

Murray Coe made no protest; he knew he'd been had. He just sort of collapsed in on himself, looking tiny and deflated. Jeffords, a big guy, cuffed the little guy's hands behind his back and trooped him out past Bryce, who was watching with horrified eyes, a splayed hand covering his mouth.

Captain Chandler, hands on his hips, fedora pushed back on his head, said to me, " 'Dimwitted dick,' am I? 'Thickheaded cops'?"

I grinned up at him. "You can't deny me the occasional small pleasure."

"What was that nonsense about Tony Carmine getting shot 'cause he was overextended with his bosses, and me staking out an underworld doctor, and hauling in the guy you shot?"

"That was color. Artistic license, we call it in the comics business."

His eyebrows climbed. "Yours should be revoked. You're right about that silencer, though—that should have told me that the Carmine kill had nothing to do with Fizer's murder."

"Yeah. It should have."

"But Carmine's murder isn't solved!"

I shrugged. "Maggie and I cracked this one. Shouldn't the Homicide Bureau do *some* of the work?"

He tried not to smile, as he headed back into the gym, where a technician waited with the tape recorder.

Maggie was still seated behind her desk, looking a little dazed.

"You okay, boss?"

"I can't help feeling sorry for Murray."

I smirked. "Feel sorry for *us*—we don't have anybody to draw *Mug O'Malley* now."

She smiled at me rather sadly. "You're all heart, Jack."

"You ever think maybe it *was* a murder? Not just legally, not just technically a murder, but Murray Coe wanting to get out from under Sam Fizer's thumb, and do the strip himself? Be in charge for a change?"

She shook her head. "No. I think he was doing Sam a favor."

"Yeah, I suppose. That Fizer was something, huh? Even had to have his own damn suicide ghosted."

"True," Maggie said. Her sigh took a long time. "But it was Murray Coe who signed the murder."

The audience at the opening of a Broadway show is anything but representative. Many attendees are relatives of the thirty performers in the company, or of the dozen stagehands or the unit manager or press agent or director or assistant director or author or . . . you get the point.

These prejudiced behinds take up enough seats to insure the weakest joke gets a guffaw and the least memorable tune performed in the most lackluster way will receive enthusiastic applause. The remainder of the backsides belong to die-hard first-nighters, current or prospective agents of cast members, New York–based Hollywood scouts, investors in the show (and family and friends), and of course the one group not laughing and applauding like parents at a school play: the jury. By which I mean the dozen in the audience who ignore the warm reception the rest of the crowd is bestowing, a panel of twelve who respect no presumption of innocence (or talent).

The critics.

Jaded arbiters whose verdict can be overturned by the public court of appeal, though that happened only rarely. It takes a lot of word of mouth to drown out a little bad ink. But now and then a *Tobacco Road* or an *Abie's Irish Rose* comes along to remind Broadway that it's part of a supposed democracy.

An opening-night tradition in theater is that the cast and other key members of a show gather at Sardi's or Toots Shor's or some other top restaurant to wait for the early editions to hit the street. After opening night on November 12, 1953, Maggie played hostess at the Strip Joint for the *Tall Paul* family.

The Strip Joint was smaller than some of those other celebrated dining spots, so my stepmother closed the place off for a private party. The beautiful boys and girls of the cast were packed in there, laughing, talking, throwing down champagne and noshing on goodies served up by Maggie's shapely waitresses in their white shirts, black ties and tuxedo pants; blue cigarette smoke drifted and the tinkle of glass and laughter rose above a pianist's subdued efforts in one corner jazz-noodling show tunes, though nothing from *Tall Paul*.

Everybody was confident—the previews had gone very well, the show had been shorn of a few excess songs and extraneous slapstick bits, and the lively remainder was clearly an audience pleaser. As long as at least some of the critics liked the show, *Tall Paul* should enjoy a long run.

Press coverage of Sam Fizer's strange suicide, including the arrest of his assistant on first-degree murder charges, had mentioned Hal Rapp only in passing. The forged and doctored *Tall Paul* strips came up not at all. Later some of that might emerge at the trial, but for now no particular pall had been cast upon Broadway's newest musical.

At the bar I spoke with Mel Norman about it.

"Rumor has it you're the guy who cleared Hal of this terrible thing," the slender, round-faced director said. He was in a tuxedo tonight. So was I, and most of the other men there.

"Maggie deserves the rave reviews," I said. "I just hauled the facts in like a trapper and let her make a fur coat out of the stuff."

"She's very good in the play, you know. Twice the age of some of the girls in the chorus, but every bit as beautiful."

I put a hand on his shoulder. "Be sure to remind Maggie she's twice as old as these girls. She loves that kind of thing."

"We already have interest from Paramount, you know. And I'm going to be the first producer of a Broadway show ever to use the entire original cast in the film version!"

He'd had quite a bit of champagne. I had no intention of holding him to that.

"Say, Jack, I heard the cops found the guy who killed Tony Carmichael."

I nodded. "Yeah. Tony had overextended himself with IOUs from the likes of Fizer and Charlie Mazurki. Got himself killed for it."

"Got to hand it to these cops."

"Yeah. They're wizards. Excuse me."

I went over to congratulate Candy Cain about her performance. She was unpretentiously dressed in a pink blouse with a yellow scarf and a black dress, and wore very little makeup, her blonde tresses up in a bun. Not a sexy Catfish Holler gal, but still a striking young woman.

"I thought you were great," I told her. "That song they added at the last minute is a lot of fun."

Sunflower Sue and Preacher Luke had a number about how Sue was over the hill because she was pushing seventeen.

"Glad you like it," she said. "Real pleasure to work with Chubby Charles . . . but I still feel like window dressing. What the heck, the audiences are having a good time, and that's what counts."

Her husband, Charlie Mazurki, ambled up, also in a tuxedo, but with a loose riverboat-gambler string tie, sporting another of his trademark pool-cue cigars. A smile blossomed under his other trademark, that generous mustache.

"I see where Tony Carmine got killed!" he said, as if his favorite team had just won a game. "Who says they only print bad news in these papers?"

Maybe he *was* funny off camera. "How many of your IOUs died with him, Charlie?"

"None, Jack." He smiled boyishly at his bride. "Ask Candy— I gave up gambling, when was it? Last year."

I moved on, stopping to say hello to Misty Winters, memorable aspects of whom were falling fetchingly out of an eye-popping black sequins dress; she introduced me to a Hollywood producer friend of Mel Norman's who'd been a guest at the premiere, and whose arm was now in hers.

I whispered in her ear: "He can only get you in the movies. I can get you in the funnies."

She whispered in my ear: "I'm already in the funnies, Jack— Bathless Bessie, remember?"

Finally I wound up over by the wall on which many a nationally syndicated cartoonist had drawn their famous characters, including Mug O'Malley and his manager, Louie, blithely happy in better days. Rapp was standing right beside a Tall Paul drawing he'd done several years ago; and Maggie, in a blue-and-beige plaid dress with navy blue gloves (Jean Desses from a recent Paris trip), was sipping champagne and chatting him up.

Rapp wasn't drinking anything, just smoking a cigarette (in holder, of course); he, too, was in a tuxedo, and smiling big, his bray of a laugh periodically punctuating every conversation in the crowded restaurant.

He was saying to Maggie, "I can't *begin* to say how much I *appreciate* what you and Jack did for me, in that tragic, *ridiculous* Fizer affair!"

She said, "You can express your appreciation by signing those contracts for *Lean Jean* we sent over to your attorneys."

"We're *looking* at them," he assured her. "I'm *positive* there'll be no problem—I'm just in the hands of a *typical* law firm: anything in a contract that isn't *incomprehensible*, ha ha ha, they immediately find *suspicious*."

I asked, "What are the chances you'll wrest *Tall Paul* away from Unique Features?"

"Good, Jack, I'd say, very *good*. I've made *unreasonable* demands for a new salary, ha ha ha, which will send those miserly bean counters into cardiac *arrest*. They're sure to realize that *Tall Paul* without *Hal Rapp* is like Charlie McCarthy without *Edgar Bergen*."

"Well," Maggie said, "in any event, *Lean Jean* will be a good start." She raised her champagne glass to him in a little one-sided toast.

Rapp turned to me and rested a hand on my shoulder. "Listen, Jack, I'm sorry I held out on you, about those forgeries Fizer did. I should've put you in touch with Ray Alexander right at the start. I guess I was sentimental about my old boss—I mean, with Sam dead, why send him out with a ruined reputation?"

I grinned at him. "Hal, don't kid a kidder—you held out on me on that score for the same reason you held out on the cops: what Fizer tried to do to you with those doctored drawings gave you the best murder motive yet."

He didn't like hearing that, but his face split in a big cartoonish grin, anyway. "You, you're an *inspiration*, Jack. I haven't done a *Hawknose Harry* sequence in a *long* time, ha ha ha, and you've just given me the *best* idea for one."

*Hawknose Harry* was the outrageous strip-within-a-strip parody of *Dick Tracy* that Rapp did in *Tall Paul* on occasion—Harry a well meaning but dim detective who blew big round holes in all the bad guys and many an innocent bystander.

Rapp was gesturing with a fluid hand. "I'll have Harry visit *all* the suspects in a case, *unwittingly* leading the killer to *all* of them—the corpses'll be stacked up like, ha ha ha, *cordwood* by the end of the story!"

"Funny stuff," I said. "Listen, something you should know."

"Yes, Jack?"

"When I was turning over rocks in this thing, half of them had you under them, pawing after some babe, including underage ones."

Maggie, who'd been taking this in, closed her eyes; to anyone else, her expression would have appeared blank—to me, it screamed pain. I was giving the top cartoonist in the business a hard time, right when he was giving serious consideration to letting us syndicate his new strip.

But she knew enough not to bother trying to stop me.

His mouth hung open, jaw slack. "Jack, that's, uh . . . a little out of *line.*"

"Hal, buddy, pal—I like girls, too. But I like them of age."

Now he was frowning, the brow deeply lined under a dark comma of Tall Paul–like hair. "That's more than a *little* out of line."

I shrugged. "Hal, I want us to syndicate *Lean Jean.* Hell, I want us to syndicate *Tall Paul.* But I don't want to wake up some morning to read about a Hal Rapp scandal worse than anything Sam Fizer ever cooked up."

He was scowling. "You're comparing me to *Sam Fizer* now? Are you *sure* you want to do business with me, Jack?"

"I don't think Sam started out a monster, Hal. I think he had to work at it, over the years. Using your powerful position to take advantage of young women isn't your most attractive trait. Be careful, or it'll catch up with you."

All humor had drained from Rapp's face, and it wasn't a pretty sight. "I better mingle. *Excuse* me, Maggie. Jack."

And he moved away from us with his familiar herky-jerky gait.

"You have quite a touch with the talent," Maggie said to me. "We'll be damn lucky if he still signs with us."

"If he signs with us," I said, "it'll be a miracle."

Her eyes grew large; for a moment there she looked like Libidia Von Stackpole. "What? Why?"

I shrugged. "I know a guy over at Unique Features. He says Rapp is just using us as a bargaining chip."

That was when the first papers made their way into the room, and the reviews were mostly stellar, Walter Kerr calling the musical "a rip-snorting ring-tailed roarer." Even the weaker notices loved the Batch'ul Catch'ul Ballet.

"Everybody, everybody!" Mel Norman called out. "We're a hit! We are a *hit*! . . . Let's all raise a glass to the man of the hour, Tall Paul's real pappy—*Mr. Hal Rapp*!"

And everybody, even me and my rum and Coke (without the rum), hoisted a glass to the creator of Catfish Holler. Rapp, not drinking, waved a hand in regal fashion and beamed a smile so broad, his cheeks seemed about to burst.

Was it just me, or were his eyes glazed and hard?

The musical *Tall Paul* was indeed a big hit, running for two years at the St. John Theatre and touring for a year after that, with much of the original cast, although Candy Cain dropped out after her initial one-year contract expired. She never thought much of the show, finding it "pleasant" at best, and almost didn't attend the Tony Awards the night she won for Best Actress in a Musical. Choreographer Richard Childe also won, presenting a soft-spoken humble speech about his "hardworking boys and girls" somewhat at odds with his Marquis de Sade rehearsal style.

And there was indeed a movie, several years later, which Candy also opted out of, though Mel Norman was as good as his word: most of the original cast returned, including Maggie, which made for an interesting Hollywood trip (but that's another story).

Misty Winters—who did well with the Fizer estate, his most recent will thrown out due to clear evidence he had not been of "sound mind" making it—was in the *Tall Paul* film, too. She soon wound up marrying a Hollywood producer (not the one she met at the musical's opening night, though) and made only a handful of features. She had several children and hers was a happy, long-lasting marriage, something of a rarity in such Hollywood circles. Ethel Schwartz really did wind up an incredible-looking grand-mother.

Mel Norman never directed another Broadway show—apparently he just wanted to prove to himself that he could do it; but he made many other Hollywood films throughout the '50s and '60s, although as the film careers of Bob Hope and Danny Kaye wound down, so did Norman's.

Cartoonist Ray Alexander kept his promise and created a detective strip, *Nick Steele*, about a suave New York private eye; he sold it to King Features, however, not the Starr Syndicate (he did send me an original strip for my collection). *Steele* was successful, but Alexander died a little over four years into its run, in a high-speed crash in one of his sports cars in the upstate New York countryside.

Coincidentally, in the same year, Charlie Mazurki also died in an automobile accident, when he hit a wet patch and then a telephone pole on a rainy night after a long, long poker game. He left Candy Cain in hock to the IRS and countless creditors, and the talented singer/actress spent years working in film, on TV and in nightclubs, digging her way out. Her most famous role, after Sunflower Sue, was as a sexy pitchwoman for cigars in a long-running series of commercials.

Murray Coe was convicted of manslaughter; though he had murdered Sam Fizer with undoubted premeditation, the circumstances were mitigating enough for the lesser charge to come into play. He served ten years and never worked in comics again, as far as I know; you can never be sure with a ghost. We found a good artist for *Mug O'Malley* and a good writer, too, and the strip lasted into the early 1970s, but everybody knew it was a pale shadow, in only a handful of papers when it ceased.

With a hit show on Broadway, Hal Rapp renegotiated with Unique Features and got a deal that would turn ownership of *Tall Paul* over to its creator in ten years; Unique also distributed *Lean Jean*, but the strip was only a modest success and was gone within five years. By the mid-'60s, when Rapp—now sole owner of *Tall Paul*—took the feature to another syndicate (no, not Starr), he swung the strip in a new direction.

After decades lambasting the follies of the right wing, Rapp shifted to their camp, offended by college protestors who looked to him like Catfish Holler residents come unfortunately to life. Their antiestablishment attitude, dope smoking and free love rubbed Rapp the wrong way. (Personally, I think he envied them.)

When he ham-handedly lampooned these long-haired kids in *Tall Paul*, he began losing papers (as well as his touch), and began a controversial series of college lecture tours, where he would take on the hippies on their home turf, making fun of them, laughing off their boos and hisses, playing Don Rickles to the counterculture. The college administrators who brought Rapp in relished the public spanking of their students.

I never saw him in those days. If I had, I would have asked him if it ever occurred to him that he had become Sam Fizer—a patriotic liberal turned right-wing zealot, a man of the people turned selfish monster.

By the early '70s, several charges were brought against Rapp for indecent sexual conduct with coeds on his college tours, which muckraking columnists brought to light. Stories dating back many years began to emerge; actresses spoke out about the celebrated cartoonist's embarrassing misbehavior, from Candy Cain and Maggie Starr to a certain princess of Monaco and an Oscar-winning graduate of *Laugh-In*.

His once revered strip dropped by hundreds of papers, stung by sexual scandal, Hal Rapp quietly pulled the plug on *Tall Paul* in the mid-'70s.

And about all that is left of Rapp's once-famous creation are amateur productions of the musical based upon it, and of course annual Batch'ul Catch'ul dances. Even now, when *Tall Paul* is almost as forgotten as *Mug O'Malley*, at high schools and on college campuses all across America, the girls chase the boys. Wishful thinking, from beyond the grave, by the tragic genius who created the greatest comic strip of all.

Barely a year after he ended the strip, Hal Rapp died of natural causes, a broken man. Unlike Sam Fizer, however, he did not commit suicide.

Or did he?

# A TIP OF THE FEDORA

This novel, despite some obvious parallels to events in the history of the comics medium, is fiction. It employs characters with real-life counterparts as well as composites and wholly fictional ones.

Unlike other historical novels of mine—the Nathan Heller "memoirs," the Eliot Ness series, the "disaster" mysteries and the *Road* trilogy—I have chosen not to use real names and/or to hew religiously to actual events. As this is a mystery in the Rex Stout or Ellery Queen tradition, the murder herein has only the vaguest historical basis, and real-life conflicts have been heightened and exaggerated while others are wholly fabricated.

Characters reminiscent of real people, in particular cartoonists in the comic strip field and performers in show business of the 1950s, are portrayed unflatteringly at times, because they are, after all, meant to be suspects in a murder mystery.

While I invite readers—particularly comics fans—to enjoy the roman à clef aspect of *Strip for Murder*, I caution them not to view this as history but as the fanciful (if fact-inspired) novel it is. The National Cartoonists Society, for example, is a real organization but I have rewritten their early history to suit this story, and do not mean to suggest that the NCS in any way endorses this fictional work.

The central conflict of this novel, the feud between two celebrated cartoonists, is inspired by that of Al Capp and Ham Fisher. "Hal Rapp" and "Sam Fizer," though obviously suggested by these real cartoonists, should be viewed as fictional characters. Many details in the novel have no parallel in history, and many aspects of the real men's lives have no parallel in this novel. Aspects of both men's personalities and lives have been exaggerated, and other traits invented, and still others omitted, to suit the purposes of this murder mystery. While Ham Fisher indeed committed suicide after his expulsion from the National Cartoonists Society, the timing of this novel is off by several years, and many aspects of the mystery have no basis in reality.

No disrespect is intended to these classic cartoonists, both of whom have been favorites of mine since childhood; the feud between two of my favorite cartoonists has long fascinated me, and I remember vividly hearing on the radio (at age seven or eight) about Fisher's suicide and being deeply troubled and confused. This novel reflects a long-held desire to address this real-life conflict, and previous notions had been to do a nonfiction work or possibly write a short story or novella about Capp and Fisher in my Nate Heller series. *Strip for Murder*, I think, represents the best way for me to have exorcized these four-color demons.

For the record, I agree with Jack Starr that *Li'l Abner* is the greatest of all comic strips, a satiric masterpiece; and *Joe Palooka* is also high on my list, a wonderfully written (and well-drawn) strip much maligned in recent years by commentators who clearly haven't read much if any of it. Whatever human faults Al Capp and Ham Fisher may have had, they were giants of the comic strip world and I continue to unabashedly admire them for their impressive bodies of work.

A few small-press *Palooka* reprints can be found if you dig for them, and a good deal of *Li'l Abner* is available. My friend Denis Kitchen's ambition to collect the complete *Li'l Abner* in book form unfortunately stalled in 1997 at Volume 27 with the 1960 strips; but the best years of the daily strip had been covered, and three wonderful volumes covering Sunday pages from 1954 through 1961 (the period when Frank Frazetta assisted on the strip) have since been published by Kitchen with Dark Horse in 2003 and 2004.

Also in 2003, Capp's classic Shmoo continuities were collected as *The Short Life and Happy Times of the Shmoo* by Overlook with an excellent Harlan Ellison introduction. The Hollywood version of the Broadway musical *Li'l Abner* is available from Paramount on DVD, preserving the play with most of the original cast in a way few films ever have. (One of my proudest accomplishments in life has been to convince Leonard Maltin to upgrade this film in his annual *Movie Guide* from two and a half stars to three stars.)

Among the many books I consulted were Kitchen's aforementioned *Li'l Abner* volumes, whose historical introductions were always helpful, in particular Mark Evanier's definitive articles on the Broadway play and the Hollywood film, respectively, in Volume 22 (1956 dailies) and Volume 25 (1959 dailies).

Also helpful were *Al Capp Remembered* (1994), Eliot Caplin; *Classic Comics and Their Creators* (1942), Martin Sheridan; *A Flame of Pure Fire: Jack Dempsey and the Roaring '20s* (1999), Roger Kahn; *Inside Story* (1974), Britt Hume; *Jack Dempsey: The Manassa Mauler* (1979), Randy Roberts; *Lotus Grows in the Mud* (2005), Goldie Hawn; *My Well-Balanced Life on a Wooden Leg* (1991), Al Capp; *Nothing in Moderation: A Biography of Ernie Kovacs* (1975), David Walley; and *Sing a Pretty Song* (1990), Edie Adams and Robert Windeler.

For New York color I again leaned heavily upon *New York: Confidential!* (1948) by Jack Lait and Lee Mortimer.

Thanks in particular to the source (who asked not to be named) who many years ago gave me copies of the National Cartoonists Society file on the Fisher/Capp dispute, including copies of legal documents, correspondence and the Capp strips as doctored by Fisher.

Thanks to the following: Terry Beatty for again helping incorporate graphic novel elements into this prose work; my longtime research associate, George Hagenauer, who gathered Fisher/*Palooka* and Capp/*Abner* materials for my use; editor Natalee Rosenstein for her patience, support and imagination (doing a mystery series about the world of comics was her notion); my agent and friend, Dominick Abel, the air traffic controller in the seat next to mine; and my wife, Barbara, my invaluable in-house-editor-cum-Daisy-Mae-look-alike.

**MAX ALLAN COLLINS** was hailed in 2004 by *Publishers Weekly* as "a new breed of writer." A frequent Mystery Writers of America Edgar® nominee, he has earned an unprecedented fourteen Private Eye Writers of America Shamus nominations for his historical thrillers, winning for his Nathan Heller novels, *True Detective* (1983) and *Stolen Away* (1991). In 2006 he received the Eye, the Lifetime Achievement Award of the PWA.

His graphic novel *Road to Perdition* is the basis of the Academy Award–winning film starring Tom Hanks and Paul Newman, directed by Sam Mendes. His many comics credits include the syndicated strip *Dick Tracy*; his own *Ms. Tree*; *Batman*; and *CSI: Crime Scene Investigation*, based on the hit TV series for which he has also written video games, jigsaw puzzles, and a *USA Today* bestselling series of novels.

An independent filmmaker in the Midwest, he wrote and directed the Lifetime movie *Mommy* (1996) and a 1997 sequel, *Mommy's Day*. He wrote *The Expert*, a 1995 HBO World Premiere, and wrote and directed the innovative made-for-DVD feature, *Real Time: Siege at Lucas Street*

*Market* (2000). *Shades of Noir* (2004), an anthology of his short films, includes his award-winning documentary, *Mike Hammer's Mickey Spillane*, and is featured in a DVD collection of his films, *Black Box*. His most recent feature, *Eliot Ness: An Untouchable Life* (2006), based on his Edgar-nominated play, is available on DVD from VCI.

His other credits include film criticism, short fiction, songwriting, trading-card sets, and movie/TV tie-in novels, including the *New York Times* bestseller, *Saving Private Ryan*. Currently he is writing the *Criminal Minds* tie-in series for New American Library's Obsidian imprint. Collins lives in Muscatine, Iowa, with his wife, writer Barbara Collins. Their son, Nathan, a recent University of Iowa graduate, has completed a year of postgrad studies in Japan.

**TERRY BEATTY** has collaborated with Max Allan Collins on various comic book series, including *Johnny Dynamite, Mickey Spillane's Mike Danger* and their co-creation *Ms. Tree*. For the past eight years, Terry has been part of DC Comic's "animated-style" Batman art team, currently inking *The Batman Strikes*. He teaches cartooning at MCAD (Minneapolis College of Art and Design), where he is currently "visiting artist."